IN HIS ARMS

"Is that it, then? You wish to remain free?"

"No! Oh, Beldon, I do love you. But I can't marry someone who doesn't love me."

Harriet glowed, love and desire shining out of her eyes, and he wondered how he could ever have thought her less than a beauty. He closed the remaining distance between them and swept her into his arms. "God help me, Harriet, I love you so much. I couldn't stand it if I couldn't have you."

He bent to kiss her and realized he was still wearing his hat. He flung it off and yanked off his gloves as well. Then they were kissing passionately, her arms belted tight around him . . .

The Lady Is Mine

Judith Laik

ZEBRA BOOKS
Kensington Publishing Corp.
www.kensingtonbooks.com

ZEBRA BOOKS are published by

Kensington Publishing Corp.
850 Third Avenue
New York, NY 10022

First Printing: May 2005
10 9 8 7 6 5 4 3 2 1

Printed in the United States of America

To the memory of Debbi,
who was the most generous heart I ever knew.

And to Rein,
who is my hero.

Chapter One

London, late May, 1811

Harriet Vernon peered around the gigantic weeping fig against one wall of Lady Sinclair's heated, overcrowded ballroom. No sign of George Briscoe, thank goodness.

"I think it's time for our dance, Harry." George spoke from behind her.

Suppressing her instinctive start, she turned toward him. *Drat!* He had discovered her hiding place.

Caught, she could only graciously agree. She gave a hand, pristinely covered by a white kid glove, to one of George's damp, spotty gloves. He led her to the floor as the orchestra played the opening to a sprightly country dance.

As clearly as if someone were whispering in her ear, Harriet heard "escape."

The word echoed through the steps of the dance. While they stood at the foot of the set, George hauled out a handkerchief and mopped his brow, murmuring, "Warm in here." Harriet tapped her foot to the music of "escape" and nodded.

Finally, the strains of the country dance ended, and he brought her to the edge of the floor. He lingered by her side, and Harriet looked up at him, wishing he would depart. George's face shone moistly. She looked again at the dark spots on the fingers of his gloves and shuddered.

Where was her brother, Arthur? The traitor had disappeared, and no new dance partner presented himself. Ever since Arthur and her eldest brother, Eustace, had narrowed their choices for her hand to two, they evinced no obligation to present gentlemen for every dance.

George brushed a bead of moisture from his brow. "Er, Harry . . . er, we've known each other a long time."

"Yes, we have," she agreed, her mind distracted with plotting her escape as soon as she could rid herself of him.

"We deal with each other extremely well."

Oh no! Her attention returned to George, and she almost cringed at the serious expression on his long face. Undoubtedly he was working himself up to a declaration. She would have sworn George had had no more notion of their eventually making a match than she had—until Arthur had planted the idea in his head.

"George, I'm most frightfully hungry," she improvised. "Could you see if the Sinclairs have any food about somewhere? You know what I like."

"Ah, er, certainly." Was that relief she spotted on his face? George wheeled about and went in search of the refreshment table.

Harriet waited until he had disappeared before she fled, struggling through the close-packed bodies clustered around the area reserved for dancing. Some time ago she had sent Lucretius Taber, Eustace's candidate for her hand, to procure her some wine. Mr. Taber would undoubtedly be looking for her, and she did not wish to encounter him.

She brushed against a number of people. At one of these near collisions she glanced up—into Lord Beldon's classically heroic features. She had admired him from afar all during the season. What if he finally noticed her now? However, he fixed his gaze beyond her with his usual expression of ennui.

She walked backward, fixing his image, his handsome face, the crisp black hair and deep blue eyes, his broad shoulders, in her mind. If her brothers would only bring Lord Beldon around as a suitor, Harriet would not wish to run away. Not that it would do, of course. She did not plan to marry at all.

And then disaster struck. She backed into a solid mass.

"Oh, there you are, Miss Vernon. You should have remained with one of your brothers. It is not proper to be without an escort." The stately tones were unmistakable.

Harriet turned toward her other suitor. *Drat*! Forcing politeness into her voice, she replied, "You may be right, Mr. Taber. However, I did not leave my brothers, but rather they abandoned me. I was dancing and when I returned, Arthur had gone and I couldn't find him."

No doubt Eustace had found his way to the rooms reserved for cards and joined a whist game, and Arthur most likely had gone out to blow a cloud with a group of his familiars.

"That is why it is most unfortunate for you to have come tonight without female companions."

"I already explained that, and surely you do not think I will come to any harm at Lady Sinclair's ball." Apparently Mr. Taber was not astute enough to notice Harriet's annoyance. Given her three older sisters, one sister-in-law, and a dutiful mother, Harriet almost never appeared in London society unaccompanied by any female relative.

Mr. Taber was near Eustace's age in his mid-thirties. His balding pate reflected the glow from the glittering chandelier overhead. An aggrieved expression crossed his face as he handed her the glass. "I do not approve of young girls drinking wine."

"Thank you," Harriet said sweetly. "I appreciate your sentiments, but the Sinclairs offer only wine or lemonade, and, as I said, lemonade has a most disagreeable effect upon my digestion." And she hoped that, by insisting upon a beverage of which he did not approve, she would forestall an offer from him.

She sipped the ruby liquid, turned to look at the dancers, and tapped her foot. "I have conceived the most violent hunger pangs. Could I trouble you to find me some little tidbits?"

A frown crossed his face. "Why did you not mention it when you sent me for the wine? It is most difficult making one's way through this crush. Oh, very well." Mr. Taber turned away.

Harriet waited until he had passed out of sight, then looked for George. To Harriet's advantage, his tallness and red hair would stand out, whereas he would have difficulty seeing her insignificant stature. No, she could not see him. Safe for the moment, she knew her respite would be brief.

This frantic need to flee her would-be suitors' attentions had increased along with her family's urgency to secure a husband for her. Her second fruitless season of seeking an eligible match had nearly ended, and Harriet still had received no suitable offer.

However, she would not consider marrying either the staid, prosy Lucretius Taber, or George Briscoe, with his stooped, lanky figure and moist hands. Both men were obviously working themselves up to a proposal. If she could but forestall them for a few short weeks . . .

Next year Astraea would come out, and no one would notice Harriet standing by her dazzling younger sister's side. Harriet planned to use this fact to persuade her parents to let her companion Great-Aunt Harriet and bypass the season altogether. She smiled.

Next year at this time, while Astraea collected scores of admirers in London, Harriet would be visiting exotic places and having adventures. A wealthy, eccentric spinster did not necessarily have to give up on having *amours*, Great-Aunt Harriet had told her, as long as she was discreet.

She had not shared her decision with her family. It was far easier to appear to go along with their design for her life than to openly rebel. Her mind returned to Lord Beldon, and her smile faded. Harriet would never simply accept a proposal unless it were a love match, and no one but Lord Beldon had captured her emotions. But he would never notice her.

Her family had said he would be a perfect match for her younger sister, but he was in town looking for a bride this season. Astraea's chance would come one year too late.

Harriet spotted George's flaming hair as he wended his way nearer to where she stood. A wave of panic struck her. The neglected wineglass still in her hand, Harriet bolted.

The tall double doors to the ballroom appeared immediately before her. The wide hallway led to other public rooms where voices resounded through open doors. No cover in any of those places. In one of those rooms stood long tables heaped with comestibles, and Mr. Taber would exit from the dining hall at any moment, bearing a plate of foodstuffs for her.

Discovery was imminent. Harriet tripped down the curving staircase, her free hand sliding along the polished mahogany banister. She paused at the bottom. The instinct to find a hiding place overcame logic, and she dashed along the corridor.

Rolleston Manning, Lord Beldon, settled a polite expression on his face to cover his boredom as he surveyed the guests at Lady Sinclair's ball.

"Have you found your bride?" the Earl of Rayfield asked. At two or so inches shorter than Beldon, he was of average height and had an oblong face with a high forehead.

"No, and with any luck she won't appear just yet. I've done my duty. Attended as many of the season's functions as I could fit into my schedule over the past six weeks. Suffered introductions to and conversation and dances with scores of young women. It's the same insipid faces at every gathering." Beldon raised a hand to cover a yawn.

"Ah, but you choose the prettiest of the young ladies. When I come to these affairs I always dance with the antidotes. Keeps all the hostesses happy and never tempts me to a greater acquaintance with them." Rayfield cast his penetrating gaze on the crowd in the ballroom, as though assessing which wallflower was most in need of rescue.

"Your family doesn't harp at you about the succession?"

"No, my mother's very understanding. 'Course, she knows I'm aware of my duty." His friend had inherited the title at a young age, as had Beldon. And though their circumstances were otherwise very different, they both had ample reason to be aware of the ephemeral nature of life. Still, Beldon had no wish to dwell upon such matters at present.

"So am I, damn it! Doesn't make a whit of difference to Grandmother. Still, I expect the search for a bride will take two or three years. By that time I'll be thirty—a good time to marry. I have high standards. My bride must be beautiful, graceful, socially adroit. Virtuous, naturally, and of course conversable and reasonably intelligent. After all, one can't spend all one's time in bed. Over the years one will occasionally have to chat with the woman."

He smiled. "Yes, if I must have a view to the necessity for an heir, I shall apply myself with dedication to doing the job properly."

Lady Sinclair approached them at that moment towing a tall, hatchet-faced young lady. "Ah, Lord Rayfield, may I present to you Miss Purdue as a suitable partner for the next dance."

Rayfield bowed and stepped away with his latest antidote. Unless Beldon missed his guess, Lady Sinclair would return instantly with a candidate for him. It was time he took his leave. He would go to his club, find a few friendly faces, take part in a game or two. Foolish to waste the entire evening.

Tomorrow he would visit Gentleman Jackson's rooms at Number Thirteen Bond Street to work off some of the restlessness and irritation at being forced to do the pretty among the ton.

At the foot of the stairs Beldon paused, looking for a footman to bring his cloak and hat, but none appeared. He felt too impatient to wait and went to get his own outerwear.

A few minutes later, cloak over his arm, Beldon returned down the dimly lit passageway alongside the staircase. He turned a corner. A fast-moving object struck him full force and bounced off his chest. A woman, he hazily realized. Knocked off balance himself, he grasped her arms to stop her fall, hearing glass shatter on the floor. From the solidity of their impact, he would not have expected her body to feel so soft against his, and his own body hardened in reaction.

He stared in complete befuddlement into the face of a young woman he had never seen before. "What the devil!"

She pulled back, ending the intimate press of their bodies, but still close enough that he felt her warmth.

"Oh, l-look what I've done! I b-beg your pardon," she said. Following her glance, he saw the girl's white gown and the white satin lining of his cloak were splashed with dark red fluid. *Blood?* The fruity scent rose to his nostrils. *No, wine.*

Beldon had not expected to encounter one of Lady Sinclair's guests, for so she appeared to be, making a mad rush through the halls and carrying a glass of wine.

She reached with a shaking hand into the tiny indispensable at her wrist, fumbling out a minuscule handkerchief, and began dabbing ineffectually at the stain on his cloak, still draped over his arm. Even through the multiple layers of cloth, he tingled at her touch, and heat spread through him. Some sort of flowery scent—hyacinths, perhaps?—wafted from the mass of silky dark blond hair beneath his chin as she bent to her task.

"Never mind that," Beldon grated at last. "My cloak doesn't matter." Despite his efforts to look away, he could not turn from the sight of her throat, sprinkled with ruby droplets. His gaze dropped lower to her breasts, their delectably rounded outlines visible against the sheer fabric of her wet dress. "It appears that your gown is ruined, however."

The girl swiped a hand at the dark stain on her bosom. "Oh, that. Now I shall not have to stay at the ball any longer. Even my brothers will see the necessity of taking me home." Her matter-of-fact tone revealed no hint of the stammer he had detected before, although some little mannerism that he could not identify remained in her speech. Perhaps a slight huskiness.

Prompted by some quixotic impulse—or the need to remove the temptation of that wine-splashed bosom from his sight—he draped his cloak around her shoulders and drew it closed.

She bit her lower lip, drawing his gaze to her mouth, full, and soft—and kissable. He stamped down the thought. He couldn't kiss a society miss unless he was courting her.

"I wonder, sir, would you mind finding my brother Eus—no, Arthur, that's better. Er, could you find Mr. Arthur Vernon and tell him his sister, ah, has had an accident, no, a slight mishap, and wishes to return home?"

He stared in shock. "*You* are one of Vare's daughters?"

"Yes. Nanny Ames always claimed I was a fairy changeling." She looked at him, a hint of challenge in her manner, and he regretted his unthinking words.

"No, I didn't mean . . . of course, you are as charming as your sisters. I only meant that you look quite unlike them."

She did look like a pixie, with a small, triangular face and her mop of unruly wheat-colored hair slipping from her coif. Her elfin hazel eyes twinkled at him.

"I know what you meant. It's all right. It's quite amusing to observe people's reactions."

"There must be a place to hi—er, wait while I find your brother."

"Yes, I suppose I should find it embarrassing to have someone happen upon me in this state. One of these doors must lead to sanctuary." She pushed open the nearest, which led into a dimly lit study empty of occupants. "I'll hide in here."

"You'll be all right?"

"Of course. I'm not injured."

He slowly backed away, his heel crunching in the broken glass. Where had she been this season? For the first time this spring, he had found someone to stir his interest. Beldon climbed the stairs back to the ballroom. Too bad Miss Vernon seemed so maladroit. Where had she been dashing so precipitously? Reaching the ballroom, he searched the crowd.

The Vernons had always been good *ton*, but he vaguely recalled some scandal connected with one of the older sisters a few years back. However, Miss Vernon's relief at being obliged to quit the party because of ruining her gown indicated a different character. Could she be merely shy?

She had a certain fresh attractiveness, but it was offset by her clumsiness and timidity. She entirely lacked the qualities he required, the beauty, dignity, and address he expected in a wife. Indeed, she appeared quite unsuitable as his baroness. He resumed the search for the younger Mr. Vernon, conscious of a lightening about his shoulders. It did not suit his purposes to unearth a candidate so soon.

After Lord Beldon had left, Harriet attempted to control her trembling. To avoid dwelling on her mortification, she thought of her arrival home, grateful that only her father would know of her latest blunder.

Scarcely aware of her actions, she hugged Lord Beldon's cloak to her, as if it could protect her from her thoughts. The room felt cool. A single candle burned on a side table near the dark fireplace. There was no place to sit except the chair behind a massive desk covered with untidily spread out papers.

She paced. Despite her efforts, her thoughts returned to her violent encounter with Lord Beldon. Running into him had been like crashing into a wall—a living wall. How could a man who appeared so trim prove such an immovable barrier?

When Harriet had looked up into Lord Beldon's startled face, she devoutly wished for fairy power to become invisible. The surroundings reeled around her and the hall lengthened eerily. She had feared she would faint, while at the same time she had longed to remain in his arms as long as he permitted.

While she looked about the study, unseeing, Harriet thought, *Lord Beldon of all people!* At least he had finally noticed her existence. Not that it could ever come to anything. She resisted an impulse to laugh hysterically.

"Good God, Harriet! What have you done now?" Eustace's voice carried its familiar scolding tones.

Drat! Couldn't Lord Beldon have done what she had asked? Both brothers stood in the doorway, confronting her. Arthur stared at her red-stained gown, his pale eyebrows lifted in amusement.

However, Eustace's face was choleric red as he railed at her, "How could you be so clumsy?"

"I didn't mean to spill the wine," she protested, then stiffened her pride to look straight at him instead of humbling herself. Eustace hardly represented perfection. In recent years, his tendency for *embonpoint* had become obvious.

Her eldest brother continued, "There's nothing for it. We must leave at once. I'll give our excuses to Lady Sinclair." He stomped away, mumbling about finding a footman to call for their carriage and bring Harriet's mantle.

His departure revealed Lord Beldon behind him in the corridor. He gave her a faint smile. "I apologize, Miss Vernon. Your brothers were together, about to search for you, I believe. I could not see any way to give only Arthur the message."

"'Tis no matter. Eustace did not mean anything, and I am used to his lectures." She blushed at Lord Beldon's witnessing still another blow to her pride. However, it hardly signified. She had wished for him to notice her, and she had made him aware of her existence, but her previous anonymity would have been preferred.

"If I might trouble you for my cloak, I'll be on my way."

"Oh. Of course." The garment was still draped over her shoulders. She tugged it off, turning the telltale stain to the inside, and held it out to Lord Beldon. As he took his cloak, their fingers brushed, and she shivered at the contact. Surely she was only chilled from losing the warmth the cloak had provided.

With a presence of mind she applauded, he seemed to sense she did not wish her brother to see the red stain. Lord Beldon tucked the cloak under his arm, bowed over her hand, and left.

Arthur smiled crookedly. "No harm done. George was disappointed, however. He looked for you. I believe he had a plate of food for you. I could find him and have him bring it."

"No! That is, I am not hungry any more."

"Well, I am sure he will call tomorrow."

Glumly, Harriet mused that her flight had accomplished nothing.

Chapter Two

Middle of June

"Oh, Beldon, your horses are such sweet goers."

A grin welled up from Beldon's chest to his mouth as the duns in question, trotting in perfect harmony, drew his curricle at a spanking pace. "Yes, they are, aren't they?" He looked at his companion, his satisfaction extending to her.

Mrs. Purvis, a curvaceous brunette with flawless peach skin and expressive brown eyes, was animated and witty. A widow, near his own age—perhaps a year or two older—she had been a loyal wife to her antediluvian husband, had mourned his death with perfect propriety, and was accepted everywhere. If, in the years since her husband's death, she had formed any liaisons, they had been conducted with circumspection. No hint of scandal had ever touched her, a consideration if word of Beldon's escort of her over the past few weeks reached his grandmother.

He could easily envision explaining that he enjoyed the widow's company, finding her more mature and sensible than the debutantes introduced to him over the course of the season, and that he had even begun to contemplate that she might do as his wife. Of course, it would take considerably longer acquaintance to make sure. Such an important matter required absolute assurances before he committed himself.

She made ideal company for a man supposed to be looking for a bride who had no wish to find one yet. Even her name, Docilla, was apt—not that he'd been given leave to use it.

"They are well behaved," Mrs. Purvis continued. "I am just dying to take the ribbons. It would be such a privilege."

"This is hardly the place," Beldon protested, looking about him at the bustling pathways of Hyde Park.

"I'm very adept at handling horses." The tempting widow brushed his arm caressingly. "My dear husband always said I should be left to manage my affairs without him and made sure I was taught many skills I might need in the years ahead. It would give me such pleasure," she smiled, her eyes promising an equal reward, "and you are right here to help me if I should need any assistance." She rubbed his shoulder.

He swallowed, his throat going dry while a surge of triumph rose in him. She had offered encouragement to his attentions, but never before had such promise beckoned.

Surely Mrs. Purvis would not exaggerate her accomplishments as a driver. And while the park bustled with activity, it was all orderly, with nothing to spook horses that were accustomed to city traffic. He handed the ribbons to her, moving in close, to guide her, of course.

"You must not sit so close. You are distracting me." Her smile took the sting from the words, and he obediently moved away slightly. She shook the reins and clucked to the horses.

Just then a small boy darted nearly under the hooves of his team. A shrieking nursemaid, following closely behind, snatched the boy just before he would have been crushed. The duns had never experienced such noise and motion. They swerved, wrenching control from the widow in a headlong charge.

Mrs. Purvis panicked, clinging to the reins and sawing at the horses' mouths.

"Give them to me!" Beldon shouted, but she showed no sign of hearing, her face so white he feared she was about to faint. Her death grip on the ribbons belied this, and he spent precious moments and all his strength to wrest them away.

Just as he gained control, the curricle rounded a turn and

Beldon saw with a sickening lurch a pair of horses on the path before him, one with a rider, and the other saddled but riderless. The second horse reared and ran away, and he saw a dark form lying on the path just beyond.

A collision was inevitable.

Still, he drew on his horses' reins and called to them. They responded to his commands, but, he feared, too late.

"Hold up a minute, Miss Harry. Pollux is limping." The groom, Elijah, dismounted and checked his mount's left front hoof. "He's cast a shoe. He'll go lame if he's rode."

"Just lead him home. I'll ride along slowly." Harriet matched her words to action, turning her chestnut mare about and suppressing her disappointment.

On such a fine spring day Harriet had wished for a full-out gallop, impossible on Hyde Park's busy pathways, but she had hoped for an invigorating trot at least. However, the number of people also brought out by the beautiful weather had forced Harriet and Elijah to a sedate walk. No sooner had they reached an opening in their path and let the horses out than the mishap with the shoe had occurred.

Harriet resigned herself to a caterpillar's crawl back home. Elijah, a small, wiry man who had been in her father's employ as long as Harriet could remember, walked along, his attention fixed on the limping gelding.

Just past a turning in the path, a fast-moving curricle suddenly bore down upon them.

Time stopped as calamity loomed. Pollux squealed, then shied and reared, tearing the reins from Elijah's hands. Knocked off balance, the groom fell, swearing. The gray took off, running between the trees.

Momentarily, Harriet froze, staring after Pollux. His headlong rush could lame the shoeless horse. Recalling her own danger, she gathered the reins to leap out of the way. But her heart nearly stopped when she saw Elijah flat on the ground, scrabbling to escape the oncoming vehicle.

He would be trampled. She must stay on the path as a barrier and pray the curricle's horses could stop in time. She held the reins firmly. Her mare's muscles quivered beneath her.

In a blur, Harriet saw the driver of the curricle haul back on the reins of his high-spirited horses, which plunged and bucked. His female passenger screamed and clung to his arm, impeding his efforts.

Harriet squeezed her eyes shut as the curricle bore down upon her. She heard the horses' hooves pound on the path and wheels crunch. The turbulence of the air blasted her.

The impact she expected didn't happen, though she could feel hot air blow against her gloved hand as a horse snorted. She opened her eyes to see the curricle stopped a hair's-breadth short of her and her mare. Miraculously, the team's sharp shoes had missed the yelling groom.

Completely panicked now, their lines tangled beyond the driver's control, the carriage horses pawed and reared again. From her own mount, Harriet reached out and grabbed the line of the left-hand horse. She dragged him to all fours just as Elijah rolled out of the way. She hung on and talked soothingly as the horse rolled its eyes and tossed its head.

The pair, exquisite, pale duns the color of antique ivory, were as terrified as any of the participants in the drama. Once she had quieted the closer one, she nudged her mare over so she could catch the ribbons of the off horse, also. Then she exhaled, feeling some of her fear drain away.

She raised her gaze to the driver. Deep blue eyes met hers—Lord Beldon! Her stomach fluttered at seeing him, despite the close call. He leaped down and came to her side, taking over the reins. "Are you all right?" he asked in a shaky voice.

"I th-think so." Her voice shook, and she turned away and dismounted to look after her prostrate groom.

Elijah lay still, his color chalky, and for a heart-stopping moment she feared he had been killed after all. He moaned and tried to rise. "Don't move! Where are you hurt?"

"I wrenched my ankle, is all," he admitted. "I be all right 'cept for that."

Lord Beldon peered over her shoulder. "May I help?"

Harriet spun, waving her riding crop, the fear that had flooded through her transformed to fury. "Yes! Race your curricle where you don't risk other people's lives. How *could* you run your cattle so recklessly? This is a public pathway. Are you lost to all concern for the harm you might do others?"

"My most sincere apologies, Miss Vernon. I take it that no one is seriously hurt?"

Ignoring him, Harriet returned her attention to the groom, who rose stiffly. "I need to find Pollux, Miss Harry. He's likely done himself an injury running away like that."

"We'll find him, Elijah. Mount up behind me and we'll go look."

"Oh, Miss, I couldn't do that. It'ud be very improper."

"Moonshine. It would be more improper for me to ride off and leave you in your condition. And you can't find the horse with your own injured foot."

"I'll help you search," Lord Beldon offered.

Harriet gave his curricle a disdainful look. "You can't take *that* where a riderless horse might go."

"Miss Vernon, your groom could drive Mrs. Purvis and you home, while I unsaddle your horse and search for the runaway."

She observed the face of Beldon's companion. The lady frowned at Beldon's offer, and Harriet replied, "Look at your team, Beldon—all lathered up, with their sides heaving from their treatment at your hands. After seeing your manner of handling horses, I would never trust *my* livestock to you."

Lord Beldon's expression became rigid. "Very well. I shan't trouble you any further, then." His back was stiff as he went back to his curricle.

Elijah helped Harriet to remount, then, with a hand from her, clambered on behind. Together they trotted after the missing animal, leaving Lord Beldon and his carelessness behind. Now that the danger had passed, Harriet's body felt boneless, as if it wanted to slip from the saddle. She was glad of Elijah's support to hold her upright. Feeling Beldon's eyes upon her, she proudly stiffened her own spine.

Beldon chuckled as he watched the two ride away. Miss Vernon had invoked an image of an angry, stamping pixie as she railed at him. His momentary amusement faded quickly, and guilt surfaced instead at the near disaster he had almost caused. He'd been a fool to give in to Mrs. Purvis's urgent pleas to allow her to take the reins.

"What an unmannerly hoyden that young woman is," Mrs. Purvis said, breaking into his thoughts.

Beldon frowned. A surge of protective instincts toward Miss Vernon shot through him at this slight. Undoubtedly her cool head had averted a greater tragedy. He did not reply to Mrs. Purvis, but a chill invaded his regard for her.

He drove the widow to her home and returned home himself, ordering the stableboy to walk his team and cool them down. Seeing their sweat-dampened coats and weary droop, a new wave of guilt washed over him.

He pictured Miss Vernon suddenly—how she had controlled her mare and kept her from bolting, standing protectively over her groom. What courage that had required. She could easily have avoided the danger of being run over by his duns, but at the cost of almost certain serious injury to her groom.

And she had gentled his horses, at the same time as she had taken him to task for his foolhardiness. She had given him an entirely different impression of her personality than in their first encounter, and he found it intriguing.

She could not be considered a potential Lady Beldon, of course. In the weeks since their mishap at Lady Sinclair's ball, he had seen Miss Vernon at a number of social functions. On every occasion she had been at pains to disappear into the background, and he had had to conclude she was devoid of poise. Indeed, even though she was reasonably attractive, he concluded he would never have noticed her but for their precipitate introduction.

In the unknown future, after he finally married, he would wish to spend some of his time in town, and entertaining his peers would be an important feature of that time. What little thought he had given to the acquiring of a wife had included the picture of receiving guests at his home, his wife, cool, beautiful, and totally composed, standing beside him. Miss Vernon would never do.

Still, he owed her an apology. He decided to send her flowers with a discreetly worded note, in case she gave her family an abbreviated version of the mishap.

The next day, a downstairs maid brought Harriet a bouquet of purple hyacinths, with a note from Lord Beldon. Apprehensively, she scanned the note, but it said only, "With regards, Beldon."

She breathed a sigh of relief. No apologetic words, or questions about her success in finding the horse—nothing she would have difficulty explaining. Upon her return home the previous day, she and Elijah had explained that Pollux had stumbled when he'd lost his shoe, causing Elijah's fall and twisted ankle.

She arranged the flowers in a vase on her dressing table. Would Lord Beldon attend Lady Caledon's musicale tonight? How could she face him again? It seemed she was doomed to disgrace herself whenever she encountered him.

Harriet's face burned when she recalled their two meetings. First she had irrefutably demonstrated her clumsiness, and then topped that by exhibiting her temper.

By good fortune, her family did not know how utterly she had disgraced herself on both occasions. Her brothers assumed her stained gown to be the only mishap at the Sinclairs', and she did not correct their misapprehension. And no one in her family knew of the near calamity yesterday.

Mama was out of town, lending support to Harriet's sister, Iphigenia, finally *enceinte* with her first child after suffering a miscarriage the previous year. A fortnight ago, when

Mother had learned that Genie had contracted a chill, she had raced to her side. Lady Vare had a genius for detecting when Harriet landed in the briars. She would not have escaped a closer examination from her dam.

She would not refine upon it any further. Lord Beldon and she had attended the same functions several times since the *contretemps* at the Sinclairs' ball, and, beyond a slight smile of recognition when his eyes met hers, he paid her no more attention than before. Doubtless he would act the same way now. If anything, he should be the one embarrassed. He had, after all, been heedless in his disregard for the safety of others.

And she should not spend so much time thinking of him—his appealing smile, the broad, athletic shoulders, the way his black hair curled. Her family had eliminated him from the list of possible suitors at the outset of the season as above her touch. Besides, she despised people who showed so little concern for the welfare of their horses. If only he weren't so handsome.

That evening, Harriet stood on the tiny balcony leading off the Caledons' music room, breathing in warm, summer-scented air. On the other side of the French doors, Lady Thomasina Towland screeched her way through a traditional ballad, though her voice was muted. Harriet had been escaping Lady Thomasina's attempts at singing as much as George Briscoe's renewed attentions.

"Lovely evening, isn't it?" Lord Beldon's baritone came from behind Harriet, and she jumped and turned. He moved to stand beside her.

Had the balcony railing been a living being, it would have cried out at her cruel grip. However, she managed to make her voice sound almost normal. "Yes, it is."

"I am sure you could sing much better than the performers who have entertained us tonight." His tone almost conveyed diffidence, had that been possible for the haughty Lord Beldon.

Harriet forced herself to relax her grip on the ornamental iron, loath to have him notice her white knuckles in the early June twilight. "Actually, I'm afraid I cannot. My voice always gives way under the strain of singing. They have even requested that I please not sing the hymns aloud in church at home. But growing up as I did surrounded by accomplished musicians, it pains me to hear a lovely melody tortured almost beyond recognition."

Now that Miss Vernon had mentioned her voice, Lord Beldon noticed again the funny little breathy catch, a huskiness that came and went. Undoubtedly it would impede her singing, but it made listening to her speak a delight. Would this idiosyncrasy become tiresome over time? Beldon thought not; it merely added character to an otherwise ordinary speaking voice, and fit her fey appearance. The last lingering light of the summer evening played upon her features, highlighting her tilted eyes and the little smile on her lips. He wanted to stay with her, basking in the sight.

"But undoubtedly you play an instrument, Miss Vernon."

She gave a little laugh. "You are confusing me with my sisters and brothers, Lord Beldon. I told you I am the changeling in my family. Eustace and Arthur both sing—Eustace in particular has a very fine voice, and Arthur has quite a talent in drama as well as painting. Pallas plays the harp; Iphigenia paints and draws; Clytie plays the pianoforte; and Astraea has a voice like an angel and dramatic ability. Even my younger brothers, Ambrose and Lionel, show signs of musical and artistic talent."

"And you have no abilities at all?" he teased.

"Oh, I am accounted a bruising rider. I can take any jump my brothers can."

"Sidesaddle? That is an accomplishment indeed." In truth he was impressed, but not surprised, remembering her expert handling of her mount the day before.

Miss Vernon must have recalled the same incident, because she blushed and visibly shrank, suddenly transformed into the shy, awkward girl he had first met. "I-I must apologize for m-my behavior yesterday, Lord Beldon. I was mortified when my t-temper had cooled, and I realized how I had affronted you. I tend to l-lose my head when I get angry, but I had no right to pass judgment on you."

"No, indeed, Miss Vernon, 'tis I who must apologize. It was the worst moment in my life when I realized the disaster my poor judgment almost caused. How is your groom?"

"He merely suffered a sprain. He will be entirely recovered in a few weeks."

"And the runaway horse?"

"Pollux is fine. What about Mrs. Purvis? I do not see her here tonight. I hope she did not suffer any ill effects?"

"To the best of my knowledge, Mrs. Purvis took no hurt. She had another engagement this evening. I believe she planned to arrive here somewhat late." He heard the stiffness in his own voice, and knew it unfair. He could not reasonably blame that woman for his own lapse in judgment.

However, the widow had not shown concern for the injured man or remorse for the potential serious harm to others. In contrast, Miss Vernon had displayed her worry for her groom and for his horses as well as her own, and even now, for Mrs. Purvis.

"May I call upon you, Miss Vernon?" The words surprised him as they left his mouth.

An incredulous look passed across her face. "Upon *m-me*?" Her voice gave a little squeak.

"Why, yes. I assure you, I do not normally abuse my horses, or put others at risk, for that matter."

She smiled, causing a flash of dimple at the corner of her mouth, and drawing his attention to her lips again—could they possibly be as soft against his own as he imagined?

"I'm sure you do not. You may call if you wish."

Momentarily, he could not drag his attention from her mouth, or attend her words. He forced his gaze out into the Caledons' garden. Night had fallen, and he could see nothing beyond the small circle cast by the candlelight from inside the house. He had spent more time alone with Miss Vernon than he should. "Good. I had better leave now, or my remaining with you will cause gossip."

* * *

Clytie and Lettice both swooped upon Harriet when she reentered the music room.

"What were you thinking to be out on the balcony with Lord Beldon?" whispered Clytie, tugging at Harriet's arm, moving them to a less conspicuous corner.

"I hear you were screaming like a fishwife at Beldon right in Hyde Park yesterday. What inspired you to exhibit your temper for all to hear?" Lettice spoke from her other side.

"What?" Harriet slowly emerged from the daze into which Lord Beldon's words had immersed her.

Clytie looked at her in concern. "He didn't make you any improper advances, did he?"

A bubble of laughter burst inside her. "Heavens, no, Clytie, this is me you're talking to. Harriet, remember? No one makes improper advances to *me!*" The plaintive note in her voice surprised her. No woman would wish to be the object of such gallantries, would she? An image of Lord Beldon enfolding her in his arms sent a wave of longing through her and gave the lie to that sentiment.

Her sister and sister-in-law looked at each other, eyes wide and mouths gaping open almost identically. "I'll find Eustace and Lord Robert," Clytie said. "Take her to the ladies' retiring room. I'll make our excuses and we'll take her home."

Lettice nodded and led Harriet away.

"I'm perfectly fine," Harriet insisted.

"You are most unwell," Lettice hissed. "You had a dizzy spell and stepped out on the balcony hoping fresh air would revive you. Lord Beldon happened upon you and attended you until you recovered sufficiently and then came to inform us."

"No, really . . . " Harriet protested in vain as her sister-in-law bore her willy-nilly to the room set aside for the ladies' refreshment. If her family made a great fuss over this, he'd never wish to call on her.

Oh, whom am I fooling? Surely his words were mere politeness. He must not have realized she was there when he stepped out on the balcony. Once he saw her, he could not withdraw without seeming rude. He did very properly apologize for causing Elijah's injury. Once he'd said that, he probably couldn't think how to end the conversation.

Harriet huddled in her chair, wrenching her body as far from Lettice as possible while they waited in the withdrawing room. The glimpse she caught of herself in the mirror assured her she was pale enough to make plausible the lie about her illness that Lettice told any guest who entered the room.

When they were at last alone, Lettice said, "You have not explained your behavior to Lord Beldon yesterday."

"How did you come to hear of it?" Harriet asked.

"Docilla Purvis told me just now how you imposed upon Lord Beldon's goodness and blamed him for the whole of it, when he went to see if he could help after Elijah's accident. I could hardly believe it of you, Harriet. Normally you are such a quiet, polite young woman. I can imagine only that you thought to bring yourself to his notice by such tactics. It won't work, you know. The best you can hope for is to give him a disgust for you with such hoydenish ploys."

How she could repair the damage Mrs. Purvis's misleading narrative had done, she couldn't imagine. If she told the whole truth now, it would only reveal how much she had omitted before, causing a great stir.

"It wasn't exactly like that, Lettice."

"Do you mean Mrs. Purvis lied? Why would she do that?"

"I didn't say she lied, exactly. It just didn't happen quite as she said. Oh, never mind." Perhaps Mrs. Purvis would not lie, but she had definitely tried to make Harriet look culpable in the near accident. Remembering how that lady had panicked and clung to Beldon while he tried to control his team, Harriet thought she was a little responsible for what had happened.

But her thoughts about Beldon were too jumbled to concentrate on defending herself.

At length Clytie returned to say the carriage awaited and the men were prepared to leave.

Once under way, Eustace turned to Harriet. "I cannot believe you would engage in such reckless behavior when we have hopes that at least one offer will shortly be made for you. Lucretius Taber will not like to have the reputation of his bride called into question, let me tell you."

"If you were in hopes you would catch Beldon's eye, you were exceedingly foolish," Clytie said. "We warned you at the beginning of the season that he will look higher for his bride."

He said he would call on me. She kept seeing Lord Beldon: the blue eyes vivid in his patrician face, the crisp curls she longed to touch, his large presence looming over her, stimulating all her senses. She went over his words, from their first encounter to "May I call upon you?" What hidden meanings could she detect? What did he truly think of her?

"Harriet! You are not paying attention!" Eustace's booming voice finally penetrated.

"What? Oh, Eustace, Lettice was right about my being unwell. I have developed the most fearsome headache." She punctuated these words by lying back against the squabs of the carriage, closing her eyes.

She sensed shock in her family's silence: Harriet was never ill. She smiled secretly. Glancing up, she caught Lord Robert's eyes upon her. He winked, and she hugged to herself the knowledge that Clytie's husband sympathized with her.

At home, Harriet escaped to her chamber, refusing offers of company or a tisane to cure her headache. She didn't have to worry about interruption, as she would have in the country, where she shared a chamber with Astraea.

She paced and recalled the discussion, when the Vernons had first arrived in town for the season, concerning which eligible bachelors to add to the list of prospects.

"Lord Beldon is in town. He's said to be looking to take a wife this season," Lady Vare had reported.

"He won't look at Harriet. Handsome as an Adonis, and with his estates and financial affairs in excellent order," Clytie had at once dismissed.

"What a pity he is looking for a bride this year." Pallas shook her head at this disappointment. "Astraea would be the ideal match for him. They would make a most beautiful couple. But we cannot tell him to go home and come back next year."

Yes, Harriet agreed, Lord Beldon's dark perfection and Astraea's luminous loveliness would make a romantic pairing. Such depressing thoughts made a disagreeable accompaniment to her solitude. Harriet wished she were a true changeling, but she had no gift of fairy magic to turn herself into a beauty.

Chapter Three

Harriet told herself Beldon did not truly intend to call upon her, and in any case had not mentioned a specific day. Nevertheless, on the following afternoon she remained home.

Although Beldon did not call, George Briscoe did, and spoke with her father in Lord Vare's study. Heart sinking, Harriet obeyed her father's summons after George had departed.

"Well, Harriet," Lord Vare greeted her from behind his desk, "it appears I am about to lose you." Despite the tenor of his words, a satisfied smile split his ruddy, still-handsome face.

"Why, Papa?" She fixed an innocent look on her face.

A testy frown crossed his features. "Do not be dense, Harriet; you know Mr. Briscoe called to ask permission to pay his addresses to you. He is a most suitable match and has satisfied me that he will care for you excellently."

"What if I do not wish to marry him, Papa?" Her father would not force her to marry George. *Would he?* Her stomach constricted at the thought.

"Nonsense, my girl." He rose and came around the desk, patting her on the shoulder. "Mr. Briscoe will be back tomorrow for your answer. If you think about the advantages, you will lose your missishness. It's natural to have doubts over such a serious step." He planted a perfunctory kiss on her forehead and turned her toward the door.

Normally not inclined to melodrama—that was her younger sister Astraea's forte—the remainder of the day was much given over to this state, picturing various scenarios should she refuse George's offer. What if Papa constrained her to accept?

She quailed to think of running away to some refuge. She knew of no safe place; none of her sisters would have any sympathy. Great-Aunt Harriet would gladly harbor her namesake, but she was traveling in South America. The next time Great-Aunt Harriet went on one of her extended journeys, Harriet intended to accompany her. For this to come about, she must avoid becoming trapped into marriage.

The previous season, Harriet had received two offers. Her refusal of the first, from a widower in his fifties, caused no stir in her family. Her father turned down the second on her behalf once the family had determined the suitor was insolvent and looked to Harriet's expectations to repair his family fortunes.

That Harriet had attracted the attentions of a fortune hunter occasioned concern among her family. To forestall such an event they had decided not to divulge her special status as Great-Aunt Harriet's principal heiress—unless such a drastic measure was required to get her off their hands. Piers Luchan's proposal had caused a flurry of worry that her expectations somehow had become general knowledge.

From her family's point of view, however, there was nothing wrong with George—except that Harriet could not stand the thought of being married to him.

A second night in a row of disturbed sleep did not give her any insights on her situation. Her wan, heavy-eyed image in the looking glass the following morning persuaded her that George would probably take himself off after her refusal with good grace and mayhap even a feeling of happy escape.

Her abigail, Mary, picked out a morning gown of pale green, trimmed at the hem with laurel embroidered in deeper green. The girl babbled excitedly about Harriet's impending betrothal as she dressed her mistress, then brushed her hair. Mary took more time than Harriet would usually sit still for, pinning up her hair, letting some curls loose about her cheeks.

"Just think, miss, after today your life will be changed. Shall I accompany you to your new home?"

Harriet returned a noncommittal answer, surprised, not that the servants knew about the proposal, but that the household assumed her acquiescence to the match. She listlessly endured her maid's attentions, dreading to think of the coming storm.

Her family left her alone in the gold salon to await her suitor. When George was shown in, she almost underwent a change of heart. When he was out of view, Harriet forgot his kindness.

"Dearest Harriet." He frowned and his mouth twisted, as though more words would issue forth if he could think of them. He crossed the room and pulled her into his arms.

She wriggled free. "Mr. Briscoe, you forget yourself."

"But Harry, we are to be married." Towering over her, he looked comically puzzled. "I would not go beyond the bounds, but surely . . . "

"You may have my father's consent to a match, but you do not have mine."

His brow cleared. "Of course! How forgetful of me. I had a fine speech all memorized, too." He knelt in front of her.

George gripped her ungloved hands, and, tall as he was, his head was level with her bosom, which seemed to draw his gaze somewhat more than her face. "Miss Vernon—Harriet—please do me the very great honor of accepting my hand and heart."

Harriet's sense of the ridiculous almost overcame her gravity, but his ceremonious words helped her to recall her lessons on replying to a proposal in form. She said gently, "Mr. Briscoe, I thank you for your offer, but fear I must decline. I do not feel for you those tender feelings that are proper between a husband and wife. I fear we should not suit."

He arose slowly to his feet. "I do not understand. Your father said . . . "

"My father does not speak for me, Mr. Briscoe. I cannot

marry you. Let us say no more about it." She held out her hand. "May we part friends?"

Involuntarily, he took her hand and shook it. "Of course, Harry—er, Miss Vernon. Friends." His expression blank with shock, he walked out of the room.

She wiped her palms on the skirts of her gown. She heard Arthur speaking to his best friend in the hall. Although she could not hear the words, she was sure he stated his assumption George and his sister had come to an agreement. "*She refused?*" His voice boomed through the door, and Harriet cringed.

Instantly, she was surrounded by her entire family—those presently in town. She closed her eyes against the accusing eyes and milling bodies. She could still hear all too well.

"What were you thinking of?" from Lettice.

Papa: "Harriet, I told you not to let missish objections interfere with your clear thinking."

Arthur: "How am I to face him again? I told him we should be brothers-in-law."

"Do you think you will get a better offer?" Clytie.

And Eustace: "Were you thinking of Lucretius Taber? I suppose he may still be brought up to scratch, but you've rather put him off with your disregard of conventions, Harriet."

"Goodness, no! If you have any influence on Mr. Taber, please keep him from asking to marry me."

The furor increased.

"I don't wish to marry at all. I'm going to travel with Great-Aunt Harriet."

"You'll do no such thing," Papa shouted. "Where did you get such a hair-witted notion? Harriet Sutton is not a proper chaperone for you. And going to all those dangerous places."

"I won't marry without love, and anyone I could love would not have me." An image of Lord Beldon came to her mind, and she firmly pushed it away.

"That nodcock George Briscoe was ready enough," Eustace said. "And Taber is close to declaring himself."

"I don't love them!" Harriet threw her hands up over her head and readied herself to run.

"My Lord Beldon," announced the butler, Bolster.

Beldon heard the Babel of voices as soon as the Vernons' butler opened the door to the salon. *Oh, oh!* He nearly backed away and fled, but it was too late, for he heard his name. He stepped into the room and paused.

The room was done in gold and white, chandeliers and gilt mirrors. A frozen tableau met his eyes, Miss Vernon in the center, looking like a vixen surrounded by a pack of slavering hounds. A blazing smile lit her face at his arrival.

"Good afternoon," he said affably. "I do hope this is not an awkward time to call."

"Not at all, not at all. Come in," said Vare. He stepped away from the rest of his family and stood more erect.

"Please sit, Lord Beldon." The brown-haired, plump woman must be Mrs.—Eustace, was it?—Vernon, wife of the heir. She matched her actions to her words, sinking onto a graceful, white-upholstered Sheraton chair with gilt legs.

He had to give the Vernons credit for social aplomb. They recovered their composure with notable speed. At Mrs. Vernon's words, they seated themselves as if they had expected callers.

"Good contest today at Jackson's, eh?" Arthur grinned and stretched his arms along the back of the settee. "You were sparring in top form. Think you could have taken Jackson?"

"In his prime? No, never." He gave Arthur a cold stare for raising a topic unsuitable in the presence of ladies and changed the subject. "How do you do, Miss Vernon?"

"I am well."

Now that he had interrupted whatever squabble had been occurring when he walked in, she beamed at him as her deliverer. What sort of scrape had she fallen into now?

"Let me ring for some tea," Mrs. Vernon said.

Miss Vernon looked at him in appeal. Hoping he correctly

interpreted, he said, "Actually, I called only to inquire whether Miss Vernon would care to go out driving with me."

"Oh, yes." She jumped up. "I'll just run and get my shawl." She hesitated and looked at her father.

"Go on, puss. Enjoy yourself," Vare said heartily.

Mrs. Vernon objected, "She isn't dressed for a drive."

"She looks charming as she is," Beldon said. "I don't want to keep my horses standing too long."

"Oh, Lettice, it will take too long to change," Miss Vernon protested.

"Let the child be," Vare said.

"Yes, Papa." Mrs. Vernon pouted.

"Thank you, Papa." Harriet hugged him, then rushed out of the room. She returned in a few minutes with a white shawl draped over her shoulders, wearing a high-crowned bonnet with green ribbons. "Shall we go?"

Beldon smiled at her eagerness, which he surmised had more to do with escape from her family than delight in his presence. He gave her his arm and helped her up into his curricle. She tucked the skirts of her gown carefully so they would not fly up. His tiger, Colley, handed him the reins to the duns, then jumped up behind as they set off.

Instead of Hyde Park, Beldon made for a road out of town. He wanted to talk to Miss Vernon, not stop and jaw at all their acquaintances. While he handled the ribbons among the heavy traffic of town, she said nothing. The breeze created by their motion and the bright sunlight caressed her upturned face, as though she let them erase her worries.

Shortly, they broke free of the busier streets and he let the duns out to trot at a spanking pace along a quieter road.

Miss Vernon grasped the hem of her gown, which had worked free and fluttered. He glimpsed her trim lower limbs, causing him to catch his breath.

"I shall have to think of you as a knight of chivalry after this," she said with a glance at him.

He grinned at her glowing, elfin face. "Fell into the briars again, did you? What was it this time?" he teased.

"It was not my fault, I assure you." The sparkle dimmed, and she looked down at her hands, folded in her lap. Her quicksilver transformation hit him like a blow.

"I believe you always say that." Beldon chuckled, trying to recapture Miss Vernon's previous carefree mood.

"That is unf-fair. You don't know me well enough to m-m-make such a claim. It *was* my fault when I spilled wine on your cloak, *not* my fault when you almost ran over my groom, and n-nobody's fault when you talked to me on the balcony."

"Got into trouble over that, too?" He frowned. "We weren't together more than a few minutes."

"Indeed, and our conversation was innocent, too, but I can never convince my family of that."

Given the surprising impurity of his thoughts toward her that night, he had to concede her family's astuteness. That night? Gad, he'd had wicked thoughts of her since the first time they'd met. To direct the conversation away from this uncomfortable track, he said, "How did you end up with the name 'Harriet' when the rest of your family has classic names?"

She laughed. "I was named for Great-Aunt Harriet. No one has said so, but I believe when Mama saw my changeling appearance, she and Papa decided they should never get me off their hands unless I had a fortune."

"Naming you after your great-aunt was supposed to ensure your receiving a fortune?" Whenever the traffic allowed, he stole a look at her. She sat primly beside him, her cheeks pinkened from the wind and sunshine, strands of honey-colored hair working loose from the confinement of their pins and her bonnet to fly about her face.

"Yes. Great-Aunt Harriet has pots of money. She was betrothed to a clerk for the East India Company. Her parents disapproved of the match, and she stowed away on a ship bound for India to join him. When she arrived, she learned her intended had perished of a fever. He had left her everything in his will, though it was just a few gems. She stayed on in India for years, learned all about gems and turned her inheritance into a fortune. It wasn't an easy life for a woman alone."

Harriet's glowing eyes gave Beldon an uneasy feeling. "Did she ever marry?"

She raised a hand to adjust her hat, looking up at him from under the brim. "No, she says marriage cages a woman and keeps her from living as she wishes. She's had adventures, traveled all over the world. She could never have done all of those things if she had married. I always wanted to be just like her."

"If you have no ambitions to marry, why are you in London for the marriage mart?"

"Oh, my family says the only proper course for a woman is to marry. For all they named me after her, they don't approve of Great-Aunt Harriet. When I don't find a husband, I expect they'll give up on me soon enough." She raised her face, alive with merriment, to Beldon's, and he chuckled along with her.

In the sunshine her hazel eyes reflected a clear green, nearly matching her gown. His whole body tightened with aching need. He must fight this temptation. A gently bred young lady like Miss Vernon could not be treated like a Cyprian. Looking about for a distraction, he recognized the area. Small villas lined the street on both sides.

"There's a small park ahead. We might take a little walk." He pulled up the horses, handed the reins over to the tiger, and helped Miss Vernon down. "Take the horses around and come back in half an hour," he told Colley.

The park was very small, intended for the owners of the villas surrounding the green. The gate into it was locked, but the fence was low, not much over two feet. Beldon stepped over it, then reached to give Miss Vernon a hand into the park.

She hesitated, her expression a mixture of caution and mischief. "If we are caught, it will mean trouble."

"If they didn't want people in their park, they should have built a higher fence," Beldon said.

With a shrug and an impish smile, she gave him her hand.

Her jaunty demeanor inspired in him a reckless mood that swamped every other thought. He strode to a tree-filled glade, still holding her hand, and she trailed along, laughing breathlessly, nearly running to keep up with his long steps. "Where are we going?" she asked.

"There's a pond here, with swans."

"You've been here before?"

"No, but what sort of park would it be if it had neither pond nor swans?"

"Oh!" They had rounded a turn in the path, and there it was—a pond, complete with a pair of swans. "How lovely. But you lied to me. You must have seen this before."

"You do not happen to have any bread to feed them?"

She laughed. "No, I'm afraid it never occurred to me to carry bread with me today. A lamentable oversight."

Beldon swung her around to face him, hands on her upper arms, and stared down at her face, enjoying the emotions that played across it, fading gradually from laughter to puzzlement.

"What is it? Do I have a smudge or something?"

"No. I just want to study you."

She made as if to turn away. "I'm not an edifying study."

"Nonsense," he whispered and bent toward her. One kiss certainly could do no harm.

She startled and made as if to pull away, but he held her firmly, his lips not quite touching hers until he felt her relax and lean toward him. It felt even better to kiss her than he had imagined. Her lips were full and soft, meeting his with a tremble, then more boldly.

He was overwhelmed by passion. He deepened the kiss and lifted her, drawing her body against his, her breasts pressing against his chest, her legs intertwined with his, their hips fitted together. She gasped at the intimate contact and pushed at him, but a moment later she relaxed. He trailed a furrow of kisses down her chin and jaw to her throat.

He was completely lost, thinking only of having more of her. He let her slide down so her feet again touched the ground. Untying the tapes at the back of her gown, Beldon pulled the neckline forward to expose her breasts. He slid his hand over the ivory flesh, sighing at the smoothness to his touch, then bent to press his lips to them.

She shivered and her eyes closed. Her head turned a little aside and a moan escaped her lips.

A wisp of thought tugged at his conscience, reining his passion. He lifted his head and gazed at her. Her lips were swollen from his kisses. The dimness of the leafy shadows restored the golden brown in her eyes, glazed with desire. He read surrender there, and that brought him back to his senses.

He recalled her tentative responses. She had not known how to kiss until he had shown her. Good Gad, she was an innocent, not some doxy with whom he could take whatever liberties he wished. There was only one honorable course for him now. He gulped and plunged ahead, giving himself no time for reflection or drawing back. "Harriet! You must marry me!"

"No, don't—" Her voice was blurred and sleepy, and she blinked her weighted lids, her expression confused.

He laid his hand alongside her cheek. "Miss Vernon—Harriet, I won't try to tell you I love you. We don't know each other well enough for that. However, I think what just happened should convince you that we shall deal with each other extremely well. I pledge myself to make you a good husband, and . . . "

"Ye-es," she said. "I will marry you." A crease furrowed her forehead. "That is . . . You did mean it, didn't you?"

"Of course." Now that the words had been said, he wasn't certain. What had he just done? Betrothed himself to a girl he scarcely knew. At the same time that a trapped feeling made him wish to draw back, unsay the words, the pulsing in his body gave him a great desire to take her back into his arms and finish what they had started.

"Would you kiss me again?" she asked.

He drew a shaky breath. "I don't think I'd better."

"Why not?"

Almost roughly he grasped her shoulders and turned her around with her back to him and refastened her gown with shaking fingers. Her body felt almost boneless and he had to support her or she would have fallen. "Because if I kissed you again right now, I wouldn't stop until I had ruined you."

"Oh," she said softly. "I wouldn't mind."

"Dear Lord," he muttered, "give me strength. *I* would. Do something with your hat; it's all askew." She lifted it and brushed back the locks of hair that had fallen from their pins. With unsteady fingers, she crushed the hat back over the curls so her hairdo looked almost neat again. Except for the spots of bright color on her cheeks, her complexion was very pale. He led her back to the curricle.

Harriet wished Beldon would say something, but his rigid posture did not bode well. He said nothing beyond curt commands to his horses, which he drove at a pace she thought reckless. Harriet stole frequent glances at him. His stern face discouraged initiating any conversation.

She knew the reason for his grim mood. He didn't want to marry her—any more than she wanted to marry him. It was all a terrible mistake, brought on by her state of bemusement from his kisses and his sense of obligation.

Now she had given her word, which put her under equal obligation. What had happened to her determination not to marry? Of course, she hadn't actually vowed never to marry, only not to marry without love on both sides. Even Great-Aunt Harriet had said she would have married her dear Milton had he not died. And although Harriet didn't love Beldon, her emotions were perilously close to it. He had stated he didn't love her, however. What should she do?

This awkward muddle was all her fault. She most certainly should have resisted his kisses. Her sisters had given her a thorough grounding in what passed between men and women, which should have prepared her for what might happen. How could anyone prepare for the powerful effect of those kisses? Once his lips had touched hers, why, she had had no thought of anything but the warmth coursing through her. Indeed, she had enthusiastically participated instead.

When he proposed, she could have laughed off their indiscretion. Nothing had *really* happened. Great-Aunt Harriet had implied a single woman might have some measure of the pleasures to be found between men and women if she were discreet. She had been unable to think at the moment Beldon had asked that crucial question.

Should she go on with this betrothal? She would work hard to make him happy and give him an heir—several heirs! If their moments in the park were an indication of what the marriage bed held in store, begetting heirs would be a most joyous duty.

Chapter Four

With difficulty, Beldon imposed dominion over his churning emotions. The narrow curricle seat almost forced him to touch Harriet, but he clung to the edge of the seat, minimizing their contact. Her touch had driven him to lose control only minutes before, and he daren't test his self-discipline again. Something about Harriet beguiled him. In fact, his arousal had not yet completely abated.

However, even had he wished for a bride so soon, she was not the bride he wanted. Not beautiful or graceful, and certainly she had no social skills. He had pictured a wife who would make every man envy him. No one would envy him Harriet.

She must have been desperate to snabble a husband to allow him such liberties, especially as untutored as she clearly was. He frowned. But she had told him she did not intend to marry.

Yet, she hadn't even waited for him to finish his proposal before she had agreed. Was that her aim all along, despite her words about not marrying? In that case she should be satisfied with this day's work. Triumphant, even.

A quick glance told him Harriet did not look triumphant. If anything, she looked close to tears. The sadness in her face tripped something in his heart.

Still, the trap he had sprung upon himself nearly suffocated him. His life was about to change irrevocably—far before he was ready.

He let his horses out, barely reining them enough for control, and giving no relief to the rage at his folly. He had already let his passions overcome his good sense. *What a coil!*

As Beldon finally drew the curricle to a stop in front of Harriet's house, his head spun with confusion. He ushered her in, saying, "I'll talk to your father now." Harriet nodded, her eyes worried, and hurried upstairs as if the devil pursued her. Did she fear her father would be angry? Beldon had no intention of revealing how the betrothal had come about.

He asked the butler to carry his request for an interview to Lord Vare and thought he detected an expression of surprise on the servant's face. If so, the man did not allow it to show for more than an instant; he was once more impassive as he took Beldon's card to the master of the house. Returning, he said, "Lord Vare will see you," and led the way to the study.

The father of his newly betrothed rose from behind his desk as Beldon entered. "Beldon. Nice to see you. Would you like something to drink? I have a good brandy here." Vare moved to a table with a decanter and raised it with a querying eyebrow.

A middle-sized man, Lord Vare still had a distinguished air despite a balding head and growing paunch. The attractions of his handsome family could be traced in his twinkling green eyes and the symmetrical bone structure of his face.

At Beldon's nod, Vare poured a measure into two glasses. Handing one to Beldon, he said, "What can I do for you?"

"I have just asked your daughter for her hand, and she has accepted."

Vare choked on his brandy. "My daughter? *Harriet?*" he said, when he had gotten his breath back.

Beldon clenched his fists. Harriet's family put little store in her endowments, an attitude he considered responsible for much of her diffidence. Hard put not to snap at the man, he replied, "I believe that was her name, yes. The same girl you gave me permission to drive out with earlier this afternoon."

"Why, the sly puss!" her father said, his expression amused. "She turned down George Briscoe today—caused a great furor in the family. Of course, if we had known she had *you* in her eye, it would have been different. George has a tidy estate—right next to the Grange. Harry would hardly have to move away from the place where she grew up. I thought she was a fool to whistle it down. Well, well, well!"

That cleared up the mystery of the commotion going on when Beldon had arrived at the Vernon townhouse that afternoon. They had not quarreled with the contentiousness his own family could manufacture.

The germ of an idea to extract himself from his situation came to him. He had always intended, when he found the suitable woman, to tie matters up thoroughly before he allowed her near his numerous, vociferous, and incompatible relations. He especially feared meeting his malicious old grandmother would ruin any chance of securing the consent of the chosen female.

"Sir, I would like to postpone making an announcement of the betrothal. Your daughter doesn't know me very well yet, and I want to make sure she won't regret her decision. The season is nearly over; I would like her to come to Langwell Towers—with her family, of course."

Lord Vare's eyes narrowed.

Beldon hastened to say, "I consider the betrothal absolutely binding on me, but marriage is more important to women. Men have other outlets—managing their estates, parliament, hunting . . . If Harriet should find she doesn't care to marry me after all, she could cry off without damaging her reputation."

"My daughter would not cry off once she has given her word. But a country house party is a good way for both of you to become better acquainted. This betrothal happened rather quickly. I accept your kind invitation. When would you like us to come up?"

"Say in a fortnight. That should give everybody time to prepare."

After finishing his brandy to seal the bargain he had made with Lord Vare, Beldon left, congratulating himself on his handling of his betrothal. No announcement would be made. He could count on his family to make Harriet flee. Then he'd be free of this tangle. He would not think of the negation Lord Vare had voiced about that hope. Beldon was sure Vare did not know of his daughter's plans to travel.

Harriet paced in her room, pausing at intervals to go to her window, which looked out on the front steps. She tried to picture events taking place in her father's study, but instead of seeing Beldon talking to Lord Vare, she could see only his blue eyes glazed with desire and feel his lips on hers.

Her face burned as she resumed pacing. Surely he would not tell Papa what had precipitated this sudden betrothal. Scarcely any time seemed to have passed before Harriet saw his form, capped by his dark hair, on the doorstep. He donned his top hat and strode jauntily to his curricle. Her heart caught at the sight of him.

Immediately, her father summoned Harriet to his presence.

Wondering whether Beldon had met with her father and departed without mentioning the betrothal, she descended to the study. Eustace and Lettice had arrived before her, allaying her doubts, but giving birth to the sinking awareness that she had just become the subject of unwanted attention.

"You little slyboots," her father began, reaching out to pinch her chin in what passed for an affectionate gesture with him. "No wonder you turned down Briscoe. Never a word! You might have let us know what was in the wind and spared us considerable worry."

While Harriet's father spoke, Lettice hugged her and Eustace gave her a hearty clap on the shoulder. They all looked in the pink of excitement, and her spirits sank still further. She had long ago given up defending herself against the reproaches of the various members of her family. In this instance she felt it would be in her best interests not to mention she had had no idea Beldon would propose, nor that she felt sure it had not been in Beldon's mind when he had invited her to go for that fateful drive.

"I can hardly believe it," Eustace proclaimed as soon as her father had finished. "Beldon, of all men. Who would ever have dreamed you'd make such an advantageous match?"

"I've sent a message to the Darwins. It's most unfortunate Clytie had to go home after you left with Beldon. Of course no one expected you would come home from your drive betrothed. What a surprise!" Lettice rattled on in her shrill voice. "And I must write Mother and the girls immediately. 'Twill disappoint them that they weren't in town. Of course Iphigenia cannot leave home, but Mother and Pallas will wish to come."

"Nonsense," Papa said. "Tell them to go to the Grange. We'll all meet there in a few days. Lady Vare will have a great deal to do. We're invited to Langwell Towers in a fortnight."

"We are?" Harriet squeaked. Everything had gotten out of hand. By now Beldon must wish he could run to the antipodes. Somewhere she must find the courage to explain this mistake to her family and save them both from an unwanted marriage. Why had she accepted when he had offered to repair his momentary lapse by marrying her?

Lord Robert and Clytie arrived, full of congratulations, and Arthur came home shortly afterward. The entire family, except Lord Robert, who must attend a political dinner, gave up their evening's engagements. Over a hastily arranged family meal they planned strategy for the close of the season, the return to Vare Grange, and their visit to Langwell Towers. As usual where family discussion concerned Harriet, her wishes were soon forgotten.

"Remember, no announcement yet," warned Vare, between spoonfuls of turtle soup. "We must carry on for the remainder of the season without giving away the news. This soup is excellent, Bolster. Convey our compliments to Cook."

"Yes, milord." The butler gave a good imitation of hearing nothing of the conversation except that which related to the dinner service.

And Harriet gave every appearance of unconcern at being the subject of the discussion, albeit uninvited to add her own opinions, as she pretended to eat. Luckily, she had practiced this role for many years and had perfected it, because otherwise the flutters in her stomach would have made it impossible to carry on intelligently.

"How can we prevent an announcement?" Eustace bellowed. "What about Taber? We can't allow him to come up to scratch, but for me to discourage him when I've made every effort to nudge him will seem most peculiar."

"Having to slink away as though we did not succeed in our efforts to settle Harriet satisfactorily will embarrass me," Lettice protested.

Footmen removed the soup and brought in the fish course.

"Seems demmed odd the man wanted no announcement," Arthur remarked as he forked up a mouthful of flaky, delicate fish. "Are you certain he won't cry off?"

"It was for Harriet's sake he wanted no announcement made," Vare assured them.

"Harriet! Why should she wish to cry off? She'll never get a better offer," Eustace said.

Harriet's heart sank. If only they knew. But of course, she must talk to Beldon before she took any steps to break the betrothal. Perhaps he had gotten over his dislike of the idea. For a moment, she allowed herself to contemplate going through with the wedding.

Glancing Harriet's way, Clytie said, "I think it was most thoughtful of Beldon. Harriet would dislike such a fuss being made over her in the final days of the season. And if Beldon leaves straightaway for his country home, she wouldn't even have his support."

Suddenly Harriet could no longer bear sitting here while they discussed her. She could only try to shore up her emotions until she saw Beldon again. Surely he would not leave for his country estate before they had talked further. She said, "May I be excused? I feel that headache coming on again."

As she departed, she heard Clytie say in lowered tones she doubtless thought Harriet would not catch, "I do hope she isn't beginning to fall in love with Beldon. I fear that can only cause her hurt."

She hurried out of the room, determined not to show any reaction. Hurt—no, she must protect her heart from a truth anybody could see. She could easily fall in love with the man, but she would not allow it. This thought hardened her resolve to hold to her conviction not to marry without love. A marriage where only one person loved would be worse than one with no love at all, leading to heartbreak for her.

When she saw Beldon, she would tell him she had changed her mind. 'Twould be far better to put away recollections of her tumultuous reaction to his caresses and concentrate on the wonders of traveling the world.

"I hear you're going out of town. Trouble at home?" Rayfield fell into step beside Beldon as he left Jackson's.

"There's always trouble at home," Beldon said, avoiding mention of the true reason for his early departure from town. "That's why I spend so much time away from it. If it ain't my mother and my aunt at daggers drawn, it's my grandmother with some complaint or other, Nicholas with a sniffle, or Great-Uncle Bartram wanting me to purchase the makings for some new fomentation for a strained hock."

"Thought perhaps you'd done the deed." Rayfield paused to let a carriage rattle by, then stepped into the street.

Beldon nearly stumbled. "What deed is that?"

"The Widow Purvis, of course. What else did you think I meant? She's been laying her trap for several weeks now. Did she bring you up to the mark?"

"No, you've got that all wrong. I've no intention of offering for Mrs. Purvis."

"Glad to hear that. Might try my luck with her myself."

"Miss—" No, of course his friend didn't mean Miss Vernon. No one had any notion of how things had progressed with her. "Mrs. Purvis? I didn't know you were thinking of marriage."

" 'Tisn't marriage I'm thinking of. There's lots of time before I have to think of that. How was the widow? Did you ever try her out?"

He'd lost interest in Mrs. Purvis after the near disaster with Miss Vernon and his curricle. "Never got that far. You're welcome to her. You'd best beware, though. It may not be marriage on your mind, but that's what Mrs. Purvis is looking for."

At first glance, Rayfield was unprepossessing, of average height. Beldon had seen him in many guises over the years of their acquaintance. He could dress in rough clothes to hobnob with thieves in the rookeries. Or he could wear the snug-fitting coats by Weston, the cravats precisely tied, and blend in with the *ton*.

However, Beldon had been in one or two sticky situations with Rayfield and knew the man gave a good accounting of himself in a brawl or a duel. He was attracted to danger as some men were drawn to gaming. Yet, for all his strange fixations, Rayfield was good company.

"There's to be a house party at Langwell Towers. Come around if you've a mind to." Beldon kept the tone casual.

"Some do of your grandmother's?"

"Er, yes, something like that."

"Perhaps I will. When is it?"

"A fortnight from now."

He parted from Rayfield.

A fortnight before he saw Miss Vernon again. At the thought of her, desire rose in him again. He quashed it ruthlessly.

Harriet's intention suffered a setback when she looked for Beldon and learned he had indeed left for his country home. Her inability to discuss matters with him left her adrift, walking through the days in a fog. She could not take any steps to end this ill-advised betrothal without speaking to her betrothed. Although he surely must regret his rash offer to her.

A message arrived from Lady Vare giving instructions for a considerable addition to Harriet's wardrobe—clothing considered suitable for a betrothed young lady to wear at a country house party, Harriet supposed. Clytie and Lettice hauled her off to the mantua maker and, with brisk efficiency, saw to the fulfillment of Lady Vare's orders. She could not help taking an interest in the new gowns, in brighter colors more flattering to Harriet's undramatic coloring, and of a more sophisticated cut than her debutante wardrobe.

The family handled the problem of Mr. Taber by an adroit avoidance of him. The Vernons attended only the most obligatory social affairs and made it known that preparations for a return to the Grange occupied their attention.

At one of the final soirees, Harriet overheard a gossiping pair of tabbies discuss her failure to bring anyone up to scratch in her second season, and felt a flash of triumph. Whenever she had heard bits of tattle about herself in the past, she had wanted to creep away. This time, she stood taller, hugging her secret knowledge to herself.

Harriet's emotions fluctuated wildly, from panic that this betrothal was all too real, to fear that only a sense of obligation drove Beldon, to elation that someone so exactly matching her most private dreams had actually offered for her, to disappointment in the loss of her dreams of adventure.

As a result, by the time the family left London, she was exhausted, her psyche worn raw. When they arrived at the Grange, her mother and Astraea greeted her with joy and congratulations. Harriet's spirits sank at needing to hide her emotions yet again, and she wished she could disappear and not have to face her family.

Astraea ran up and flung her arms around her next-older sister, causing Harriet a double dose of guilt. Astraea, with hair a pale gold that caught light and reflected it magnified to glory, her face a perfect oval and her complexion like living marble, outshone the whole family for beauty. Further, she delighted in everything around her, and her heart had nothing mean or spiteful in its makeup.

"Oh Harry, I'm so *thrilled*! Aren't you excited? They say Beldon is so handsome, and rich. It's like a fairy tale!"

"Indeed," Harriet said dryly. The sight of her younger sister's shining face recalled Pallas's assertion that Astraea and Beldon would make a perfect match. Why had she not thought of that as she faced her dilemma?

If she married Beldon, he and Astraea would perforce meet. How could he not fall in love with her? Astraea, too. She could never meet such a beau ideal as Beldon. They would fall in love with each other—and there would be Harriet in the middle. *Oh, no!* She could not bear to think of it. Her heart ached as though she had already lost him to her sister.

And their suffering would be equally intense.

She couldn't marry him.

Her mother's greeting was more sedate as she expressed Iphigenia's disappointment in being unable to travel to offer her felicitations in person. "At least the dear girl has progressed past any worry about miscarrying again," Lady Vare said. "She has made it to eight months, so if she is brought to bed any time soon, the child should survive. Harborough is overjoyed that it seems he will finally have an heir."

Harriet looked at the still-beautiful face of her mother, the blue eyes and distinguished silver hair. Now that face, which had so often reflected worry and exasperation when she looked at her strange, changeling daughter, beamed upon her with pride and triumph. Harriet wished she deserved that pride, but Beldon had not wanted to offer for her. She did not believe the marriage would take place.

That night as she lay in bed with a sleeping Astraea, Harriet pondered the misfortune that had led Beldon to offer for her when he, by his own admission, did not love her. She must arrange for Astraea and Beldon to meet. If the two were destined to fall in love, Harriet would have to step aside.

It was the perfect solution. Once Astraea and Beldon found each other, Harriet was sure her family would not stand in the way of her plans for her own life.

Luckily, Harriet did not love Beldon. What she felt could not be love, merely a temporary infatuation. Naturally, she had noticed him at many of the same affairs she had attended during the season, but had never allowed herself to imagine he would become interested in her. She had firmly quashed any deeper interest in him once they had become acquainted.

And she most certainly had not built any dreams upon the kisses they had shared. Oh, those kisses—and the other things he had done, she thought, her face heating. She must put such thoughts out of her mind, and not imagine it was Lord Beldon instead of Astraea lying in bed beside her. Indeed, if her plan succeeded, the opposite would be true, and she would be the one in bed all alone.

Somehow, thoughts of the adventures she would have traveling with Great-Aunt Harriet no longer seemed so exciting compared with the picture of Astraea enjoying Beldon's kisses.

Chapter Five

Seated at the head of the immense table in his dining hall, Beldon cast a satisfied look down the long line of his relations. It had been an inspired idea to invite Miss Vernon to Langwell Towers. *Good Gad!* Any woman of sense who took a gander at his family would run screaming at the thought of allying herself to them. His betrothal was as good as ended.

At the foot of the table, his grandmother, the Dowager Lady Beldon, grumbled, "Don't see why you had to invite the gel's whole family. They'll be nothing but trouble." Her eyes, the deep blue of Beldon's own, flashed a scathing glance his way.

Beldon set down his soupspoon. "I could scarcely invite Miss Vernon without a chaperone. You've always enjoyed playing hostess to a house full of people."

"Not any more. I'm getting too old for such exertion. Why do you suppose I insisted it was time you took a bride?"

"I thought it was for the succession—that's what you told me." Beldon glanced down the table to his cousin, Oswald Manning, his heir presumptive. The young man ate as though he had been deprived of food for months, a fact disputed by his soft, round physique.

Grandmother noisily slurped her soup. "That too, though you had to be reminded to do your duty. Why can't Miss Vernon entertain her own relations and leave me in peace?"

"I explained to you, the betrothal is not to be made known yet. It's a little premature to expect her to serve as hostess for her own entertainment."

Beldon pictured Harriet Vernon sitting in his grandmother's place at the foot of his table, and found the vision surprisingly pleasing. He frowned and shut away the thought.

Servants cleared the soup course and brought in the fish. At the dowager's left, her brother, Sir Bartram Paige, spoke up around a mouthful of roast beef. "I do hope you realize I will be occupied with training Pasha, and will be unavailable to entertain your male guests."

"The only male member of the family to accompany Miss Vernon will be the oldest brother, the Honorable Eustace Vernon. Lord and Lady Robert Darwin, her sister and brother-in-law, have an invitation to some political allies but may join us later.

"The duchess is bringing her two sons"—Beldon turned to his mother, Mrs. Willoughby, seated to his right—"who are close to Nicholas in age. He should enjoy the company."

"Rolleston, you know he will find any boys his own age to be his intellectual inferiors." His mother was still slender and attractive. However, the cares imposed on her by two marriages, first to an ailing man who had left her a young widow, and then to a sea captain who was gone much of the time early in their marriage and now invalided and despondent, left her fretful and often petulant.

With an effort, Beldon kept the irritation out of his voice. "A Master Nicholas Willoughby will not find the Marquess of Calder and Lord Peregrine Savage, sons of a duke, beneath his touch, no matter what their respective intellectual gifts may be. It will do Nicholas good to associate with boys his own age. He is too much alone." His mother had thus far resisted his persuasions that his half-brother should be sent to school.

On her other side, her husband, Captain Willoughby, gave a mumble that Beldon took to be agreement, but it was unclear with whom he agreed. For a naval hero, the man had remarkably little heart to stand up to his wife. The captain downed his wine, and Beldon frowned. His stepfather was drinking too much, as usual. Glancing at the empty sleeve pinned to Willoughby's uniform jacket, Beldon felt a tug of sympathy.

His gaze swept around the table at the various faces to whom, in one manner or another, he felt love or obligation. Yet he could stand them only in small doses, and Miss Vernon must certainly find their constant company insupportable.

Beldon's glance returned affectionately to Marianne Manning, his cousin, seated between Sir Bartram and Captain Willoughby. Serving as her grandmother's companion and aide-de-camp, Marianne carried far too many of the burdens of the household. She would fall heir to most of the work of this house party, despite the dowager's complaints.

Marianne seemed to have settled into spinsterhood, although he did not know why. She was attractive enough. However, after her single season a few years before, she had returned home changed, quieter and with an air of resignation. Since then, she had refused to go to London, ignoring her mother's sighs and frequent references to wasted chances.

"Beldon, I think it vastly unfair that you didn't manage to secure any young men for this house party. How am I to amuse myself with these dull people?" The captain's daughter, Miss Lucy Willoughby, pouted. She had a mouth made for pouting.

"You are too young to practice your wiles upon young men. Miss Vernon has a younger sister accompanying the party. As Miss Astraea is also not yet out, you will be responsible for entertaining her."

At Lucy's *moue*, Beldon added, "and if this plan does not meet with your approval, you can help in the nursery. Mr. and Mrs. Eustace Vernon will also be bringing their young children."

Lucy tossed her head. "I'm not a child."

"At fifteen you are most certainly not a woman, either. If you want me to believe you are grown up, try behaving like it."

His mother defended her stepdaughter. "Indeed, Rolleston, you refine too much upon Lucy's youthful high spirits."

"High spirits, is it?" interposed his aunt, Mrs. Manning. "The child entirely lacks conduct. I have never understood why you allow her at table with the adults. You certainly do not give her the guidance she needs—or Master Nicholas.

"*I* would never have countenanced my children behaving thus, and you must admit you will never see such pretty manners as dear Marianne and Oswald exhibit." Aunt Manning beamed fondly at her offspring. Oswald continued eating, ignoring this exchange, but Marianne blushed at this renewed attempt by her mother to push her forward.

"Indeed, your children are the pattern cards of manners, dear Mrs. Manning," Mother cooed, "and as dull as pattern cards as well. They never have a word to say for themselves. I should much rather see lively spirits in a child."

"Well, I never!" Aunt Manning's outrage presaged a long evening of squabbling between the two long-time rivals, who before the deaths of their husbands had been sisters-in-law.

Lucy blushed and jumped to her feet, drawing near to Mrs. Willoughby in a defensive pose. "Don't you insult my mother," she shouted, hands on her hips. At the same time, Marianne went to her mother's side and bent over, whispering, "Mother, please. It does not become you to engage in this useless wrangle."

Lucy turned to her stepmother and said, "Pay no attention to her. Everyone knows you are the best of mothers." Since her own mother had died when she was too young to remember her, she had little basis for comparison, but Mother smiled and patted the girl's hand.

The old dowager looked silently upon the fray, a smug smile playing across her face. Beldon often thought she fed upon the discord in the household.

Beldon stood, his anger masked. "I think we gentlemen will excuse you, ladies, while we indulge in our port and cigars."

Conversation ceased abruptly as the ladies stood to leave. He couldn't resist adding, "I would take it very ill should you engage in this kind of display before our guests."

What was he thinking? He counted on his family's squabbling to end the betrothal.

His mother hastily reassured him. "Rolleston, you know we would not *think* of such a thing."

He grinned. Luckily, they would never remember—their rivalry had stood too long for them to give it up now.

"Beldon has invited the girl and her family to a house party at Langwell Towers," Docilla Purvis said to her caller at her London townhouse, struggling to keep the indignation from her voice. How had that insignificant mouse stolen the man *she* wanted, practically from the altar? After her years of cosseting her invalid husband, and still more lonely years of putting out lures for someone younger, handsome, and virile, she had found the perfect man. It was intolerable!

"If it's such a secret, how did you find out?" Piers Luchan reclined on the delicate sofa in Docilla's salon, looking very much at ease, an annoying habit of his.

"I managed to worm it out of Lettice. The poor woman thinks she's the soul of discretion, but she can't keep a secret." Docilla arose to renew the brandy in his glass, then seated herself opposite him.

"Perhaps it's time to give up the chase." He sipped at the brandy, looking at her with an expression of speculation.

"Nothing is settled yet, I'll be bound. There's been no notice in the papers. I've put too much effort into this to give up so easily. I was this close to hooking him"—she gestured with thumb and forefinger—"when that girl and those stupid runaway horses ruined everything."

"I thought you had planned the runaway and falling into Beldon's arms when he rescued you." He grinned at her.

"They weren't actually supposed to run away."

"Foolproof plans often run awry, Docilla." He crossed one leg over the other and swung it idly, swirling the brandy.

She resisted the urge to strike him. His smugness was infuriating. "You have an interest in this, too. I expected you to be eager to accompany me to Langwell."

"You forget, I was warned off a whole year ago. I have no interest any more."

"You still need to marry an heiress, do you not?"

"That was my plan. Unfortunately, the guardians of all the heiresses seem to know my sorry state, and so far have successfully kept their young ladies from my clutches."

"This is a house party. Guardians don't keep their innocent charges so closely under their wings at such affairs."

"There's only one slight problem." Luchan hesitated. "We haven't been invited."

"We'll never succeed if you only look for problems." Docilla leaned forward, giving Luchan a glimpse of cleavage with her low-cut gown, as added insurance of her persuasiveness. "I intend simply to show up and behave as though I were invited. Beldon's too polite to call me a liar and turn me off."

Luchan cleared his throat and looked away. "Why do you need me? It sounds as if your plan is in place."

"I need you to distract the girl. I thought you'd be happy to have another chance at her fortune."

He frowned. "It's out of the question, Docilla. I can't go to Langwell Towers."

The flat finality of his tone set her back for a moment, but she went on, "I realize you don't have enough acquaintance with Beldon to pretend an invitation. I've thought of a solution for that. Lucretius Taber is Beldon's neighbor."

Luchan stared. "What has that to do with anything?"

"Miss Vernon's brother Eustace was trying to promote a match between them this past season. I'll wager he kept a closer mouth than his wife did, and Taber has no idea what's in the wind. It would be easy enough to get him to return home, and you will be *his* house guest."

"Docilla, please! You may think you have matters satisfactorily arranged, but it's all a mystery to me. I have no more acquaintance with Taber than with Beldon. Don't even want to know the man, to tell the truth. He sounds a consummate bore from what I've heard."

"Sheep!"

"What?"

"Taber raises some kind of sheep—supposed to grow very fine wool, or some such. Don't you need sheep for your crufters up in Scotland?"

"Crofters. And yes, if I had any money to buy sheep."

"He doesn't need to know about your poverty-stricken state. Arrange with him to go look at sheep. And then I'll tell him what a fortuitous coincidence it is that he's going to his country place, because I hate to travel all alone to Beldon's house party. See!" she finished in triumph.

Luchan groaned.

Harriet caught her breath at the first sight of Langwell Towers through the Vernon carriage window. It deserved its reputation as one of England's loveliest country homes.

Its Palladian front, the formal garden blooming in a revelry of colors, neat hedges along the cobblestoned drive curving up to the doorway, the whole framed by majestic oaks, created a breathtaking vista. The beauty of the surrounding countryside, lush forests interspersed with rich farmlands, all laid out upon gently rolling hills, had impressed her as well.

Footmen hastened to assist them in dismounting from the coach, and a rigidly proper butler stood at the doorway waiting to welcome them. Immediately upon his heels a motherly-looking woman hurried forward. "Welcome to Langwell Towers. I am Mrs. Goodman, the housekeeper. Hester," she instructed a round-cheeked young maid, "take the children up to the nursery. Perhaps you will wish to accompany them to see them comfortably settled, Your Grace, and Mrs. Vernon?"

The respective mothers of the younger members of the party nodded, and Mrs. Goodman continued, "I will see that you are shown to your chambers after you have satisfied yourselves as to your children's comfort. If the rest of you will follow me . . . " The housekeeper's words trailed behind her as she ascended the grand staircase.

Harriet hardly had time to glance around the lofty entrance hall, gaining only an impression of rust-colored marble, gilt mirrors, and huge spaces.

She and Astraea were shown into a large, comfortable chamber containing a huge four-poster bed covered with a bright yellow counterpane and hangings. Light-colored wood paneled the lower half of the walls, white wallpaper with a pattern of tiny yellow flowers above. Airy white curtains at the pair of tall windows, bracketed by heavier drapes in a green- and yellow-flowered design, completed the cheery atmosphere of the room.

After the housekeeper had explained that tea would be served at four and then departed, Astraea asked, "Is the house so small that we must share a room?"

"Perhaps Lord Beldon wanted only to make sure no hint of scandal would follow from my staying in the same house as he," Harriet suggested.

"Or perhaps he doesn't trust himself to stay away." Astraea's eyes brightened at this thought. "Oh, Harriet, you are so lucky!"

Harriet sighed. Even remembering the occasion when Beldon had become carried away, she could not give any credence to Astraea's theory of Beldon's overwhelming passion toward her.

Beldon returned home from business about the estate some half hour before teatime and hastened to change his clothing. He hurried downstairs to the drawing room shortly before four. His family had already gathered, obviously eager to meet his betrothed despite their complaints. None of the Vernons had come down yet, however.

They came *en masse* at the stroke of four. Beldon stepped forward to greet them, disappointment overcoming him. His memory had softened his images of Harriet, invested her with greater claims to beauty. Now she looked plain indeed walking in on the arm of what must be the youngest Vernon sister.

Miss Astraea's vaunted beauty had not been exaggerated in the least—her appearance stunned the senses. To an impartial eye, the Duchess of Moorewood's riper beauty, and even Lady Vare's mature, assured demeanor pleased the eye far more than did the reserved prettiness of his intended.

As he exchanged courtesies with the members of Harriet's family, he drew his gaze back to her and recognized the worry in her hazel eyes. Although his acquaintance with Harriet was of short duration, some strong connection between them led him to awareness of her anxiety about his family's reaction to her and her doubts of his feelings.

Equally he knew, as a result she would stammer and behave awkwardly. He wished in that moment to hold her, carry her away from anything that would hurt her. He enclosed her arm in his and led her into the drawing room, to his grandmother, seated in state upon an armless Sheraton chair.

"Grandmama, may I present Miss Harriet Vernon. Miss Vernon, Lady Beldon."

Harriet murmured some words, too softly to hear; he felt her tremble beside him. As he started to introduce the other members of her party, the dowager fixed a gimlet eye upon him and said, "You've done a fine day's work, Beldon. You've gone and promised yourself to the only Vernon with no pretensions to beauty."

In the shocked silence that ensued, several things occurred. Beside him Harriet shrank and attempted to pull free from his grasp. Her family, to a one, moved closer to Harriet, although, perhaps bound by politeness to an elderly woman, none of them spoke. He felt a momentary relief that despite the Vernons' lack of respect for Harriet, they were prepared to shelter her.

And he entirely forgot that he had invited Harriet to Langwell so that his impossible family could drive her to break their engagement. He was swamped by an overwhelming surge of protectiveness toward his betrothed. He took a few moments to collect himself, not trusting he could remember his own obligation to honor his grandmother.

He tightened his hold on Harriet, then looked her up and

down slowly, as though considering Lady Beldon's words, then said, "Oh, do you think so? I really don't see much difference." A further pause. "Of course her coloring is not the same as her sisters'. But then those pale blondes have not been much in vogue for several seasons."

Chapter Six

Harriet stood rooted to the floor. The smile with which she had prepared to greet Beldon's relations froze on her face like a mask. She would appear even more conspicuous if she turned tail and ran from the room. If only she could simply disappear. Fairy dust would come in handy.

The maliciousness in the old woman's eyes burned rational thought out of Harriet's mind. She felt Beldon's arm warm on hers, heard him speak to his grandmother but couldn't focus on what he said. Tension in the room relaxed.

Beldon gently pulled her toward the rest of his relations and continued introductions. Harriet gathered impressions of a multitude of faces as she stammered her responses. *Drat!* Why must that plaguey stammer return whenever she became nervous?

The presentation of the two families took a long time. Finally, led to a chair, Harriet sat. Handed a dish of tea and some biscuits, she balanced them on her lap, knowing her throat would close against any attempt to swallow. Conversation swirled around her, sounding like gibberish.

She gathered her faculties and looked again at Beldon's family. Except for the dreadful old woman, his grandmother, she could not remember one name. Was the faded blonde Beldon's mother, or was it the smartly dressed brunette with the dramatic white streak at her left temple? Perhaps the brunette, she decided, based on her hair coloring, although she could detect no other similarity to Beldon in their features. The brunette's eyes were a smoky brown, unlike Beldon's intense blue.

His eyes matched Lady Beldon's. The color presented a startling contrast to her withered old face, but she must have been ravishing in her day. However, she was horrid. Harriet belatedly realized that the old harridan's words insulted Beldon as much as Harriet. How could he endure her spiteful tongue?

When she married Beldon, she would have to suffer that tongue, just as he did.

If. She caught herself, remembered her purpose here. Harriet most likely would not marry Beldon. If Astraea married him, *she* would have to put up with the dowager. But the old lady would surely find Astraea a more pleasing granddaughter-in-law than Harriet. She sighed, her gaze returning to Beldon.

She had forgotten to note the reaction of her sister and Beldon to each other when they met. She had intended to keep a close eye on them to tell if attraction instantly grew between them. Now she must watch for clues during the next fortnight.

A young woman approached. "May I join you, Miss Vernon?"

Harriet gave her consent and the woman sat next to her.

"I am sure you do not remember me. I always have trouble putting all the names to faces when I am introduced to so many people at once. I am Marianne Manning, Beldon's cousin."

She was beautiful, with dark chestnut-colored hair and the Manning blue eyes. "I must apologize for my grandmother, Miss Vernon. I am very fond of the old dear, but she likes to shock people and say outrageous things. She does not mean any harm."

"Oh, indeed?" Harriet took care to keep the skepticism from her voice. Was Miss Manning making mock of her? No, Beldon's cousin had such an open smile upon her face, Harriet could not doubt her sincerity.

"Perhaps tomorrow, after you have had a chance to settle in, you would care to look about Langwell Towers? I would be very happy to give you a tour."

"Oh, yes, I should like that, Miss Manning."

"Please call me Marianne. We are to be family, after all."

The tightness in Harriet's neck and face eased at the friendly welcome of Beldon's cousin. The next fortnight might not be the ordeal she had feared. "Then you must call me Harriet," she responded.

Just then the butler entered with three newcomers.

Beldon watched as Harriet sat erect on the straight-backed chair, the cooling dish of tea balanced on her lap. His earlier sympathy turned to vexation. He could not escape the renewed conclusion that she would make a most unsuitable peer's wife. It was not that she lacked beauty. She merely did not show to advantage among the rest of her stunning family. Indeed, in most company she would be thought an attractive woman.

However, she had not even a modicum of aplomb or social address. She made no effort to converse, but looked as though she would be happier mucking out stalls in the stables than visiting with her affianced husband's relations.

Marianne left her grandmother's side and came to sit by Harriet. From his location across the room, Beldon could not hear Marianne, but Harriet unbent and responded to his cousin's attempt to draw her out, even giving a tentative smile.

A disturbance in the hall interrupted his thoughts. Soon thereafter, his butler opened the door. "My lord, you have some callers," he announced in a tone that hinted at his puzzlement.

On his heels three people entered the room. The arrival of his neighbor, Lucretius Taber, produced no surprise, as they called on each other occasionally when residing at their country homes. What were Mrs. Purvis and Piers Luchan doing here?

"Oh dear, we're late, I see," Mrs. Purvis said, glancing at the tea paraphernalia. "It is all my fault. Mr. Taber wished to start early, but he was left cooling his heels in my parlor for the greatest time while I decided what to pack."

Beldon congratulated himself on his mild tone as he said, "What brings you here, Mrs. Purvis?"

She looked at him, her eyelashes lowered flirtatiously.

"Why, you invited me, Beldon." With an affected pout she added, "Don't tell me you have forgotten."

He gritted his teeth. He had most certainly not forgotten an invitation he had *not* extended. Short of declaring the woman a liar, however, he could not think what to do.

"I'm afraid it must have slipped my mind. Since you traveled with Mr. Taber, perhaps you could stay with him."

Shocked, Taber exclaimed, "You can't mean it, Beldon. My house is a bachelor establishment. Mrs. Purvis would be ruined if she stayed there. I already have Mr. Luchan as a guest."

That was another mystery. What commonality between Luchan and Taber could have occasioned Taber to invite him? Taber was a stuffy old stick, while Luchan was widely known as a fortune hunter. The situation smelled smoky when he reflected upon it.

Unfortunately Taber had the right of it, as far as Mrs. Purvis was concerned. She could not stay at Taber Manor; Beldon was saddled with her.

He turned to his butler. "Usherwood, ask Mrs. Goodman to prepare a bedchamber for Mrs. Purvis. Oh, and please see that fresh tea—and some more victuals—are brought in."

"Of course, my lord." Usherwood bowed and left the room.

"Come in," he said to his unwanted guests with a heartiness that concealed his dismay. "Do you know everybody here?"

He saw his consternation reflected in Miss Vernon, who looked alarmingly pale. Marianne, he noticed, was put out of countenance also. Although she had not been in London this past season, she doubtless kept informed of events and knew Beldon had escorted Mrs. Purvis about. The expressions on the faces of Harriet's family also showed various degrees of chagrin.

"Hullo, Taber," Harriet's brother, Eustace Vernon, said tonelessly. "I recall your country home is nearby."

Taber and Mrs. Purvis walked over to Eustace. "Yes, Beldon and I are neighbors. Live just a mile away."

"Hello, Lettice. I did not realize you would be here," Mrs. Purvis said.

"Docilla," Mrs. Eustace Vernon responded, her expression as sour as if she had drunk undiluted lemon juice instead of tea.

The only face in the room that appeared undaunted by the new arrivals was the dowager's. Her eyes sparkled gleefully. Fresh fodder for her machinations, Beldon thought.

"That vicious old lady! I wanted to scratch her eyes out." Astraea paced indignantly around the bedchamber.

Harriet groaned and lay on the yellow counterpane, her head pounding. She never had headaches—or never used to until she had made Beldon's acquaintance. What a muddle. If she had been prone to faint, the moment Piers Luchan and Lucretius Taber walked into Beldon's drawing room would have been the time for it.

She had seldom thought of Mr. Luchan since the previous year when he had dangled after her and her father hinted him away. Lord Vare wanted no fortune hunters for one of his daughters, even a daughter whose chances for a match he doubted.

Mr. Taber would pursue his somewhat irresolute courtship of her. She could not cope with two erstwhile suitors while matters remained so unsettled between her and Beldon.

Mary came in to dress her two charges for dinner.

"How can you bear it, Harriet?" Astraea sat before the dressing table while Mary brushed her golden locks. "That mean old woman will probably live for years and years yet, and she will make your life miserable."

Astraea could not know Lady Beldon's needling paled in significance before the problem the new arrivals presented, and Harriet would not inform her. With Astraea's penchant for drama, she would magnify this latest *contretemps* into a tragedy.

"Astraea, do not distress yourself. I admit I was taken aback by the dowager's comment. However, now I am forewarned, and I shall have no difficulty managing. I shall proceed just as I do when I receive a scold from Mama, and say, 'Yes, Ma'am' and 'No, Ma'am' in my vague manner that no one takes any offense at. Then I shall just go my own way as usual."

Astraea giggled at this, and the anxious frown cleared from her unlined brow. "Are you sure you do not mind?"

Mary finished Astraea's coiffeur and Harriet took her place. "I can cope with the old harridan, I assure you," Harriet avowed. She hoped for a change her hair would obey Mary's attempts to create a masterpiece.

"Perhaps it is a good thing after all that you and I are sharing a room. If more unexpected guests arrive, Langwell Towers' bedchambers will be filled." Harriet stood to have one of her new, more sophisticated gowns dropped over her head. As Mary did up the back, Harriet examined herself with gloom. The dull gold satin brought out golden highlights in her eyes and hair, and the draped bosom artfully emphasized her curves. Still, she looked like herself, not transformed into the beauty of any of her sisters.

Mrs. Purvis—what a complication. Harriet was determined to give up Beldon for her sister, but not for that aging *coquette*. Perhaps it was unfortunate no notice had been published of the betrothal. That should certainly have forestalled Beldon and her becoming besieged by former admirers.

"Who is Mrs. Purvis?"

"I believe she is a friend of Lord Beldon's. You should ask Lettice, however, as she and Mrs. Purvis are bosom bows. What did you think of Lord Beldon?" Harriet held her breath while she awaited the answer to this all-important question.

"Oh, he's most handsome. I believe you are the luckiest of all my sisters. Of course I quite like Lord Robert, but Pallas and Genie's husbands are nothing out of the ordinary, even if Pallas's is a duke."

Harriet couldn't tell whether any note of partiality toward Lord Beldon invested Astraea's voice. Naturally, Astraea would try to dissemble if she had been struck with love for her sister's betrothed. Beldon would also be too noble to admit to what he would regard as a dishonorable feeling. Harriet must be vigilant in the next days to determine the true reactions of these two whose happiness she had taken in hand.

She clasped Astraea's arm and they descended for dinner.

Beldon frowned at the vision of Harriet in the low-cut gown. Curls artfully framed her pixie face and clung to her slender neck. He had wanted nothing more all evening than to kiss every spot those curls touched. Instead, he was surrounded by chattering people. Harriet was clear across the room, a smile on her face as she listened to some nonsense spouted by Luchan. And Beldon's efforts to find a moment's privacy with her had been stymied.

Before dinner, he invited Harriet to step out into the garden, and several of her relatives joined them.

He showed them all the features of the garden, behaving with civility and reminding himself that he was not supposed to find Harriet so tempting. The reminder didn't help, and he wondered whether he might go through with the match after all. But the idea gave him a pang of loss—loss of the dream of the tall, poised lady, whose face he could almost see, by his side. Next to this dream woman, the thought of Harriet, passionate in his arms, seemed a betrayal. Such thoughts did not make his desire vanish, however.

Taber and Luchan showed up, uninvited, just before dinner was announced. The meal had to be put back while two more places were set. During dinner, Harriet sat nearly at the opposite end of his place at the head of the table. Afterwards, he cut short any attempt by the men to linger over port and cigars and joined the women in the small salon.

Now, as Harriet laughed at a sally of Luchan's, Beldon had taken enough. He rose from his chair and started across the room. Taber stepped in front of him. "I say, Beldon, can't you set up a table for cards? It's a dashed flat evening."

Beldon noticed for the first time bored expressions on the

faces of several guests. With an inward sigh he summoned Usherwood to set up card tables and bring decks of cards.

"Care to join me in a game of whist, Lady Beldon?" Taber said. "How about you, Vernon?" He nodded at Harriet's brother.

"Er, yes, I wouldn't mind," said Eustace, glancing at his wife as though for permission.

"Marianne, you will partner me," ordered Lady Beldon. "Help me up."

His grandmother was perfectly capable of rising from the sofa upon which she sat, but Marianne came to lend her arm to the old lady.

Amid the bustle as the card players settled themselves, Beldon noticed Marianne shoot a look over to where Luchan and Harriet sat and quickly glance away.

Thus reminded of his interrupted purpose, Beldon set out to attain Harriet's side again.

"Oh, Beldon." Mrs. Purvis's dulcet tones stopped his progress. An imperious gesture from her made him change direction to join the widow.

"I vow, your house is lovely," she gushed. "I have heard it's one of the loveliest homes in England, and I certainly can agree with that judgment after seeing it."

"Thank you, Mrs. Purvis."

Beldon stepped away, to be brought up short by a new sally from the widow. "I would so desire to be shown around."

"I'm sure that can be arranged. In fact my cousin Miss Manning has arranged a tour of the house tomorrow, I believe, to any guests who have an interest in seeing it. She is a most accomplished guide. You must ask her what time the tour is to begin." He turned again.

Mrs. Purvis tapped him with her fan. "Why, Beldon, if I didn't know better, I would think you are anxious to be rid of me. But we both know the particular attentions you paid me this past spring."

A sensation like dropping into a pit swept over Beldon. What was she saying? Did she imply he had made any sort of declaration to her? He most carefully had done no such thing. A few embraces, invited by Mrs. Purvis, and not relished half so much as the brief episode with Harriet, either. In fact, he had been conscious of a perception that he'd stepped in a field laced with traps every time he had seen Mrs. Purvis.

"I am glad you found my company enjoyable this *past* spring, Mrs. Purvis." He glanced at Harriet again. She watched him, her eyes large and wounded-looking. Luchan now stood behind Lady Beldon, pointing out a card in her hand. Sir Bartram was with Harriet, talking in an unusually animated fashion.

Mrs. Purvis frowned. "I'm eager to hear what plans you have for our entertainment while we are at Langwell Towers. Is there to be a ball, perhaps? I do enjoy meeting everybody's neighbors when I visit the country. Don't you find country people refreshing? I vow, they are almost like foreigners." She had a hold of his arm now, tugging him to sit beside her.

Beldon resisted. "I hope you enjoy your stay," he forced himself to say. "As host, I must see that all my guests' needs are met. If you'll excuse me . . . "

Lucy came dashing up to him, with the youngest Miss Vernon trailing behind. "Please say we may have a picnic tomorrow, Beldon. Mama claims the weather is to be too damp, and Aunt Manning says we mustn't be so much bother to the staff. But Mama doesn't know anything about the weather. She says she got it from Papa and that he is never wrong."

"Why don't you wait until tomorrow and see how the weather is? If it is fine, then you may plague Cook and Mrs. Goodman to your heart's content."

"As if I would let a little rain stop me!"

"Perhaps your guest does not feel the same way. You must learn to be a good hostess, Lucy."

"Oh, you are such a prosy bore, Beldon."

"You surely aren't going to let this minx speak to you that way, are you, Beldon?"

Just when he'd been on the verge of cutting short his conversation with Docilla Purvis, she had inserted herself into it again. He gritted his teeth.

Thoroughly annoyed, with Lucy and the whole lot of people at Langwell, he said, "Come here, young lady." Grabbing her arm, he led her from the room and sent her off to bed. He'd hear from his mother for this piece of highhandedness, but it was worth it to have gotten rid of Mrs. Purvis, temporarily at least. He stood watching Lucy flounce up the stairs, then turned to find Harriet's younger sister standing behind him.

"I apologize, Lord Beldon," she said. "I tried to tell her not to plague you, but she was most determined."

"Think nothing of it, Miss Vernon. Lucy can be a little headstrong. If the adults in her own family cannot control her, it is expecting too much of yourself to do so."

He led her back into the room and immediately noticed Harriet's eyes widening at his entrance with her sister. What did she believe, that he was making up to an infant? He started toward Harriet again, to be stopped once more by an imperious command from his grandmother. "Beldon, I'm feeling chilled and Marianne is the dealer for this hand. Go fetch my shawl."

When he returned from this errand, he noticed with relief that Mrs. Eustace Vernon sat with Mrs. Purvis. However, now Captain Willoughby sat next to Harriet, and from his appearance, he was in his cups again. Beldon had to get to her, but this effort was in the nature of a rescue. As he handed the shawl to his grandmother, she cast a look up at Luchan, who still stood by her chair, apparently flirting with the old beldame for all he was worth.

Beldon glanced at Marianne, noting she looked rather pale. "Are you feeling quite the thing?" he asked her, and immediately regretted it, for if she were not, he would no doubt be stuck playing whist in her place.

"I'm fine," she assured him, and as he turned to rescue Harriet from Captain Willoughby, Marianne added, "No, I do believe I don't feel well. Will you excuse me, please?" Not waiting for a reply, she jumped up and hurried from the room. Luchan made an instinctive move, as if to go after her, but instead excused himself to Lady Beldon and returned to Harriet.

"Beldon, sit and finish Marianne's turn," Lady Beldon demanded. It was no use to deny her. She had trained Marianne and Beldon to her exacting standards in the game of whist, and she insisted no one else could serve as her partner.

His dander was up now. He *would* find a way to speak to Harriet alone before this evening was over. He no longer knew why he wanted to do so, but it didn't matter. After all, for the moment she was his.

Would the evening never end? Beldon now partnered his grandmother at cards but had spent time with everyone save Harriet, she fumed. Why had he invited her to Langwell if he was only to ignore her? She was quite sure all his relatives noticed his discourtesy, as her family did. And there was Mrs. Purvis, who no doubt gloated that she had garnered much more of Beldon's attention than Harriet had. The very thought made her stomach shrivel.

This evening she scarcely had a chance to speak to Miss Manning, who had been friendly to her at tea and while they waited for the gentlemen to join them. Then Miss Manning had been appropriated by her grandmother to play cards, and later, she abruptly excused herself and departed.

After dinner Mr. Luchan made her the object of his attentions. He was entertaining, and she tried her best to be diverted by his flirtation, but she could not help observing Beldon's interactions with Mrs. Purvis and other guests. Mr. Luchan noticed her distraction, made a smiling reference to it, and drifted over to the card game.

A middle-aged man wearing a rather soiled naval coat had stumbled over and sunk heavily into the chair by Harriet, the glass in his hand, which appeared to contain whiskey, sloshing over as he sat. He had imbibed several glasses of wine at dinner, Harriet had noticed.

"Hear you're going to marry m'stepson." At Harriet's nod—he must be Beldon's stepfather—he went on, "Good lad. Took in m'family—and me, of course—when I was landlocked." He took a deep draught of his whiskey. "Nothing more useless than a sailor away from the sea."

"I am sure that is not true," Harriet murmured, but he gave no sign he heard her, instead sinking into whatever melancholy reflections occupied his mind. He was pitiable, but Harriet could not console anyone in her present mood.

When it became clear he had no further conversation in mind, she arose and went to sit with Astraea, who sat alone after Lucy Willoughby had left. Lucy must be the daughter of the man with whom Harriet had just conversed. Astraea chattered gaily, but Harriet had trouble concentrating on their conversation, compulsively watching the card game, though she wanted to look anywhere but at Beldon.

After what seemed an eon, Beldon's butler finally wheeled in a tea tray, signaling that the festivities were nearly over. Harriet concealed a yawn behind her hand.

Mr. Taber and Mr. Luchan declined to partake of tea, Mr. Taber claiming they must get back to his house. Beldon saw them to the door and did not immediately return to the salon.

Finally, Lady Beldon asked her grandson to ring for her maid to help her to bed, and her departure was the cue for everyone to head up the stairs to their chambers. As Harriet reached the staircase, Beldon approached her for the first time in the entire evening and slipped her a folded piece of paper. Surprised, Harriet did not think quickly enough to refuse to take it. Once in her room, she could not help reading it.

Please meet me in the library in one hour.

What bold-faced brass. She crumpled the note. Did he think that after he had spoken scarcely two words to her all evening, she would come running to his summons?

Very likely he wished to call off the betrothal. Yes, that must be it. Why else would he have paid no attention to her ever since her arrival? What should she do? This was too soon—although he and Astraea had spent a little time alone together, it was not sufficient for their love to become fixed. If the betrothal were called off now, her family could not remain the fortnight that had been planned for this country house party.

Three or four times during the evening, Beldon had looked as if he had wished to speak to her. If so, someone else had always waylaid him before he could seek her out.

Suddenly, Harriet realized that, despite all the evidence and her own common sense, she harbored a small hope that he would yet come to love her. Hope would only get her hurt, but it refused to be quashed, and she knew she must meet Beldon, to find out where matters stood.

She paced while Mary helped Astraea remove her gown, brushed out her hair, and made her ready for bed. When she came to help Harriet with her gown, Harriet said, "Never mind. I am not ready to sleep. I think I will go down to the library and see if I can find a book."

Mary snorted and gave her a disbelieving glance but left the room.

Astraea looked at Harriet eagerly. "What is it? I saw Beldon hand you the note."

"It is nothing. Said he will see me tomorrow." It was not a lie. The small mantel clock said it was a quarter to twelve; by the time she went downstairs, it would be the next day.

With a miffed expression Astraea climbed into bed and turned her back on Harriet. Harriet paced some more. The little clock chimed midnight.

At twelve-thirty, Harriet could not wait any longer for the hour to pass. Surely everyone was sleeping by now.

Lifting the candlestick from her bedside table, she crept out of the room. She paused at the bottom of the stairs, not knowing which room was the library. She contemplated a cowardly return to her room, but a door along the hall opened, and Beldon beckoned to her, then placed a finger to his lips in warning.

Harriet hurried to the library door. When she approached, Beldon grabbed her hand and drew her in. He took the candle from her and blew it out, leaving them in darkness, and closed the door behind them. Immediately his arms went around her, imprisoning her against the door.

Her heart raced at his closeness. "Why did you want to see . . . " she began, but his lips fitting over hers stopped the words. All thoughts and speculations fled from her mind as the feel and taste of him took over every sense, melting her at her core. Eagerly she wrapped her arms about Beldon's neck, shivering at the contact of their bodies.

As his kisses deepened she welcomed him, and then murmured, "No," when he broke away from her lips. He pressed his lips against her throat and the bared skin of her cleavage, and she wriggled against him, desperately seeking more intimate contact.

He pulled her away from the door, all the time kissing her face and neck. She found herself on his lap, spilled across a huge overstuffed chair. He possessed her lips again, while his hands stroked her through the clothing. She tingled at the touch of his fingers on her breasts. "Oh, my," she whispered.

He stopped. "This was a mistake. I never meant to let myself get carried away again."

She still lay in his arms, her eyes closed, struggling for control. It seemed she was equally helpless against the temptation he represented. "I must get back to my room." Her voice sounded higher than usual, almost squeaky. "Astraea will wonder what happened to me."

For a moment longer, Beldon held her. "Yes, you must." He helped her to her feet and tugged her toward the door.

She resisted. "I told Astraea I was getting a book."

He pulled a book at random off the shelf and handed it to Harriet. He relit her candle and passed it to her, holding her hand for an extra moment. Then he said, "Good night," and gently pushed her out the door.

She made her way to her room. His regret over their renewed passion showed he didn't want her. She must admit that there was no chance for love between them and begin her campaign to ensure that Astraea and Beldon noticed each other. She would have to be subtle. Although they might fall in love unwittingly, she was quite sure neither would respond well to a deliberate attempt to throw them together.

In her room, Harriet glanced at the book he had given her. She laughed.

Astraea sleepily stirred in the bed and blinked her eyes open. "What do you find amusing at such a late hour?"

"Oh, I didn't mean to awaken you"—Harriet set the candle back on the bedside table—"but as long as you are, you may as well help me take off my gown." She walked over to the dressing table and, laying the book down, reached to unfasten her dress.

Groaning, Astraea threw back the covers and went to help. "Was your sojourn in the library worth our loss of sleep?"

"Yes, I suppose so." Harriet allowed her thoughts to dwell on those moments in Beldon's arms. She could almost accept the thought of marriage to him even though he didn't love her. But he would soon tire of her. No, she would not permit herself to even think of making this temporary betrothal permanent.

Astraea leaned across her sister's shoulder to look at the book, her blond braid swinging forward. " 'An Authentic Account of An Embassy from The King of Great Britain to the Emperor of China. Including Curious Observations made, and Information obtained, in Traveling through that Ancient Empire and a small part of Chinese Tartary. Together with a Relation of the Voyage undertaken on the Occasion by his Majesty's Ship the Lion, and the ship Hindestan in the East India Company's Service, to the Yellow Sea, and Gulf of Pekin; as well as that of the return to Europe; with Notices of the several places where they stopped in their way out and home.' Why, Harry, do you still plan to go traveling with Great-Aunt Harriet?"

Chapter Seven

Harriet squirmed. She had hoped Astraea wouldn't show any curiosity about the book. Then she realized she had overlooked a potential ally in Astraea by not confiding the truth to her—some of it, at least. She felt the younger girl's cool breath on her back as she finished untying the tapes of her gown.

"I've never given up my plans to travel." Harriet stepped out of the dress and turned to the wardrobe to hang it on a hook, then removed her corset and chemise. She dropped her nightshift over her head and turned to Astraea, who looked stunned at Harriet's revelation. "I have tried to think how to tell you, but you were so pleased with my match. I regretted agreeing to marry Beldon almost as soon as I said the words."

"Oh, Harry, how could you? He is so handsome and I, well, I thought 'twas a love match."

Harriet chuckled. "It's far from that. I admit, at first I was dazzled when he proposed—he is so handsome and he was the greatest catch of the season." She sat at the dressing table and pulled the pins from her hair.

"But, he loves you, doesn't he? Why else would he choose you amongst all the girls on the marriage mart this season?"

"No, he doesn't love me. He said as much when he proposed. He spoke of things we had in common." Harriet ran the brush through her curls, comparing, as she always did, her shorter hair with its drab color to Astraea's glorious locks.

"What things?" Astraea looked hopefully at her, probably trying to salvage some romance from the situation.

Harriet blushed. Her main thread of commonality with Beldon was the inconvenient lust they had for each other, but she would not say that to Astraea. "Oh, he was not specific. We've talked of a number of matters, so I'm not sure exactly to what he was referring."

Astraea took the hairbrush from Harriet and stroked it through more gently than Harriet had done. "You must tell him at once and be released from the betrothal, Harry."

"It isn't that easy. What will our parents say, especially Mama? For probably the first time in my life, she is actually proud of me. They will be so disappointed—and so embarrassed. I have been hoping I could perhaps, well, set the date for several months from now, and when the time came close, pretend we have just discovered our incompatibility. Or something.

"I think Beldon regrets his declaration as much as I do. I have been afraid, ever since we arrived, that he intends to tell me he doesn't think we should suit after all."

"That's the solution. Just tell our parents Beldon has changed his mind. They cannot blame you for that."

"No, I cannot. He would be regarded as a blackguard of the worst sort if he cried off. His only hope is for me to do so. And you know even if he could tell me he no longer wanted to marry me, our parents would still believe it was my fault. I have to make sure the betrothal stands through the house party. You must help me, Astraea!"

Beldon sat alone in the darkened library, inventing creative epithets to describe his mishandling of the situation.

Harriet's ardent response to his kisses and caresses argued against her ending the betrothal. His own conscience nipped at him for his behavior. Perhaps attempting to manipulate one's bride-to-be to end a betrothal was less dishonorable than backing out oneself, but it was surely only a matter of degree.

He must try to make something of this misbegotten match. He had told Vare he wanted time for Harriet and himself to become better acquainted. He must make a beginning at that aim.

For that, he must get her alone. He would never get next to Harriet, between those actually inimical to the match—Mrs. Purvis, Aunt Manning, those cursed suitors of Harriet's—and those who considered it their privilege to make free with his time—Lucy, Uncle Bartram—and his grandmother numbered in both groups. All seemed in a conspiracy to keep them apart.

And if they succeeded? Was there still a chance she would cry off?

Temptation rose in him to avoid the whole matter, much as he avoided his family by staying in Town as much as possible. He rose from his chair, lit a candle, and headed for his chamber. No, if he were doomed to wed Miss Vernon, better to make every effort to at least begin the marriage on terms of compatibility.

When Harriet and Astraea left their room the next morning, Harriet flinched at the thought of facing Beldon's family at breakfast. She had not yet sorted them all out. Last night, at dinner and afterward, her mind had dwelled almost exclusively on Beldon's lack of attentions to her, and she had not even made an effort to remember the others. Now she could not help wondering how many of them agreed with old Lady Beldon's remark about how ill she compared with her beauteous sisters.

And would she encounter Mrs. Purvis? During the endless evening just past, she had not had any exchange with this woman she knew was inimical to her, but her luck was bound to change. Had Beldon invited the widow in hopes that her presence would induce Harriet to cry off from the betrothal?

At the foot of the stairs, a maidservant gave the sisters the direction to the breakfast room, and they found their way. The expansive room was paneled in oak, with several still life paintings upon the walls, and at one end a large bow window looked out on a grassy garden fringed with flowering shrubs. Harriet stopped short upon viewing the seeming multitude of faces in the room and belatedly realized that not all of Beldon's relations were present.

Eustace and Lettice sat among the other occupants at the long table. Undoubtedly Mama had requested a tray in her bedchamber, and Pallas always breakfasted with her sons when they resided within the same walls, wishing to spend as much time with them as she could.

The distinguished older gentleman, to whom Harriet had spoken yester evening, sat at the table. Sir Somebody or other. The rest of the people in the room consisted of the rather plump young man; Beldon's stepfather, the naval officer; Miss Willoughby; and the faded blonde who Harriet had decided last night was not Beldon's mother. She need only determine who the middle-aged lady was, and the rest of the unknown people too.

Astraea and Harriet each took breakfast from the sideboard, toast and a boiled egg for Harriet. Astraea filled her plate with thickly sliced ham, kidneys, a concoction that appeared to consist of eggs and cheese, and pickled pigs' feet.

They sat at the long table, and a footman stepped forward with a teapot. "Tea, madame?" His stiff posture and the pompous tone of his voice made Astraea giggle as she assented.

Harriet glanced at her sister-in-law's cup, which contained some dark liquid. "Is that coffee you have, Lettice? Oh, good. I'll have some, too."

Astraea had sat next to Miss Willoughby and fallen immediately into an animated conversation with her. The girl appeared a year or two younger than Astraea, and from her awestruck expression had conceived a deep admiration for Harriet's sister.

Harriet chose a chair as far from anyone as possible, not wishing to be drawn into a conversation that might expose her ignorance of everybody's identity. Nevertheless, the elderly sir, seated opposite and down two chairs from her, asked suddenly, "Do you hunt, Miss Vernon?"

"Why, yes, I do!" Taken by surprise, she forgot to conceal

her not-quite-proper pastime, receiving frowns from Eustace and his wife.

"Splendid!" He beamed at her. His white locks curled luxuriantly, and deep lines criss-crossed his bronzed face. "I raise and train hunters, you know. I've been working with a promising youngster—Pasha. Perhaps you would like to visit the stables. I would be most pleased to show you around."

He launched into an obviously favorite subject and appeared ready to continue for some time. The lady who was not Beldon's mother broke into his speech. "Sir Bartram, I have asked you not to bring stable talk to our meals. It quite puts me off my food, Miss Vernon," she said in an aside to Harriet.

Hurriedly, Harriet said, "I would like to visit the stables sometime, Sir Bartram, but it is impossible this morning. Miss Manning has offered to show me around Langwell Towers. That is, she is not here—perhaps something has come up and she is not able . . . " She glanced around the table seeking enlightenment on the whereabouts of her would-be guide.

"My daughter is busy in the mornings," said the older lady. "She assists her grandmother, Lady Beldon, with duties concerned with running this considerable household. Marianne has been groomed from childhood to become chatelaine at Langwell Towers. Nevertheless," she condescended, "I believe she said she would hold herself ready to give you a tour of the house later. She will meet you at two o'clock in the downstairs hallway."

"Y-yes, of course. I-I would not w-wish to put M-Miss Manning to any t-trouble."

"It will be no trouble," Mrs. Manning assured her grandly. "Marianne always does her duty. If some of your family wish to accompany you on the tour, they are welcome." The older lady smiled at Eustace and Lettice as she rose from the table and strode out of the room.

"Must be about my business, too," Sir Bartram said. He gave Harriet a formal bow. "Let me know whenever you have time to make the acquaintance of my horses."

Harriet gave up on eating, managing only to swallow some coffee. Miss Manning had seemed congenial yesterday afternoon, and she hoped she had found a friend in Beldon's lovely cousin. Now it seemed Harriet's betrothal had blighted Miss Manning's expectations of a match with Lord Beldon, and any friendship between them must be tainted with Miss Manning's disappointment, however dutiful and pleasant she might be to Harriet.

She listened to the conversation between Astraea and Miss Willoughby, who was saying, "I will be sixteen by next season, and Mama has said *she* doesn't mind helping me make my bows, but Beldon says I may not go. Everybody in this family toadies to him. It isn't as though he is even my brother, not really." She shot a resentful glance at her father, who continued to eat, impervious to her insinuations.

"Undoubtedly Lord Beldon knows what is best for you, Miss Willoughby," Eustace abruptly said. "Young girls introduced to society too soon are likely to make a misstep, in some cases to their ruination. And if your mother approves this notion, she is far too lenient. My mother was most insistent that her daughters wait until they were eighteen to make their debut."

"Indeed, you must not think of such a thing as a come-out in London at your age," Lettice agreed. "There are so many pitfalls. Even our dear Harriet, who is a tractable person for the most part, found it difficult to remember all the rules. If I should have daughters, they will be well prepared before I allow them such a challenge, I assure you." She rose and beckoned Eustace to follow. "We shall meet you at two for the tour of Langwell, Harriet. I look forward to seeing this lovely house in more detail." Lettice departed the room with her husband.

Into the militant quiet that followed Eustace and Lettice's intrusion into the girls' conversation, Astraea said, "I understand precisely what you mean, Lucy. I used to believe I would never reach the age of eighteen. In my family, it was an inflexible rule that no one of the sisters could make her come-out until the next older sister was spoken for, which usually meant that we were eighteen anyway by the time it was our turn. But you know, a house party such as this one is an opportunity to make the acquaintance of some other young people."

"That's very well when there are some young men among the company, but Beldon has invited only your family—and that other friend of his, Mrs. Purvis." Miss Willoughby's pouting mouth matched the bitter tone of her voice.

"Your speech is most ungracious and inhospitable, Lucy," said the fleshy young man, who had been silent all this time. "It would appear you do not welcome our guests, and I am sure you do not wish to create this impression."

"Oh, you are horrid, Oswald. You never used to be so prosy until you took holy orders, and now you think you are superior to the rest of us! Everybody has advice for me, and nobody understands how *I* feel!" Miss Willoughby jumped up and ran from the room in tears.

"Oh dear," said Astraea. "I wished only to give her thoughts a more positive turn, but it seems I added to her feeling of being disparaged."

"It is very kind of you to worry, but not at all necessary," Oswald said. "Lucy likes to dramatize herself. Her storms quickly appear and are just as quickly over."

"Perhaps I ought to find her," Astraea mused. "I have some books of fashion plates. They might cheer her up."

"That is a good idea," Harriet assured her sister, and Astraea sprang up, hugged Harriet, and left the room.

The young clergyman watched Astraea go and then turned to Harriet. "Miss Vernon, I do not wish to intrude, but you looked somewhat distressed after your conversation with my mother. I assure you that any consideration of a match between my cousin and Marianne was only in my mother's mind. The two people most concerned in the matter have never thought of it, believe me."

"Thank you, Mr. Manning." Harriet smiled at him, not certain whether to believe him, at least as to Miss Manning's feelings. Harriet's own brothers were the last persons to whom she would ever have confided her infatuation with Lord Beldon, and Miss Manning might feel the same. Here was another pair she would have to study for clues to their feelings.

However, if Miss Manning felt an unrequited love for Lord Beldon, Harriet did not think her breaking off the engagement would turn his thoughts in that direction. Her life was growing ever more complicated, besieging her with the difficulties she had encountered since her arrival at Langwell Towers.

Shortly before, Harriet had wanted to flee the breakfast room, but now as Mr. Manning exited, leaving her alone with the silent Captain Willoughby, the room seemed a haven where she did not need to face the troublesome household.

At two, Harriet and some of her family gathered in the downstairs hallway. Mama awaited the tour eagerly, having an interest in architecture. Lettice and Eustace also waited.

Others joined the group. Mrs. Purvis expressed her ardent desire to see the house. And, before the time appointed, Mr. Taber and his house guest, Mr. Luchan, had called on the residents at Langwell and also joined in.

As they were about to begin, Lord Beldon walked by. Harriet had not seen him since the library the previous night. She had to squelch a strong desire to run to him.

Beldon paused. "Why should you wish to waste your time on a tour of Langwell, Taber? You've seen it any number of times."

"I've never had the tour," Mr. Taber replied.

Beldon shrugged. Giving a last, intimate smile for Harriet, he continued on his way. She felt herself blushing.

If Miss Manning was surprised to see so many waiting when she appeared, she did not reveal it, either by word or expression. "If you'll follow me, I'll show you the cellars first," she said. "Langwell Towers was built in the late seventeenth century by the second Lord Beldon. The architect was Robert

Hooke. Additions and renovations were undertaken in the eighteenth century at various times."

Although Harriet harbored doubts she would ever be mistress of the estate, she had every intention of paying heed to Beldon's cousin's explanations of the house features. However, as Miss Manning conveyed them to the kitchens, the pantry, the buttery, the wine cellars, giving a smooth explanation of the running of the house at each station, Harriet found herself distracted. Mr. Taber and Mr. Luchan had quickly taken up positions on either side of her.

"Your family was very enterprising to obtain the invitation to Langwell Towers, Miss Vernon," said Mr. Taber. He smiled.

Harriet frowned. "I do not know what you mean, Mr. Taber."

His smile widened. "Why, Eustace knows I am a neighbor of Beldon's."

Oh, dear. Could Mr. Taber think they had contrived the invitation to further Harriet's proximity to him, in an attempt to obtain a proposal? Harriet could not explain the truth to him, when no betrothal between her and Beldon had been announced, and she was so doubtful it would continue. But if this was what Mr. Taber thought, he was likely to feel very badly used when he learned the true situation, since she would refuse any offer from him no matter what happened with the betrothal. She must speak to Eustace. Perhaps her brother would be able to hint Mr. Taber away.

"Now we will go up to the second floor and tour the bedchambers, and work our way downstairs, finishing on the ground floor with the public rooms," Miss Manning said.

Mr. Luchan leaned over Harriet and said, "Miss Vernon, I suppose you are wondering that I never formed one of your court this past season, since I was so attentive last year?"

Harriet stared, no words coming to her mind to rescue her. She knew why Mr. Luchan had stayed away.

The question apparently was rhetorical, however, for he continued, "Actually, it was because of your father, Miss Vernon. Lord Vare informed me my suit would be unwelcome. If you had shown any sign of partiality, I would not have allowed myself to become so easily dissuaded. But indeed, upon reflection I decided 'faint heart' and all that, and came to put my fate to the touch again. No, don't say anything. I want no answer from you until we have more time to become acquainted."

What was she to do? No matter what happened between her and Beldon, Harriet did not wish for any other suitors. Miss Manning eyed her with annoyance, no doubt vexed that her kindness to Harriet was being repaid with such inattention.

They entered the small nursery. Eustace and Lettice's two young sons played under the watchful eye of their nanny, Mrs. Miller.

Pallas asked Mrs. Miller, "Where are Calder and Lord Peregrine?"

"They went with Master Nicholas, Your Grace. I heard some talk of fishing."

Pallas paled. "I hope they will be careful. Did Mr. Draper accompany the boys?"

"I'm sure I don't know." None of the Vernon servants cared for the tutor to Pallas's boys, Harriet knew. Too starched up by half, and she suspected he spied for his relation, the duke.

"Mr. Oswald was with the boys, Your Grace. He'll look after them," Hester declared. "He tutors Master Nicholas."

After the nursery, the group returned to the first floor.

"The wings with their round towers were built in the mid-eighteenth century," Miss Manning continued when they had reached the first floor. "Robert Adam designed the additions and a new front for the whole building, and much of the interior design was completed at that time. We will begin with the grand dining salon at the back of the house."

As the tour proceeded, Mr. Taber and Mr. Luchan kept close to Harriet, vying for her attention. Subtle attempts she made to disengage were squelched. Perhaps she was too subtle. However, Lady Vare maintained a lady could always find a polite way to rid herself of unwelcome attentions.

They viewed the large drawing room, music room, and a suite of apartments made up into a bedchamber, of which

Miss Manning said, "Queen Anne is reported to have used this apartment in 1703. Unfortunately for any who prefer to see the chamber as it was then, it has been refurbished since that time, although the family attempted to reproduce the furnishings as closely as possible to those the distinguished guest would have used."

As they left Queen Anne's chamber, they passed another set of rooms. "These are Lady Beldon's rooms," said Miss Manning. "She always rests at this time of day, so we will be unable to view her apartment." In an aside to Harriet, she said, "It is the master apartment, but Lady Beldon has refused to give up the rooms since Grandfather died. As Beldon has not resided at Langwell all that much, he has not pressed the issue.

"Now we will go down to the ground floor where we will conclude the tour," she said more loudly, for the whole party.

The visitors dutifully plodded down the stairs, where they viewed the library, ballroom, gallery, conservatory, and chapel. By the time the tour concluded, the attentions of her would-be suitors had exhausted Harriet.

She repaired to her chamber for a few minutes' rest before dressing for afternoon tea. It was unfair that she could have all the attention of Mr. Taber or Mr. Luchan, but the man she really wanted to spend time with her was so elusive.

Chapter Eight

Harriet presented herself in the drawing room at the stroke of four, as prepared as she could be to face Beldon's family and the troublesome other guests. Astraea had helped her with her toilette—after the maid had left their chamber, as Mary would not have approved of the changes to her own handiwork. Astraea was most adept at applying a paint brush to a lady's face in such a way that her artistry was undetectable.

Thus, Harriet felt at her best, attired in a tea gown of pomona green, with curls clustered most becomingly about her face, and the elfin tilt of her eyes and her full lips artfully highlighted.

That Astraea's efforts had succeeded was obvious in the appreciative looks bestowed on Harriet by Piers Luchan, Sir Bartram, and even Beldon's sober cousin Mr. Manning. Mr. Taber unbent sufficiently to say, "You are looking well, Miss Vernon," although she thought his expression faintly disapproving. Perhaps the paint was not as invisible as Astraea had claimed.

However, the person whose approbation she sought, Lord Beldon, did not appear. Although he had expressed regrets that he had kissed her in the library last night, she later had reflected there might be cause for hope in the very fact that his passions could be stirred by her.

There was not enough reason to hope to justify throwing away her dreams. She should not worry about what he thought. She should strive, through the remainder of this visit, to aid Astraea and Beldon to fall in love, and then proceed with her plans for her own life. Oh, but she could not help harboring the wish that Beldon would prefer her over her ravishing sister.

She looked toward the door just one more time, and Miss Manning, who had taken a place on the settee beside Harriet, said, "I believe he is much taken up with estate business, Miss Vernon. He has not been home to Langwell for some time, and he always finds a number of matters have awaited his attention when he first returns."

"Yes, of course." Harriet tried to keep the disappointment out of her voice.

Mr. Luchan drifted over. "Good afternoon, ladies. How do you lovely ladies do this gloomy afternoon?" He waited only for them to attest to their well-being before he turned to Miss Manning. "I wish to thank you, Miss Manning, for the most interesting and educational tour of your home. Did you not find it most illuminating, Miss Vernon?"

"Indeed, I did, Mr. Luchan. I have already thanked Miss Manning for her kindness in showing us about the house."

Miss Manning had stiffened when Mr. Luchan came near. She set aside her tea things and rose. "I really must see how Grandmother does. If you'll excuse me?" She walked away.

Mr. Luchan watched her, his face almost mournful for a moment, before he turned to Harriet. "I seem to have that effect on all the young ladies. No doubt it is what comes of my ill repute. You shall not abandon me, Miss Vernon, shall you?"

"No doubt I *should* do so, Mr. Luchan. However, I think I am safe among so many people in this room, no matter how ill you intend to use me. I will risk your company for a short while."

Mr. Luchan took the place on the settee that Miss Manning had abandoned. Shortly, Mr. Taber joined them, sitting at Harriet's other side.

Mr. Luchan and Mr. Taber continued to hover over her all during tea, paying her attentions that would have been flattering if she had cared in the least for their opinions. Trying not to reveal her boredom, Harriet looked around at the others. In truth, most of the people in the room looked bored.

Her mother sat with Mrs. Manning. Mama had her patient expression while Mrs. Manning held forth on some emphatic opinion, nodding her head and gesturing with her hands. In another part of the room, young Reverend Mr. Manning sat by Miss Willoughby and Astraea. He, too, wore a patient and slightly amused expression while Miss Willoughby chattered animatedly.

Eustace and Lettice stood by Mrs. Purvis close to the fireplace, which had a cozy blaze going, in honor of the drizzly day, though it was by no means cold. All three cast occasional disapproving glances Harriet's way. She lifted her chin and stared at them. If Eustace would but drop a word in Mr. Taber's ear, Harriet knew she would lose one of her suitors.

Miss Manning sat with her grandmother and Sir Bartram. Lady Beldon looked at Harriet sternly, no doubt disapproving of her sitting with two unattached young men. She refused to be cast down by guilt at Lady Beldon's disfavor. To whom would she talk if her supposed fiancé would not make an appearance?

Pallas was not of the party, no doubt spending the time with her sons. And Captain and Mrs. Willoughby also had not joined the group for tea.

Just before they disbanded, Beldon strode in and went directly to Miss Manning. "Marianne, could I see you in my study, say half an hour before dinner tonight? I wish to go over the household accounts with you."

"Why, yes, Beldon, if you wish." Marianne frowned slightly, and her voice sounded surprised. Was this unusual behavior on Beldon's part?

He came over and bowed to Harriet. "Miss Vernon. I shall see you at dinner. I will excuse myself now—I'm all covered with dirt from the stables." With a bow to the rest of the company, he left the room.

His abruptness, almost discourtesy, topped Harriet's gloom.

As soon as she could, she escaped from her gallants, saying she must dress for dinner. In truth, as she made for her chamber, she knew not what to do, whether to cry or to storm and throw things about.

* * *

Seated at his desk, Beldon barked "Come" when Marianne knocked at his office door. She carried a heavy ledger. "I had to borrow this from Mrs. Goodman. She was somewhat indignant at being excluded from any discussion of her accounts."

"Yes, just set it down somewhere and sit down. I had to think of some excuse to talk to you."

She laid the account book on his desk before taking the chair. "You don't need an excuse to talk to me, Beldon. We've talked whenever we wished since we were children."

"Life is more complicated now." He waved a hand in emphasis. He stood up, unable to sit still any longer.

"I need you to ask Harri—er, Miss Vernon, to accompany you after dinner to somewhere private, the conservatory, perhaps."

Marianne raised an eyebrow. "How should I do that?"

"How should I know? Make up an excuse—you can think of something, I'm sure."

"I don't understand, Beldon." Her brow wrinkled as she gazed at him.

"I need to talk to her alone, but I can't get near her."

"Do you think that's wise?"

"Of course it is!" There he was, losing control again, his voice rising. This never happened to him. He calmed himself, leaning with his hip on his desk. "We have things we need to discuss, but I can't get near her in the crowd. Just do this for me, will you please?"

She rose slowly, her brow still furrowed. "Yes, I'll do it."

"Good." Beldon strode to the door.

"Is that all? No discussion of accounts?" Marianne rose and reached toward the ledger.

"No. Tell Mrs. Goodman I changed my mind. We'll talk about them later." He walked out of the room.

At dinner, Beldon looked halfway down the length of the dining table, where Harriet Vernon sat, and frowned. Who had arranged the seating at this confounded meal, anyway?

Of course, it was Marianne, who had suffered the tutelage of old Lady Beldon on the subject of precedence. So, he had the Duchess of Moorewood at his right, and Harriet was placed between Luchan and Taber.

She wore a gown of a soft orangey color that lent her a glow, and even with all the beauties at his table, hers was the face to which his gaze was drawn.

He'd had a damned difficult time staying away from her all day. 'Twould only be a repeat of last evening, however, hanging about but being unable to get near her in the crowd.

He must remember, putting his hands on her, kissing her, as he longed to do, was forbidden. When he met her later in the conservatory, he intended to do nothing more than invite her to go riding with him, early in the morning before anybody was about. It was an innocuous way to further their acquaintance.

He'd not make up one of her court, following and mooning about her like Taber and Luchan. He could hardly picture a more unlikely pair than those two. What were they about, anyway? Harriet had not been so besieged with suitors in London, so far as he'd been able to tell. He glared at the two men, vying for her attention as though she were the most important person in the room. What was it they found so fascinating, anyway? He sent another glare in their direction, but neither of them took their attention away from Harriet long enough to notice.

Harriet, however, looked his way in mid-glare, and a shocked expression crossed her face.

Damn! He had to talk to her. Alone. He hoped he could count on Marianne to follow his instructions.

After dinner, the women settled into the salon in a perfunctory fashion. Harriet had not heard of any entertainment planned for the evening, and the individuals in this disparate group had little in common with each other. Pallas fell into conversation with Lettice. Mama talked with Mrs. Willoughby—planning Harriet's nuptials with Beldon, she feared. Miss Manning kept by her grandmother's side, joined by Mrs. Manning. Astraea and Lucy Willoughby disappeared quite soon from the group, and Mrs. Purvis paced restlessly, making no attempt to look interested in the other women's conversation. Harriet could hardly blame her; she found very little to hold her interest in the oddments she heard.

Fortunately, the men came in soon. However, again Beldon was not among them. Harriet hardly knew whether to be furious or discouraged. She could no longer entertain even the slightest thought that Beldon intended to make their attachment real. And neither could she hope that Beldon and Astraea would make a match, if they were never together in one place.

In the future, she would at least have to insist that Astraea remain with her when the whole group gathered. Then if Beldon did deign to show his presence, there might be some chance of a romance blossoming between them.

Mrs. Purvis, lacking Beldon to work her wiles on, made up to Mr. Taber, to Harriet's relief. Eustace had told her when they first came down for dinner that he had finally taken Mr. Taber aside and informed him of Harriet's changed circumstances.

Mr. Taber had sulked when he had approached Harriet before they were seated at the table and said in the tones of one who considered himself ill-used, "Why did you not tell me of your betrothal to Beldon? I mislike making such a figure of fun."

"I apologize, Mr. Taber, but I could not speak of it. The betrothal is not yet official."

He had at least been gracious enough to speak to her at dinner, relieving her a little of Mr. Luchan's attentions, which showed no signs of abating. Either Mr. Taber had not yet had the chance to share the news with him, or Mr. Luchan chose to ignore Harriet's affianced status.

Mr. Luchan made his way to her side promptly when the men joined the women, and without Mr. Taber to act as a buffer, Harriet found his attentions wearing.

She was rescued by Miss Manning's coming over and saying, "Miss Vernon—Harriet—could I ask for a private word with you?"

Harriet abandoned Mr. Luchan with a promptitude which could not have given his consequence any boost. When he made as if to follow the two women, Miss Manning fended him off with, "I need to speak privately with Miss Vernon, Mr. Luchan," and he drifted off to join Lady Beldon and Mrs. Manning.

Miss Manning led the way out of the room and down a long corridor. Harriet, trying to remember the details of the house layout from her tour, had no idea where they were headed. "What did you wish to speak to me about?"

"In a moment." Miss Manning's face was serious, and Harriet suddenly had a sinking feeling she intended to ask her to give up Beldon so his cousin could have him. What would she tell Marianne? The truth, she supposed, gloomily. She did not possess Lord Beldon to give away.

They entered the conservatory, a large, high-ceilinged room filled with plants, fruit trees, and flowers. Light came through tall windows along the outer walls, the setting sun turning the leaves to golden. Farther away from the windows, the room was dim. Out of the shadows came Beldon. "Oh!" Harriet stepped back involuntarily.

"He asked me to bring you here," Marianne said. She frowned uncertainly. "He said he needed to talk to you. But, if you don't want to see him alone, I won't leave you."

"No, that's all right." Harriet spoke slowly, her attention fixed on Beldon. She needed to talk to him; she knew that, but could not remember why.

"If you are sure." Marianne backed toward the door, looking reluctant to leave, but then turned and hurried away.

Holding her gaze with his own, Beldon moved to Harriet and swept her up in his arms, banding her so tightly she could hardly breathe. Or perhaps it was his touch which had that effect. He bent over and pressed his lips against hers. Her mind emptied of thought and sensation took over as she melted against him. For several minutes she was lost in his kisses, and then his lips moved over her face and hair. Harriet leaned into him, needing ever more.

Beldon pulled back, taking Harriet's hands. "Go riding with me tomorrow, early in the morning."

"What?" She blinked, coming back with a thud from that place his kisses always carried her.

"First thing, before anyone else is stirring. I want just the two of us, alone."

Harriet stared at Beldon, sheer happiness at the thought of riding with him contending with warnings that it wasn't wise to be alone with him. And Astraea, shouldn't she invite her, give her more of a chance for her romance to develop with Beldon? But Astraea was at best an indifferent rider, and somewhat timid around horses. She would not be at her best in such circumstances. Besides, Harriet wanted to have this chance to be alone with Beldon.

"When I issued the invitation for this house party, I told your father I wished us to become better acquainted. We cannot do so in the crowds always around us. Someone else always demands either your or my attention. Please say you'll come."

"B-better acquainted?" Harriet tried to interpret the expression on Beldon's face. Was he anxious for her answer?

"Why, yes. Our betrothal happened so suddenly, we scarcely know each other. Do you feel you know me well enough to commit to spending our lives together?"

What did he want of her? Was he looking for her to back out of the betrothal? Surely, asking for time together must mean he still had thoughts of going through with it. "Yes, it's true I hardly know you," she said. "I'll go with you tomorrow."

"Good. I'll meet you in the stables at dawn." He kissed her again, a hasty leave-taking this time, then walked briskly from the conservatory.

Harriet, not at all sure she could find her way back to the salon, stared after him. He could at least have offered to see her started the right way. She walked along the corridor, hoping to see a landmark she recognized. Luckily, she had not gone far when she saw Marianne lingering in the hallway—far enough from the conservatory not to be suspected of eavesdropping, but close enough to assist if Harriet needed her. She felt her lips curve up in a grateful smile.

"I thought you might need a guide."

"Thank you. I was wondering how to find my way back."

Marianne leaned to peer at her. "Are you all right?"

"Of course. Why should you doubt it?"

"You are rather, er, mussed. Perhaps you should go tidy yourself before you go back in the salon."

"Oh, my." Harriet could feel the heat rise up her neck and face. How embarrassing that Marianne could tell Beldon had kissed her. Was she jealous? She scanned her expression, but could detect no emotion other than, perhaps, amusement. Still, she did not want to deal with the others. And besides, she wished to be rested for her early morning horseback ride. "I think I will just retire for the evening, then. Could you please make my excuses and say that I was very tired?"

"Of course."

"Good night then. Thank you for . . . everything." Harriet dashed upstairs. Once in her room, she looked into the mirror. Indeed, she wasn't mussed so much as flushed, with lips that looked swollen and darkened.

Why, this was exactly the effect of the cosmetics Astraea had so expertly applied earlier. No wonder people considered face paint shocking. A few tendrils had worked loose from their pins, and, Harriet admitted, anyone with eyes could have seen she had been engaged in passionate love play. No, not love, she reminded herself. Something very close to it on her part. She felt breathless and dizzy, rather like when she took a jump and realized as soon as her horse left the ground that she was off-balance and headed for a fall.

She had to do a better job of guarding her heart. Still, her thoughts leaped ahead to imagine, with their spending more time together, Beldon's actually falling in love with her.

Chapter Nine

Harriet searched the deserted stableyard, hollowness growing in her midsection. No one seemed to be about. Beldon must have forgotten about their riding engagement. She shivered in the mists of dawn and wrapped her arms about her. The stable doors were ajar and she peered into the darkened building.

At the far end, she discerned movement. Definitely she heard soft whistling. An early rising stableboy. Nevertheless, she entered the stable, moving quietly toward the sound. If she discovered only a groom at work, she would attempt to sneak off undiscovered and save herself from embarrassment.

Once Harriet's eyes adapted, windows at the ends provided sufficient illumination to see a dark bay horse in the corridor, with two human legs behind it. The man spoke in an Irish brogue, "Ah, 'tis a beauty you are and no mistake."

Harriet turned to flee the stable, but just out of the corner of her eye Lord Beldon's face became visible over the horse's back as he stood fully. "Good morning," he called.

"Oh, good morning." Harriet approached the horse, heat rising in her face. "I-I thought you w-were a groom. You were speaking in an Irish brogue."

Beldon burst out laughing. "And be sure I was, for this is an Irish horse. Come and meet her."

Harriet came forward eagerly. "Oh, she's exquisite!" Perhaps "exquisite" was not quite the proper word to describe her; the mare was tall and solidly built, not some dainty ladies' mount. Her conformation was perfect, with a deep chest and strong, well-muscled legs. Harriet could easily picture her flying over jumps as though they were mere pebbles on the path.

"Isn't she, though? Harriet, meet Witch. Witch, this is Harriet. Pardon me for the familiarity, but we don't stand on ceremony in our stables."

Harriet waved away the inconsequential use of her given name. "Did you say her name is Witch?"

"Yes, and it fits her, too. She is planning your downfall as we speak." Beldon's voice held laughter, and, given the considering look in the bay's eyes, Harriet could believe his words. "I took your word that you are a bruising rider. There isn't another horse in the stable that you will enjoy riding so well. She floats over the ground like an angel, but you'll have to show her who's boss."

"Why, Lord Beldon, that's the best compliment anyone has ever paid me!" Harriet pulled off her glove and held out her hand to Witch, eager to touch the velvety nose. "I wish I had something for you, lovely girl, but I don't." The horse snuffled at her hand, then tossed her head, obviously displeased to find no offering there.

Beldon, beside her, whispered, "Here," and handed several lumps of sugar to her surreptitiously, so the horse wouldn't see. Harriet turned her head to smile her thanks before placing the sugar on her palm and offering it again.

Delicately, Witch nibbled the treat off Harriet's hand, then permitted her to stroke her soft nose. "You are a beauty, aren't you," Harriet murmured. Her attention half on Beldon, feeling his gaze on her, she rubbed the horse's face, tracing the small star on her forehead, combed her fingers through the coarse hairs of her forelock, and then patted the sleek neck. Beldon drew in a sharp breath and a shivery sensation shot through Harriet. Would he kiss her? She tingled at the thought. He made no move to come closer, though.

"I think we're friends, now." Harriet looked at Beldon.

He stared at her hand, looking lost somewhere in his thoughts. Hastily, feeling almost as if she had disrobed in front of him, Harriet tugged on her glove again.

He shook himself and turned to lay aside the curry with which he had been grooming the mare. Harriet noted with approval that he set it on a shelf with other grooming supplies. Then he exchanged the halter for a bridle, and placed a sidesaddle on Witch's back. While he cinched the saddle he said, "She'll try to shake you off when you first mount her. If you let her have her head at the first opportunity and run off her fidgets, she'll do anything you ask of her after that."

"I'm sure we'll get along," Harriet assured him, eager to ride the lovely creature.

Beldon took the reins in his hand and turned toward the shadows at the back of the stable, where Harriet now realized another horse stood tethered. Beldon collected the big, rangy, dark gray gelding, already saddled and bridled, and walked the two horses to the stable door. Harriet followed. As they left the building, an older man rounded the corner and stepped into view. "Ah, Higgins, we were just about to go riding. This is Higgins, my head groom." Beldon turned to Harriet.

"You're putting her up on Witch?" the man asked, raising an eyebrow.

"Yes." Beldon handed the man the reins to his horse and turned to help Harriet mount.

At the exact moment Harriet settled her weight into the saddle, Witch hopped to the right. Harriet had fortunately felt the brief gathering of the horse's muscles and prepared herself. She saw a quick impression of Beldon reaching to catch her fall, and then her attention was taken up with reacting. She instinctively threw her weight in the same direction, gripped the leg rest, and firmed her hands on the reins. Before the horse came to rest, a deep, gravelly voice came from Harriet. " 'Ere now, stop this nonsense!"

Witch whipped her head around to stare at her, and Beldon and his stable man stared in equal shock. She chuckled. "Our old groom who taught me to ride spoke that way. I learned to imitate him to discipline the horses." She looked at Beldon. "You talk to your horses in an Irish brogue; I speak Cockney!"

Higgins laughed. "She'll do. I think our Witch has met her match."

Beldon swung up on his own horse. "Yes, I think she has." He led the way out of the stableyard.

The morning sun was just cresting the horizon, further gilding Harriet's gold riding habit. Beldon had already noted how her eyes appeared golden in the habit, and the ridiculous little concoction made up of feathers that perched upon her head like a bird. What a contradiction she represented.

She found the horse's rhythm quickly. Beldon admired her sureness with the horse, the lightness of her touch. He shivered, thinking of that touch as she stroked the horse, how he had suddenly imagined her small hand stroking him the same way. It had taken all of his willpower to keep from taking her in his arms and ravishing her on the stable floor.

The pathway led around the back of the stables. "See that archway of trees just ahead?" he called out to Harriet, riding slightly ahead of him. "There's an open, level stretch where it's safe to let out the horses."

"Oh, good!" She put Witch into a canter, and soon they entered the trees, still deeply shadowed in the dawn. Almost at the same moment they gave their horses their heads. Harriet had a slight lead as they started racing, but his horse had a longer stride and pulled ahead. Before the hall of trees ended, however, the lighter weight Witch bore gave her a telling advantage, and she nosed out Beldon's horse. Harriet was laughing as she pulled the bay mare up. The arched lane gave onto a broader path, and Harriet looked both directions before she turned to Beldon and asked, "Which way?"

To the right, the path led around the back of the house and to his tenant farms. The path to the left took one to a wood, his eventual destination, but he found he wanted to prolong the day, so he said, "Right."

Harriet turned her horse in that direction and continued at a trot on the still-fresh horse. Beldon rode up beside her. Harriet's eyes sparkled from their race, and her face had a becoming pinkness.

"Oh, she's a delight!" Harriet leaned over to pat Witch's neck. "Thank you for letting me ride her."

Beldon gradually slowed the pace so they traveled at a walk. "Consider her yours."

The path took them up the slope of a rounded hill. At the top, the vista to the north looked over the extensive gardens behind Langwell Towers, with its artificial lake and the Grecian temple at lake's edge.

The house gleamed, its white stone turned to rose by the rising sun. It had been constructed with the intent of making the view from the back as inspiring as that from the front. Handsome leaded glass windows, arched at the top, gave those in the house a vantage point to see the famous gardens, and lent architectural interest to the view from the outside, along with the circular conservatory at the west side of the house. Terraces led from the three separate sets of doors at the back, down into the formal flower gardens and on to the naturalistic landscape around the lake.

Beldon always gazed with pride and reverence upon the panorama at this point of the path, and he looked at Harriet to see her reaction to it.

"Oh, how beautiful!" she breathed, and then her face took on a wistful expression.

She sat for some time gazing at the house, and Beldon could not guess what she was thinking. Was she musing that Langwell would soon be her home?

The cool, classic beauty of Langwell reminded him again of the matching beauty he had pictured as his wife. This pixie, this fairy changeling, was not the proper mistress for his house, no matter how much he desired her.

The sense of entrapment caught him again. His chest constricted and for a moment he found it difficult to breathe. "We had better move on."

While they descended the hill, Beldon mulled over his options. She had claimed she wished to travel and had no interest in marriage—but that was before he had proposed. However, it was worth a try.

"Have you heard from your great-aunt recently, Miss Vernon?"

"No, she is traveling somewhere in South America at present. We do not expect her return for some weeks yet."

"Do you think she will be disappointed to hear you have deserted her?" he asked, trying to sound casual.

"Deserted her, Lord Beldon?" She frowned in puzzlement.

"Perhaps those are too strong words. Did you not have plans to travel in her company, Miss Vernon?"

Her eyes went wide, and he thought she paled, but as her skin was cast in a peach glow by sunshine, he could not be sure. She looked down at the ground by Witch's hooves, as if needing to pick her way on the downward slope. "Our plans were always rather vague," she said. "I cannot imagine that she will be much discommoded. She has always traveled alone."

Damnation! No help there, it seemed. He must count on his family to make the match undesirable to Harriet.

"Miss Vernon, I have had no chance before now to apologize for the remarks my grandmother made. She is—difficult. My family has become somewhat accustomed to her blunt manner of speaking, but I know it must have been hurtful. I should no doubt have warned you about her."

"There is no need to apologize, Lord Beldon. Her words were insulting to you as well, if I recall."

"Yes, but as I said, we are accustomed to her manner of speaking and take no note of it. Indeed, my whole family is of a quarrelsome cast. It is one reason I have spent so little time here at Langwell. But naturally, once I am married, my wife will reside here with my family."

At the foot of the hill, the farm of one of Beldon's tenants nestled. The Anders family and their employees were just starting their day when Beldon and Harriet approached, and two small children dashed out the gate and intercepted them.

The elder, a tow-headed boy of four clad only in a shirt

which came past his knees, ran nearly under the feet of Beldon's horse, yelling, "What did you bring us, Your Lordship?"

The little girl, just two, and entirely naked, ran more slowly on short, unsteady legs, but her lungs had as much capacity as her brother's. She echoed, "B'ing us?"

Their mother erupted from the house and picked up the girl, covering her small body with the apron she whipped off from around her middle, and stood blushing. "I must apologize, Your Lordship. I try to teach them manners, but the lessons don't stick when you come around."

Beldon laughed as he dismounted. "Of course they forget their manners around me. They know I always spoil them." He came around and helped Harriet dismount, then led her toward where the whole Anders family was gathering.

He picked up the small boy and tossed him overhead, to squeals—of delight from the lad and "Me, too!" from the baby.

"Oh, no, you don't," said young Mrs. Anders. "It wouldn't be proper and you without a stitch on."

"What do you have for us?" the boy repeated once Beldon set him on the ground again.

"Let's see." Beldon reached into a pocket inside his coat. "You probably have not broken your fast yet . . . " he looked an inquiry to their mother, who shook her head, "so candy would not be good. What about this?" He handed a sixpence to the lad.

"Gee!" The boy's eyes grew huge. "Thanks!"

Beldon looked at the little girl, who was stretching her arms out to him. "You are too young for money, I think. You would probably just try to eat it. What about this?" He drew a whistle out of the pocket. "You will probably have to show her how to blow it," he said to young Mrs. Anders.

The woman smiled at him and took the whistle. Placing it in her mouth, she gave a hearty blow. At the satisfying noise the whistle made, the girl said, "Me want it!" and reached for the treasure. Her mother handed it to her, laughing.

As they rode away, Harriet cast a glance at Beldon. "You

were very good with the children. It's obvious the entire family likes you. My father is not so easy with his tenants. I mean, he is a very good landlord. They respect him, of course."

Harriet's smiling face and glowing eyes started an immediate response in Beldon to bask in her admiration, immediately superseded by discomfort as he realized he did not wish to increase her regard for him. He must find a way to counteract her assertion.

"Do you mean my tenants do not respect me, Miss Vernon?"

"Oh, no, indeed. It's clear that they respect you as well. It's rather a puzzle to me," a small frown crossed her forehead, "for Papa is wont to say that a landlord may have his tenants' liking or their respect, but not both." She smiled at him. "I daresay Papa was wrong."

"No, Miss Vernon, he is probably right. My grandfather always used to tell me I had no notion of the dignities of my position and would be taken advantage of by the tenants. However, I grew up with Henry Anders, and 'tis difficult to stand upon ceremony with him and his family."

The sun had risen well above the horizon by the time they entered the shaded forest. The springy carpet of moss and grass under the feet of the mare smoothed her ride and muffled the sounds of hoofbeats. The scents of leaves and earth warmed by summer sunshine made Harriet feel at home.

She was falling in love with Beldon, a terrible state of affairs. She should not have come out riding with him alone. This whole morning, her mind had scrambled to think how to bring Astraea into the conversation. Their time together had seemed a perfect opportunity to make sure Beldon knew all of Astraea's finer qualities, in addition to the great beauty which he could hardly help noticing. However, she had managed to say not a single word about her sister. Every opening she thought of made her intentions too obvious.

The situation was complicated by the fact that she dared not claim her own disinterest in him too soon. If she ended up no longer betrothed to Beldon before he became attached to Astraea, there would be no further reason for the family to prolong the visit, and all would be ruined. To make everything even more difficult, this morning she had not been able to tell whether Beldon was trying to improve their acquaintance, as he had said, or whether he was trying to discourage her.

If he wished to end their betrothal, the merest whisper on her part would see the bond broken in a trice. However, if he was beginning to care for her, perhaps any effort on her part to bring Astraea to his notice was doomed to failure—and she could not help the wistful desire that this would be proved so. What was wrong with her to let her foolish hopes loose again?

If only he did not show so many admirable traits in addition to the handsomeness that had first attracted her. Naturally, she would not wish to promote a match between him and her sister if Beldon did not have qualities that would make him a good match for Astraea.

"You spoke of your distance from your family," she said, "but I observed you seem close to your cousin, Miss Manning."

"She is several years younger, and we seldom spent time together while we were growing up. I have the greatest respect for her. She oversees the household, cares for our grandmother, and is the greatest help to me in managing the estate."

"It must be a comfort to you to have her. I cannot think what I would do without my sisters—and Arthur, too. He, Astraea, Genie, and I were inseparable while we were children. Less than six years separates the four of us. Pallas, Eustace, and Clytie were several years older, so I understand how that makes a division that is difficult to overcome.

"Astraea and I have grown especially close since Genie was married three years ago—and Arthur, of course, has been away at school a good part of the time. I am sure many people look at Astraea and think she is too beautiful to be good, too, but I do not know a kinder, more compassionate person."

Harriet continued, "And your younger sister and brother are a good many years younger than you, so you have not had the experience of sharing your childhood with a sibling."

"Lucy is not my sister, Miss Vernon. Her mother was Captain Willoughby's first wife, who died when Lucy was but an infant. Mrs. Willoughby and my mother were girlhood friends, and when Mother heard of her death, she wrote a letter of sympathy to the captain. He confided that he needed to go to sea and was distraught at having no one to care for his daughter. Mother offered to take Lucy. She had been widowed several years by that time. Lucy remembers no other mother, and she and my mother are most fond of each other."

A clearing opened before them, with a picturesque cottage centered in it, two stories, half-timbered, with a thatched roof. A profusion of vines grew up the walls—honeysuckle, roses, wisteria, grape, and ivy tangled together with indiscriminate intimacy. The gardens were similarly overgrown in riotous confusion, vegetables and flowering plants crowded together, with any paths which had once wound among them fallen victim to their unrestrained propagation. So many colors and scents overwhelmed Harriet's senses. She was utterly charmed.

Beldon rode his horse toward the door of the cottage, turning back to Harriet to ask, "Would you like breakfast?"

"Breakfast?"

He dismounted and lifted a bag tied behind the saddle. "Bread and cheese. There's a well in back of the cottage, so we'll have water to drink. We're missing breakfast at home."

Chapter Ten

"Breakfast would be just the thing. I'm quite ravenous!" Harriet declared, and Beldon helped her dismount.

"There's a small stable in back." He led the horses around the house, and Harriet followed.

"Won't the people who live here mind our using their home?" Even as she said the words, she noticed the unused, neglected air of the cottage. Nobody lived here now.

Beldon confirmed her guess. "It's unoccupied. My old nanny lived here in her retirement."

The stable held two stalls, and was made up with straw bedding. If no one lived here, the place was still not completely unoccupied, Harriet thought. She eyed Beldon as he made the horses comfortable. He looked up and grinned. "Nothing disreputable. If I *have* to be home, which I must sometimes to tend to business, I have to have someplace to go away from my family. Can't stand them for very long at a time."

She smiled nervously. She was suddenly aware that, in the cottage, they would be quite alone. What might happen between them? She would be able to stop matters from going too far, she assured herself.

He took a key from behind a feed bucket on the shelf and led the way to the house, unlocking the door and holding it open for her to precede him inside.

They entered a small kitchen, stone-floored and cool. Beyond a thin layer of dust over the surfaces, the room was clean. With complete familiarity, Beldon set the bag of food down on the table and picked up a white stoneware jug sitting on a shelf. "You can look around, if you like, while I get water."

Harriet removed her gloves, then examined the blackened stone fireplace, the utensils in a small cupboard, a tin sink. She found a small store of cloths in the cupboard.

Two rough wooden chairs bracketed the rickety table in the center of the room, though she suspected he never would have sat in the kitchen with his old nanny. There must be a parlor, and his former servant would have considered it improper to entertain the master in this room.

She dusted the table, shook out the cloth, and laid it next to the sink.

Beldon walked back in, water droplets condensing on the jug he carried. He had removed his coat and rolled up his shirt sleeves, apparently to save them from becoming soaked with water. The forearms thus revealed were surprisingly muscular, riveting Harriet's attention.

He found two mugs and plates in the cupboard and set them on the table. "Breakfast is served."

Harriet took one of the chairs and watched the muscles in his arms move beneath his skin as he sliced bread from the loaf with a well-worn knife. Black hairs curled crisply on his arms, tempting her to reach out and touch them. Her breath stilled.

He laid two thick slices of bread on Harriet's plate, then turned his attention to the wheel of yellow cheese. Mechanically, she picked up a slice of bread and bit into it. "How long ago did your nanny die?"

"Who said she died?" He laid slabs of cheese on each plate, then placed cheese on a piece of bread and took a bite.

Her gaze on Beldon's throat as he chewed, she said, "Oh, I thought . . . You said she didn't live here any more."

"No, she married a farmer—a widower with six children—two years ago."

"Were you close to her?"

"What child isn't close to his nursery maid? I spent most of my time with her when I was small. Grandfather soon took me in hand to see I learned what I needed to know as his heir." He poured water into the two mugs and set one in front of Harriet. Again, she was mesmerized by the motions of his hands and arms as he worked.

"Your father had already died?"

"He died when I was four. He had been sickly all his life—wasn't even expected to live long enough to produce an heir."

"You were four when your grandfather dismissed your nursery maid and began to teach you how to be a baron?"

"Oh, she wasn't dismissed. And I didn't spend all my time with my grandfather. He'd not have countenanced that. But Birdy—Miss Birdsell as she was then—was nursery maid to Marianne and Oswald, also. She didn't retire until Oswald went to school." He finished his bread and cheese and took a long drink of water.

Harriet sipped from her cup, cool water relieving her parched throat.

"What do you think of my hideaway?"

"It's charming. Would you show me the rest of it?" Harriet could not eat with Beldon so close to her. Watching him move, the strength in his muscles, the maleness in him, was too distracting.

"Certainly, if you wish. Are you done already?"

She nodded and he packed the food. Leaving the leather pouch on the table, he took her arm and showed her the other room downstairs, a small parlor, decorated with handworked lace curtains and needlepoint chair covers.

At the far side of the parlor, a door opened to a short hallway leading to the front door. From the hall a narrow wooden stairway rose steeply, probably to the servant's bedchamber.

He took one of her hands in his. "I've been wanting to do this." Raising it to his lips, he kissed the tips of her fingers.

Shivering, her legs suddenly weak, she pulled her hand away and escaped to the staircase. He followed. Partway up, she paused and looked down at Beldon.

He drew a lock of hair that had escaped from her coiffeur into his fingers, and she shivered at the slight tug on her scalp.

They reached the top of the stairs, and he reached to pull

her into his arms, but she evaded him. "You said we would see the house, Beldon."

"My name is Rolleston. Can you not call me that?"

Harriet giggled. "Rolleston? Oh, no, I couldn't."

She darted into one of the two rooms on the upper floor. It stood empty, dust thick on the floor and a dingy pair of lace curtains, the same type as on the ground floor, hanging limply at the small window the only objects in the room.

Beldon followed her. "It isn't *that* bad a name!" He took her hand, and she shivered.

"There's nothing wrong with the name. It just isn't . . . isn't how I think of you." She moved toward the window, and he, still holding her hand, allowed her to draw him along. Their passage stirred up the dust, which swirled around them. Harriet coughed. The window looked out into the surrounding forest, offering little view.

A strange mood had invaded her, an intense awareness of their isolation in the cottage, in part an eagerness to take the opportunity, in part wariness. When he trapped her against the window casement, however, she came willingly into his arms for his kiss.

His lips plied hers, his own warm and urgent. She returned the kiss eagerly, her breath stealing away and surrender overrunning her body. He finally released her, resting his forehead against hers, and a lock of his sable hair tickled her sensitive skin.

Harriet sucked in a lungful of dust-laden air and coughed again. Beldon pulled back and looked around as if newly aware of their surroundings. "This is just a lumber room, used for storage." His voice came out hoarse, and he cleared his throat. "Mrs. Popplestone probably emptied it out when she married—or else my steward did. Let's go."

"No, I haven't seen the whole house yet." Harriet darted out the door and crossed the short hall to the remaining door. Swinging it open, she stopped short, momentarily disconcerted at the fully furnished bedchamber that greeted her. However, her embarrassment quickly vanished at the charm of the decorations. And, if any stray question had occurred to her as to whether Beldon entertained his *chere amies* in the cottage, the narrowness of the bed banished such thoughts.

The room's ceiling sloped. The walls were whitewashed; a colorful handworked rag rug lay on the floor next to the bed. More lace curtains hung at the small window tucked under the eave, and a lace counterpane covered the bed. He wrapped his arms around her from behind and nuzzled the back of her neck. Heat speared through her. He pressed kisses into the curve of her shoulder, cupping her breasts with his hands. She leaned against him, her legs suddenly seeming boneless.

She didn't know whether he turned her or she managed on her own, but her arms went around his neck, and she and Beldon were kissing passionately, her body crushed against his. She inhaled his aroma, mixed with leather and horse.

They had somehow moved inside the tiny chamber and continued toward the bed. Beldon's fingers worked at the fastenings on her riding jacket. The jacket fell open and he pushed it off her shoulders as they collapsed together on the bed.

Only her chemise and stays covered the upper part of her body, and the next moment he took her nipple with his lips, sucking through the fabric of the chemise. Harriet gasped at the intense tingle that arced from her breast to her lower abdomen. She twisted, stretching up toward him and grasping his shoulders to pull him close, then slipped her hands upward to ruffle his hair, reveling in the texture, crisp and smooth, beneath her fingers. He changed his attentions to her other breast and she gripped his head tighter, filled with a boundless need to have him closer.

Far too much clothing came between them still, and she pulled his shirt free from the waist of his breeches and burrowed her hands under to feel his hard, muscled chest and the contrasting downiness of the hair growing there.

He groaned as she touched him and returned to kissing her mouth. She opened to the roughness of his tongue probing the sensitive, moist surfaces inside. She became aware of the desperate, almost purring noises she was making.

Beldon was tugging the skirts of her riding habit upward until finally she felt his fingers caressing her stocking-clad thigh, then finding the skin above the stockings. She sucked in a breath at the myriad sensations and wriggled, wanting his fingers to discover even more intimate places.

He pulled himself back from her and she murmured in protest. Then she silenced, watching through dazed eyes as he fumbled with the buttons at the flap of his breeches, his own eyes glazed.

Ah, she wanted this, wanted to know the secrets her sisters had told her of, to see what was hidden under his clothing, to feel him piercing her, then advancing inside. She continued caressing his chest, urging him with her body to hurry.

Her sisters! *Astraea!* Her fingers went still. "No," she whispered, "we can't do this."

For a few moments the issue hung in the balance. Beldon was in another place, far from the reach of her quiet words. If he continued his seduction, she would welcome him. She had used up her small store of resistance.

Slowly, though, the tension left him and his eyes filled with shock. He sat on the edge of the bed, cradling his head in his hands. "Oh, God!" wrenched out of him in an agonized groan.

Harriet became aware of her own uncomfortable state, lying on her bundled-up jacket and with her skirts twisted about her waist. The cooling moistness of her chemise prickled her tender skin. She pulled away from Beldon and scooted around him off the bed, hastily rearranging her clothing and donning her jacket.

Beldon didn't move while she crossed the room to a small mirror hanging on the wall. He almost appeared to be in pain.

Her appearance was a disgrace, her hair sticking out in all directions from the neat chignon she had begun with that morning. She would have to let it down and hope it would look better if she combed it with her fingers, for she didn't have a comb. Perhaps she could pretend she had not taken the time to arrange it before her ride this morning.

Her face would give her away, however. Her cheeks had a

deep flush and her lips were swollen, almost bruised looking. And her riding habit was sadly wrinkled. She could only hope that the ride back to the Towers would restore her appearance and not give rise to suspicions from her family, or Beldon's.

She covered her face with her hands. She had to ride in company with Beldon, but how could she ever face him again?

With an effort, Beldon pulled himself to his feet, avoiding even a glance at Harriet. He had to get out of there. Walking unsteadily, he headed for the door, passing too close to her. He didn't trust himself to speak to her.

Downstairs, he fumbled with his clothing, straightening his shirt and rebuttoning his breeches, or at least as many as he could fasten; the breeches had become a great deal tighter than that morning when he had donned them, and stretched uncomfortably over part of his anatomy. After attempting to arrange his coat to cover his embarrassing state, he snatched up the bag holding the remnants of their meal and stomped out the door to the stable.

He ached all over and his head hurt. Forcing his mind to other matters, he tightened the cinches on the two horses' saddles and led them out into the open area behind the cottage.

There was no sign of Harriet. Where was the blasted girl, anyway? She had led him on, and then stopped him when her ruin was all but inevitable. What was she thinking of?

She had stopped him. If she had not, their wedding would now be assured, with no possible exit for him. Whatever had made him think he could be alone with her and not lose control over his desire?

She might not be remotely the image of the wife he wanted, but she drew him as surely as a magnet draws iron. Whether they married or not, he could not ruin her. He would have to stay far from touching range from now on.

Harriet stepped out the door and tripped toward him, wearing a strained smile that appeared as falsely fastened to her face as a clown's mask. His body tightened anew in response to the vulnerability barely hidden beneath her brave show. 'Twas fated to be a confoundedly unpleasant ride home.

"You ready?" His voice sounded rough, as though dust clogged his gullet, and he cleared his throat. She nodded. He shouldered past her, locked the cottage, and returned the key to its hiding place. Coming back out of the stable, he realized his resolution to avoid touching her was impossible. There was no mounting block to assist her into the saddle. He would have to lift her. The alternative, to ride off and leave her standing there, would be inexcusably rude, tempting as it was.

He strode over to the mare and stood impatiently, and Harriet finally moved to allow him to boost her into the saddle. She stepped into his cupped palms and settled her weight, looking beyond him so their eyes would not meet.

He backed away hastily, mounted his own gelding, and urged him forward. Harriet fell in behind; the path through the woods was too narrow to afford them to ride abreast. She was blessedly silent at first; only the muffled clopping of her horse's hooves on the soft footing of the path and the shift of leather reminded him she was still nearby. The sudden thought of the saddle cradling Harriet's bottom shot a shaft of pain straight through Beldon. He gritted his teeth.

Shortly, they left the forest behind, and the lane widened. She drew level with him, and he felt her gaze probe his face.

"I suppose you have n-noticed how beautiful my s-sister Astraea is," she ventured. "That is, no one could fail to notice. Everyone says she is the most beautiful girl they have ever seen, and even in my family, w-with all my s-sisters having remarkable beauty, she is accorded the prize." She paused, waiting, and Beldon supposed he should offer some comment, but the effort was beyond him. He nodded.

She went on, the stammer smoothing out of her voice as she spoke, but that damnably appealing little catch, or hesitation, whatever it was, continued. How had he never noticed how erotic the effect of her voice was?

"Astraea sings like an angel. She also draws and paints in

watercolors. And she loves amateur dramatics. She always does her part in any family entertainment. I am sure, once she makes her debut, she will be in great demand. That is only a few months away now.

"Did I tell you how kind and gentle she is? She has been the greatest comfort to me any time I am perturbed or dispirited. I am sure I do not know what I would have done, many times while I was growing up, without her companionship."

Would Harriet not shut up? What was this sudden prattling about? She seemed determined that he would not have any peace. He squirmed, trying to find a less constricting position. God! He thought his family knew the ultimate in techniques of torture. They couldn't compete in the same arena as she. How would he ever survive the ride home?

He looked up at the sky, noting the gathering clouds. The brief sunny period appeared to be at an end.

The house was at last in view when her voice turned tentative and the brightness in her eyes dimmed. "Lord B-Beldon . . . I do not know how to say this, but I think it best if we do not meet in private any more, not during the duration of my stay at Langwell Towers. I c-cannot—neither of us—can answer for the consequences if we do."

He nodded. "I had already come to that conclusion, Miss Vernon. I must apologize for my behavior."

As they rode into the stableyard, a crack of thunder resounded around them.

Chapter Eleven

At the knock upon his study door, Beldon frowned. Immediately the door opened and Marianne poked in her head. "May I come in?"

Since she quickly followed by stepping into the office, the question seemed to be rhetorical. He scowled more deeply. "The door wasn't locked."

"Oh, was it supposed to have been?" She raised an eyebrow.

Beldon leaned back in his chair and glared at her. "What do you want, Marianne?"

"When do you plan to come out of here?" Her tone was even, but the hand that smoothed the already smooth dark brown knot at the back of her head showed her irritation.

"I have a lot of work to do."

"Look out the window, Beldon."

He didn't need to. "It's raining. Has been for two days. That's why this is a good time to catch up on paperwork."

"You also have a house full, including the woman you intend to marry. Your guests are moping around with this rain. Even a stroll in the garden is impossible. You should be devising activities for their entertainment."

"I'm no good at that type of thing. You've always been far better with games and whatnot than I." He stared at the paperwork untidily piled on his desk, hoping she would take the hint and leave.

"We've performed musical numbers, or played charades and cards, to exhaustion the last two days. We need something new." She sounded suddenly weary, and a wave of guilt stabbed him.

She sat in the high-backed chair on the other side of his desk with a swirl of her skirts. A furrow on her brow, she leaned toward him and asked, "What are you about, Beldon? You'll drive your bride away with much more of this neglect. Grandmama has constantly nit-picked at Miss Vernon; Mama and Aunt Matilda are at each other's throats; Lucy is going into a new decline every half hour because her life is being ruined by your cruelty. And you are not there to deflect any of it."

He turned in his chair to look at the unremitting, gloomy view outside his window. He could not be within view of Harriet without his desire for her overwhelming him. Since he could not satisfy his lust, he had to stay away. And so he had hid out in his study, pretending to work, all the while castigating himself for his cowardice.

This was exactly what he had hoped for when he'd devised this house party. A few more days of this and his unsuitable fiancée would run from him and his family. Except he was no longer certain that outcome was what he wanted. His body still hardened in response every time he thought of Harriet half-undressed and more than half-willing in the cottage.

However, Beldon now suspected marriage to him was not what Harriet wanted. He growled under his breath when he thought of her transparent efforts to interest him in her sister Astraea. He didn't want any damned baby for a wife, and if Harriet thought he could not find a bride without help once she took herself off on her travels, she was mistaken.

Was that her plan? He could only assume that she believed merely breaking her engagement to him would bring down her family's wrath, or perhaps that it would take losing him to her sister to ensure their approval of her scheme to travel. Whatever her purpose was, his pride would not allow him to beg her to keep to their agreement.

Every time he went near Harriet, the constant ache in his

loins intensified to an almost unbearable pain. And if he joined his guests, Docilla Purvis instantly besieged him. Beldon uncurled the fists he had unconsciously clenched, looking down at his calloused knuckles. He could not box his way out of this dilemma.

He turned back to Marianne. "I have no idea how to amuse these guests. You think of something."

Her lips thinned. "Not if you aren't willing to take a hand in the entertainment."

It *was* his duty. He had come up with this harebrained scheme. "I'll be there at dinner tonight, and stay with the party through the evening."

She stood up. "And through the rest of this house party?"

He gave her a weak smile. "No promises. I'll do my best."

She shook her head at him, her expression solemn. "No, Beldon. That's not good enough. I do have an idea that will ensure everyone's entertainment through the next fortnight. But I won't help you without your promise."

He waved his hand dismissively. "Yes, I promise. Do whatever you like."

"This isn't easy for me, Beldon." The strain in her voice made him look more closely at her, noting for the first time the faint shadows under her eyes, like fading bruises.

He wasn't being fair to her, leaving her all the responsibility for this misbegotten house party. How had he made such a mull of things? But he could not confess to the little cousin who had always looked up to him that he didn't know what to do. "I'm sure you'll do just fine," he said gruffly, picking up a paper at random from his desk and making notations on it as though completely absorbed in his work.

Beldon looked up at the soft snick of the door closing behind Marianne. Drawing in a deep, labored breath, he snapped the quill in his hands and threw it against the window. Ink splattered on the pane and dripped, making a murky blur with the moisture condensed on the glass.

* * *

"What are you doing here?" Marianne tried to keep her voice steady, but it quivered, matching the tremors that wracked her insides.

"You should know. You asked me at luncheon to meet you in the conservatory." Piers Luchan leaned against a potting table, arms loosely crossed. He looked far too casual, but Marianne spotted a certain wariness in his green eyes.

Rain struck forcefully against the windows, and the large, glassed-in room, which usually sparkled with light, was shadowed and gloomy. Water caused by condensation dripped from eaves all about the room. The dampness in the air carried a chill. She shivered in her light muslin gown, drawing her shawl more closely around her shoulders.

"You know I don't mean here in the conservatory. I mean *here*. Why did you come to Langwell?"

"That should be obvious enough, Miss Manning. I am pursuing an heiress." The words were said lightly but carried a bitter undertone.

"You planned to catch yourself an heiress five years ago." The words made an icicle stab through her heart.

He gave her a weary smile. "Yes, I have chased any number of them since. They have proved remarkably elusive prey."

"You should not have come here. I have finally achieved some measure of peace and you have torn it up again." She turned away to keep him from seeing the tears in her eyes, walked a few steps, then stopped, her back to him and head bowed. Confronting Piers was impossible. Why had she let Beldon dragoon her into planning amusement for his houseguests?

He was behind her in a flash, not touching but close enough that she could feel his warmth. "If you've found any peace in the last five years, you are luckier than I." His voice sounded rough, almost savage, and it ripped at her.

With a sense of inevitability, she whirled and stepped in to him. His arms came around her. Groaning, he pulled her close.

She sank against his chest, feeling the last five years melt away at his touch. Grabbing the lapels of his coat, she burrowed her face into the cloth, absorbing the smell and feel of him, the lemony scent of the soap he always used, the lean tautness of his body.

Tears poured forth despite her efforts to hold them back, and he held her tighter and murmured soothing sounds. Then he was kissing her. "Don't cry," he said over and over between kisses. She claimed his lips to still the words, passion igniting in her.

Piers returned the kiss feverishly, his lips brushing hers and then burning against her throat for a timeless space. He dragged his lips away and leaned his forehead against hers a moment, then pulled back, setting her a little away from him.

"Nothing has changed." His voice shook. "I still own a Scottish village, farms, land. There are still people who depend on me, half-starving and with their shelters falling down around them. More than a hundred people who have no hope of bettering themselves unless I can come into possession of a great deal of money."

"I know," she said. Hungering for his touch still, she controlled herself, stepping farther away, into the shadowy embrace of the branches of an orange tree. The tall plants that surrounded her seemed almost menacing, predatory. She picked up the shawl that had slipped while she was in his arms and clutched it around her.

"Have you ever chased butterflies, knowing you don't really wish to catch them, and you find at the last moment you withhold the proper swoop of the net so that you miss? That is how I've been chasing heiresses. All the time I castigate myself, because my people still suffer."

"You must do your duty. We decided on that course five years ago." Tears welled behind her eyes, and she blinked to hold them in, lowering her face so Piers would not see.

"I don't want to, Marianne. I didn't come here for Miss Vernon. I knew it was *your* home and I couldn't stay away."

She didn't dare reply to this. It was the same circle they had gone 'round and 'round before. There was no answer that did not either break both their hearts or force him to break faith with those who needed him.

She changed the subject. "You know Miss Vernon is betrothed to my cousin?"

"I know she is supposed to be. Have you ever seen a betrothed couple behave as they do?"

Marianne paused, recalling Miss Vernon's thoroughly kissed appearance after she and Beldon had met in this same room. "I don't know. There is *something* . . ."

"He should be offering to break my neck for the attentions I've been paying her. He should have kicked Mrs. Purvis's pretty behind right back out the door when she showed up. She knew she wasn't invited. She counted on Beldon's being too courteous to call a lady a liar. I think a little less courtesy was called for in the circumstances." He pounded a fist into his hand.

"I would almost enjoy trying to steal Miss Vernon out from under his nose—except for you, and except that I believe Miss Vernon is hurt by his neglect."

Marianne caught her breath. It was small and mean of her, but she hated the tenderness she heard in his voice when he spoke of Miss Vernon. "She hasn't seemed to mind your attentions."

"She is acting. Her eyes follow Beldon when he's in the same room. Then Mrs. Purvis cozies up to him and Miss Vernon smiles and flirts with me. She isn't the answer for me anyway, Marianne. She has only 'expectations,' not an actual fortune. Unless I could shake loose some money from the great-aunt who's named her as heir, we'd have a long wait to be able to help my village. The aunt is more likely to cut her off altogether for marrying a fortune hunter."

She should not feel so happy at his words. Curse it, anyway, she should want him to find the wealthy wife he needed, anything to get him away from her, away from the constant pain his presence caused. "I didn't know. Beldon hasn't even mentioned she is an heiress."

He had gone back to leaning against the potting table, his auburn hair the only contrast to the dark, mist-enshrouded green of the room. "The fortune is likely not important to him, damn him anyway. She's a nice little thing. I hate to see her hurt."

Silence fell between them as Marianne fought the jealousy his words evoked. Then she said, "This wasn't why I asked you to meet me, Piers. You are still involved in drama, in pantomime?"

"Yes, pantomime is an abiding passion of mine." He crossed his arms and quirked an eyebrow at her.

"Could you put together something, a pantomime for the guests to plan for and perform? Beldon invited these people with no notion of actually providing any entertainment. If we have any more days like the two we've just gone through, we'll all be ready for Bedlam."

He shook his head. "No, it couldn't be done. What would I use for actors, for a stage? There are tricks and mechanics. The musical accompaniment. Pantomime requires actors who are equal parts dancer, acrobat, musician, and thespian—*and* who can wittily improvise. There's no Grimaldi here."

"I wasn't thinking of a professional pantomime, Piers. Just something that would occupy and amuse the guests. I understand the Vernons are a talented family, musicians and artists. You could find out what they could each contribute, build your play around their skills."

"There isn't time enough. There are costumes, sets, props. A thousand details. I couldn't mount a pantomime in two weeks. Two months would be cutting it close."

"Could you not make a try at it? My God, the atmosphere has gotten so thick in these last two days, I keep expecting some of the people here to come to blows." She did not mention that the bitterest feud was between her mother and aunt. And they certainly weren't the only ones who looked a little tense.

"Let me think about it. I'll try to do something."

"Thank you, Piers. I was sure you would be able to do it."

"I'll need a great deal of help from you. I hope you are prepared to make a sacrifice of your time for the cause of peace at Langwell Towers."

Time? To work side by side with Piers? She couldn't! If she

had any hope of avoiding heartbreak, she had to keep a stern grip on her emotions as long as he was at Langwell. Oh, but how she wanted to take advantage of the excuse to spend time with him.

"I have a great many duties. I won't be able to take much time away."

"I see. In that case, I don't see how I can possibly carry out your request." His eyes glinted with mischief.

"That's extortion!"

He smiled, a parody of a leer; then his gaze slid away. He suddenly looked very vulnerable, as if her answer meant a great deal to him.

"Very well, I'll help as much as I can." Her heart beat faster at the thought of working with him, though she knew the eventual pain would be worse than the momentary pleasure.

Harriet stood at the French doors of the drawing room, staring out into the rain-washed garden. The paving stones of the pathways had a thin film of water and looked like islands in a mud-choked lake. Water sluiced down from the sky in an unrelenting torrent.

She would not relieve her restlessness with a walk outdoors today. The past two days had been interminable. She could not stop thinking of what had happened in the small cottage. She had been a fool to imagine she could control her responses to Beldon. After all, she had had prior evidence that she could not.

She could not sort out the emotions that had driven her. Most likely, she wanted to have as much of Beldon as she could before she gave him up to her sister. Perhaps she even hoped for a different conclusion—one that would have forced them both to go through with the marriage. His relief it had not come to that was shown in his avoidance of her in the past two days.

Behind her, the tension in the room was thick. The other ladies all looked the picture of industry, occupied with needlework. However, fretfulness and irritation underlay their busyness.

Mama knitted a sweater for Genie's imminent baby, and Lettice worked a crewel seat cover, part of a set she had labored over sporadically for some months.

Mrs. Purvis ostensibly worked on a net handbag, but actually sighed, squirmed, and shot frequent hopeful glances at the door.

Mrs. Willoughby, also occupied with needlework, looked up frequently with a slight frown on her face. Mrs. Manning sat with Lady Beldon, and had several times offered such services to the old lady as reading to her or sending for tea, which so far the beldame had refused with a snort.

Lady Beldon appeared to be the only one who actually had any enjoyment. Her gaze roamed from one occupant to another and a satisfied smirk lit her face.

Harriet's teeth clenched. Between Lady Beldon and Mrs. Purvis, she was under siege almost constantly. Lettice occasionally acted to deflect Mrs. Purvis, but for the most part Harriet was on her own to bear up however she could.

Sir Bartram had left to go to the stables not long before, wearing an oiled raincoat and large-brimmed hat to protect him from the deluge. She had been tempted to ask to go along, but did not possess any raingear.

Beldon might be in the stables. She was too ashamed to face him after nearly yielding to him. Remembering their intimacy at the cottage, the heat expanded to her chest. She fanned herself with her hand. Surprising how, despite the chill outside, the room seemed so warm.

She had not seen him since they had parted at the stables the day before, except briefly, in company with everyone, at dinner last night. She should be grateful he made himself scarce. She did not love him, so it was puzzling how she kept hoping he would show up. She was the one who had said they must keep their distance. All the same, it hurt that he had so easily taken her at her word.

There was no escape into the half-flooded garden. With a

sigh, Harriet ambled back to her chair and the abandoned book. The travels of the "Embassy from the King of Great Britain" through the empire of China and Chinese Tartary did not hold her interest as thoroughly as such accounts usually did.

Mrs. Purvis drifted over to where Harriet sat. "What are you reading, Miss Vernon?"

"It's a book I found in the library." Harriet hugged the book to her chest, hoping to deflect Mrs. Purvis's attention.

The other woman leaned over to look at the cover of Harriet's book and raised her eyebrows. "Geography? What an odd choice of reading matter for a young woman. I was sure the book would be a novel, or some improving work. Does your mother approve of your interest in such a subject?"

Harriet glanced at her mother to determine if she had heard this exchange. Lady Vare did not forbid her interest in traveling, but neither did she wholly approve. "She allows it, m-ma'am."

Mrs. Purvis pursed her mouth as though she tasted something sour. Harriet shrank into her chair, hating to be thought an oddity and hating even more that she could think of nothing to curb Mrs. Purvis's attacks on her.

"I suppose you must find something to pass the time. However, I cannot conceive what your mother is about, to encourage such peculiar diversions in a daughter with little to attract the male sex. I do not wonder she still hasn't fired you off after two seasons. I notice your admirers are not about this afternoon. But you should beware of losing their interest altogether, with such unfashionable tastes."

The old cat. Harriet was sure Mrs. Purvis knew as well as anyone at Langwell that Harriet was supposed to be betrothed to Beldon, even if it had not been officially announced.

Harriet looked up to find Lady Beldon's malevolent gaze upon her. The old woman's expression seemed to know and approve of the stinging assessment she had received from Mrs. Purvis. Harriet understood Mrs. Purvis's motivation—she hoped to capture Beldon for herself. But why had the old lady disapproved of her before she even came to know her?

She shivered and closed her book, every instinct crying out to flee from the room.

She had not seen Marianne enter the salon, but she now stood near Harriet. Marianne must have heard the end of Mrs. Purvis's speech, for she said, "Mr. Taber had some business to attend at home. He mentioned he would return in time for dinner. Mr. Luchan is around somewhere, I believe. No doubt, as it is almost time for tea, he will make an appearance soon." She smiled at Harriet, warming her.

Marianne moved across to Lady Beldon and fussed over her a bit, arranging her shawl and adjusting a pillow at her back. Then she ordered tea to be brought in.

Other members of the house party wandered in as the tea tray was brought. Eustace sat down beside his wife. Sir Bartram came in, his silvery hair slicked back and slightly damp. Pallas and Mr. Manning entered together, having apparently both been in company with the older children. Astraea and Lucy Willoughby bounced into the room, full of good spirits. Mr. Luchan walked in the door just as the tea was passed around. Mr. Taber was not with him. And of course Beldon did not join them, though Harriet's gaze kept returning to the door.

Once everyone had settled with their tea, Piers Luchan stood and announced, "I have been asked to provide entertainment to help pass these rainy days. I spent some time this afternoon making notes and plans for a pantomime, which I shall write this evening and perhaps part of tomorrow. I hope I may induce everyone to take part in rehearsing and performing it by the time this house party is ended."

"Oh, what fun!" Astraea said, then bent to whisper to Miss Willoughby. The other girl had a sulky pout on her face, but that changed to a wide smile at whatever Astraea imparted. The two girls hurried over to Lady Vare, and Astraea spoke urgently to her mother. Lady Vare shook her head.

Astraea kept talking, although Harriet could see by the firm line of Mama's lips that whatever Astraea asked, Mama would not change her mind.

In the meantime, Luchan made the rounds of the room, starting with Lady Beldon. He leaned near the old lady in a caressing, flirtatious manner. She simpered as though she were a young woman and shook a finger at him. Grinning, he moved off, talking to everyone else in the room in their turn, ending before Harriet. She quickly opened her book and pretended to be engrossed, guessing what Luchan would say.

"I hope you will participate in the pantomime, Miss Vernon."

"I will help where I can," she hedged. Knowing that what she offered was not what he was asking, she added, "I cannot act. I won't take a part in the play, but I will sew costumes or paint backdrops—whatever help I can be behind the scenes."

Luchan's smile did not falter. "I believe you are too modest, but I will accept any help willingly given. It will be difficult to mount an acceptable production with the small number of guests at Langwell Towers."

Astraea and Lucy Willoughby joined them. "It is unfair, Harriet. Mama says I may not take a role in the pantomime, as I am not out. She also won't write to Arthur to join us. She said he made it clear he wanted to pursue his own interests. The pantomime won't be any fun for Lucy and me if we may not participate."

Luchan said, "Miss Astraea, I believe I can persuade your mother to let you sing a song or perform an instrumental piece. There will be several such in the program, and it is an acceptable way for you to be introduced to such entertainments."

Beldon walked into the room, and all Harriet's attention focused on him. Her heartbeat picked up its pace and her skin tingled, as if it remembered his touch. Lucy Willoughby dashed over to him like an ungainly gazelle. "Oh, Beldon, you'll never guess what is to take place. We are going to have a pantomime. I'm going to take part in it!"

"A pantomime!" Beldon looked over at Marianne, frowning. "Is this the entertainment you got up for our guests? Never mind, if everyone is agreed, I have no objection. But you will not be performing in it, Lucy. You are much too young. And, don't count on my involvement, either. I have too much to do." His gaze sought out Harriet, going through her like an arrow.

It's because of me. He will avoid being in my company. A dull ache spread through her at the thought.

Marianne hastened to Beldon's side and drew him away, talking urgently to him. He nodded and left the room.

She rejoined Luchan and Harriet and smiled at Luchan. "He will take part. I reminded him of his promise."

What promise had Beldon made to Marianne? Harriet suddenly felt quite ill, with the beginnings of a pounding headache.

If he were to be involved in the pantomime, all the more reason for Harriet to keep clear.

Chapter Twelve

Beldon came out of the stable after turning Pasha over to a groom for cooling down. He stopped to breathe the cool, fresh air of early morning. The stable smells—hay, horses, manure, and leather—mingled with the scents of moist earth and rain.

Uncle Bartram had supervised the training of Pasha, a three-year-old colt, but at the age of nearly sixty, he could no longer put a hunter through its paces. Beldon was becoming more involved with the horse-breeding business than he had foreseen when he had fronted his great-uncle the money to take it up.

Mud spattered Beldon's boots and well up onto the legs of his riding breeches, making him feel unpleasantly damp. The weather continued wet, although today it was more of a persistent mist than the downpour of the previous two days.

However, taking the hunter for a hard gallop and over some modest jumps had eased some of his restlessness and frustration. The young horse was not ready yet for serious work, but he showed promise of becoming an outstanding jumper at maturity.

He rounded the corner of the stables and was intercepted by Carstairs, his gamekeeper, towing his half brother, Nicholas, and two other boys, whose stumbling steps and frowning faces expressed their reluctance for this meeting. Carstairs carried two shotguns in the crook of his arm, giving Beldon a clue to the nature of the boys' offense.

"Caught these boys out in Langwell Wood, my lord. Shooting at birds, they were," Carstairs said.

"Where did they get the guns?"

"Out o' the gun room up at t'house."

"I know where the key is kept," Nicholas contributed. He glanced up at Beldon from under a curtain of black hair, then flushed and looked down.

"Did they bag any birds?"

"Couple of crows and a pigeon" was Carstairs's disgusted rejoinder.

"I knew we weren't supposed to shoot at any game birds in the summer," Nicholas said.

"Luckily you managed not to kill each other," Beldon said. "All right, Carstairs, thank you for bringing the boys to me. I'll handle this now." He took the guns from the gamekeeper.

"You know you are not to take a gun out without an adult along," he said to Nicholas.

"Calder and Lord Peregrine said the d—, er, their father taught them how to shoot," Nicholas volunteered.

Beldon doubted the Duke of Moorewood had taught his sons to shoot. By all reports, he left the boys in the care of their mother and scarcely saw them from one year to the next. He studied the three boys without speaking.

Nicholas, twelve, had the black hair he and Beldon had both inherited from their mother. Nicholas's eyes, however, had the same dark stormy gray color as the captain's.

Both the duchess's sons were handsome lads, the elder light blond, the younger sandy-haired.

"Where are your tutors?" Beldon asked.

"Cousin Oswald went to call on a friend today. We said Mr. Draper would look after us," Nicholas said, "but he's sleeping."

"He sleeps when he is supposed to be watching you?"

"He is up nearly all night," Lord Peregrine said. "Spying on Mama."

Beldon barely restrained himself from showing his disgust at the thought of the boys' father hiring a tutor to spy on their mother. He didn't want any part of this conversation, but he couldn't let the matter of their stealing the guns pass.

Calder shot his younger brother an annoyed look, but Lord Peregrine ignored him. "That is his real job, you see. Tutoring us is only a ruse."

"He tutors us," Calder defended. "We know Greek, Latin, mathematics, history—all that stuff."

"Yes, but we've learned nearly all of it on our own," Lord Peregrine countered.

"Let's keep to the subject, which is that you boys stole guns from me and went out shooting at birds," Beldon said.

"We won't do it again, sir," Calder said, drawing himself up as if to look older than his thirteen years.

"If you teach us to box," Nicholas immediately added.

"What?" Beldon could scarcely follow the lightning-quick shifts of the boys' minds.

"I told them you are better than Gentleman Jackson. They—we all want to learn how."

Beldon hid his smile, amused in spite of himself. "Let me see if I understand this. You boys have just committed some serious mischief, and you want me to reward you for it with boxing lessons? Does that convey the idea?"

The boys nodded, their faces innocent. "It will keep us out of trouble, sir," Nicholas added.

"It seems to me more likely to cause trouble."

"No! Honestly," Lord Peregrine said. "We will just practice sparring. We won't get into any real fights, or put toads in Lucy's bed, or black pepper into old Draper's tea." He looked down, scraping his boot in the dirt.

"Toads and black pepper? Are those tricks you've already played, or just ideas you've contemplated?"

"We wouldn't actually do anything like that!" Calder's voice was full of indignation. But Beldon caught a guilty blink of Nicholas's eyes. *Oh, oh!*

It was none of his business. His mother didn't appreciate any interference with Nick, and likely the duchess would agree.

"In the first place, I'm not better than Jackson." Beldon

backed away, determined to make his escape without committing himself to any follies. "In the second place, I've never taught anyone to box and have no idea how to teach such a skill."

"You can just show us how you do it. We'll practice on our own." Nicholas shot him an ingratiating smile.

He looked at the three boys. Some quality tugged at his emotions, a hunger in them for a man's attention, and his wish to avoid being drawn in dissolved. "Absolutely not. If I am to teach you, you must give me your promise you won't ever box with each other or anybody else unless I or somebody I designate is around to supervise, you won't ever hit each other or anyone else in anger, and you will behave like gentlemen at all times." How did he end up saying such a thing?

"We promise!" they chorused with eyes wide and solemn.

"I mean it. If any one of you breaks the promise, lessons stop for all of you." This was worse and worse. It seemed he had committed himself to teach three boys to box.

"We'll be good," Nicholas said.

"All right, then, meet me in the stables after luncheon. The small indoor arena should be a good place to box." And it would be wise to keep the lessons out of the house, where a mother might happen upon them.

Whooping and slapping each other on the backs, the boys ran for the house.

What was he to do now? How did one go about teaching boys to box? Beldon tried to remember learning. His first lessons had been at school, administered by older boys—and without the adult supervision he demanded. At the time, he was ignorant of the serious injuries that could be inflicted. He was wiser now. Not, apparently, wise enough to resist the importunities of a trio of half-grown boys. He shook his head and slowed his steps. He couldn't help the laugh that welled up from inside. He felt lighter than he had since his home had been invaded by Harriet and her relatives.

* * *

Harriet walked into the library to return the book she had been reading. Seeing Piers Luchan seated at the table, she stepped back. "Excuse me, I didn't mean to interrupt."

"No, please." Luchan leaped up and took her hand, drawing her into the room. "Interruption is just what I need. Would you listen to what I have so far and tell me what you think?"

She held back, aware of the impropriety of being alone with him, and not wishing for a renewal of his amorous attentions. "No, I shouldn't be in here alone with you. It isn't proper. I don't know anything about pantomime, anyway."

Luchan kept her hand. "Please, Miss Vernon. We'll leave the door open. I have no wish to compromise you. And your opinion is just what I need. I already know what a professional in the theater would say—he would tell me it is complete claptrap. I shall call together all the guests and residents at Langwell this afternoon after luncheon to go over preliminary plans. Before I expose my efforts to everybody's mockery, I want to know whether a playgoer, someone such as yourself, would find it entertaining."

He led her to a chair and gave her a gentle push. She shrugged and seated herself, laying her book upon her lap. "Very well, Mr. Luchan, inflict your 'claptrap' upon me."

He laughed. Going back to the library table, he sorted through the confusion of papers upon it, some of which looked as if they had been crumpled and then smoothed again. "Here," he said. " 'The Lovers' Knot.

Within this salubrious sylvan bower,
Where my weary heart sees only purgatory,
I entreat you to while away an hour.
Here I divulge my woeful story.

With motley coat and pointed chin,
I give you pitiful Harlequin.
He preens and struts, his efforts wrought.
Languishing, he sighs, but lovers, not
Those sanctified by parental approve,

Seek to escape the tangled coil
Wov'n by foolish Pantaloon
When thus with Columbine foil
The plots and devices of a poltroon.

Follow your heart; it leads you true.
If love it finds, joy follows thereto.
I pray you pleasure find in the tale I wrought
Of loves true and untrue, a lovers' knot.' "

Luchan set aside the paper on which he'd scribbled the lines and looked anxiously at Harriet.

"Why, I think it quite good, Mr. Luchan. Quite as much so as the pantomimes I have seen at Sadler's Wells. Is that what you will call the play, then, *Lovers' Knot*?"

"It will be *Harlequin and the Mermaid, or Lovers' Knot*. He came around the table again and leaned one hip against the front corner, uncomfortably close to where Harriet sat.

"I particularly wished to speak to you, Miss Vernon. I do not agree with your analysis of your talent. I have danced with you on several occasions and found you to be light on your feet. There are only two women in this party young enough to take the two main female roles. I intend to ask Miss Manning to portray Columbine and her alter ego, Glissanda. I need you to play the Mermaid Princess, Halcyone."

"I couldn't. Surely, Mrs. Purvis, or Pallas . . ."

"They aren't young enough. I will find roles for them if they wish. Mrs. Vernon also—they are all over thirty, and not able to convey that youthful air I need." He pushed away from the table and walked to Harriet's chair, bending his knees to squat so his face was level with hers. His green eyes held a seriousness at odds with his usual nonsensical attitude.

"I shall play Clown, of course. I believe Mr. Vernon will make an excellent Pantaloon. Lord Beldon, despite his reluctance, must play Harlequin. There isn't anyone else among this party to handle that role."

At least, if she took the role of the mermaid, she would not have to play opposite Beldon. But . . . Astraea! It would be a wonderful opportunity for the two to spend time together. She must help Astraea persuade their mother to allow her younger sister to take the role. "I believe my sister Astraea would make an ideal Columbine," she said. "Then Marianne—Miss Manning could play the mermaid."

"No, Miss Vernon. I spoke with Lady Vare, although I concur with her opinion that a young lady not yet out should not appear in any entertainments but those which include just one's family. Lady Vare will not change her mind about Miss Astraea's taking a role, but she is considering still the possibility of allowing her to sing a song or perform upon the pianoforte.

"And before you suggest Miss Willoughby, she is not up to the discipline necessary to learn a role and practice it, even were Beldon to allow it.

"There is no help for it, Miss Vernon. You must play the mermaid. She is a relatively small role, but very important. You will not have many lines to say, but the mermaid has a dance number with Clown, and will be the catalyst for my young lovers to metamorphose into Harlequin and Columbine." He stood and walked behind the library table.

Harriet heard noises in the front hall—the distinct sounds of an arrival. "That could be Clytie and Lord Robert," she said, jumping up and hurrying out of the library to greet them.

Instead, she beheld a spectacle of confusion. Several trunks were piled in the entry. Beldon's butler and a couple of footmen stood with eyes wide in shock. In the midst of the chaos stood Great-Aunt Harriet, wearing a several-strand necklace of feathers, bones, and shells, and with a multicolored feather headdress perched atop her head. Behind her was her bearded Sikh servant, Aseem Singh, looking just as usual, turbaned and with his sword hanging at his side.

Harriet just stared. It could not be. Great-Aunt Harriet was not expected back in England for several weeks. But there was no doubt it was she. Laughter bubbled up in Harriet. Trust her great-aunt to make a memorable entrance!

"Oh, there you are, dear," Great-Aunt Harriet said. "I understand I am to wish you happy."

Harriet rushed to hug her favorite relative. "When did you get here?" she asked, pillowed against Great-Aunt Harriet's ample bosom. "The last I heard, you were in South America."

"I am home now, and never so thankful to be on English shores. I could not travel freely on the continent as there was much unrest. Several countries have demanded their independence from Spain. Brazil was different. The Portuguese royals rule there. I visited the court. On the voyage home, our ship was stopped by an American man o'war. I thought for a while we would become prisoners. I do not understand such ill feeling by our former colony. People say there will be war." She hugged Harriet again and stepped back. "Enough of that. Let me see you. It's been more than a year, I believe."

Harriet stood, blushing under Great-Aunt Harriet's scrutiny. "Hmm," she said. "You don't look much like a bride. Where is that glow? You have dark rings under your eyes."

Her face on fire, Harriet said, "Nothing is exactly settled yet, Great-Aunt Harriet."

"I will wish to learn more about that. For now, I must see to my baggage. There is more outside still."

Harriet moved to the door and gaped. Great-Aunt Harriet's luxurious traveling carriage stood on the drive, and next to it a large cart piled to overflowing with more boxes and trunks underneath an oiled canvas cover to protect them from the rain.

"Did you come straight here from your ship? How did you know where to find us?" Harriet asked.

"No, went to the Grange first. Vare said you were all here. But all my belongings are mixed together and I didn't want to take time to sort things out before seeing you."

Harriet laughed and hugged her great-aunt again. With her here, matters would soon be settled satisfactorily.

* * *

Before tea, Beldon stepped into his library for a measure of peace prior to sacrificing himself for the entertainment of his guests. He had just finished the boxing lesson.

The boys had exhausted him, although he congratulated himself it had gone well, given he hadn't the faintest idea what he was doing. He considered it a stroke of genius that he had thought to protect the boys' hands by wrapping them. He remembered a boy at school—Atwater, his name was—who had broken several bones in his hand when a punch had caught his opponent wrong. The hand had healed badly, leaving him crippled for life.

He did not wish to be responsible for such an injury to a future duke, nor any of the boys. He would never hear the end of it from his mother if Nicholas had a permanent injury. For that matter, the boy was destined for a life at sea—it was the Willoughby heritage—and a maimed hand would ruin his future.

Equally, a blow with a bare fist could do serious damage to other parts of the anatomy. He'd seen men whose thought processes were askew for life from repeated blows to the head, and heard of deaths from a punishing blow to the guts.

He hoped his stringent directives to the boys not to box without supervision and not to hit anybody in anger would be observed. However, he believed he had sufficiently laid out the dangers to the boys. They were probably better prepared to avoid harm than untutored boys fighting without any knowledge. And boys *would* get into fights.

A book on the floor beside one of the armchairs caught his attention. As he picked it up, he recognized the dark red cover of the book Harriet had carried about for the last three days.

He turned it over to read the title. "An Authentic Account of An Embassy from The King of Great Britain to the Emperor of China. Including Curious Observations made, and Information obtained, in Traveling through that Ancient Empire and a small part of Chinese Tartary. Together with a Relation of the Voyage undertaken on the Occasion by his Majesty's Ship the Lion, and the ship Hindestan in the East India Company's Service, to the

Yellow Sea, and Gulf of Pekin; as well as that of the return to Europe; with Notices of The several places where they stopped in their way out and home."

The air in his lungs seemed to rush out as if he had taken a blow to the gut. Harriet wanted out of their betrothal. Travel exerted as great a pull as ever. He should be elated, but he felt only a sense of loss.

With her great-aunt now here, Harriet might long to go with her on the next journey. Did he stand a chance to persuade Harriet not to go? That was nonsense. Of course he didn't want to stop her. He sank into the chair and bent over, his head in his hands. He had never been so confused in his life.

How had Harriet managed to find the volume in his library? Beldon only vaguely remembered seeing it on the shelves.

"Oh, good," she said. "You found my book." Harriet stood in the doorway, dressed in a day gown of jonquil muslin, her hair arranged in curls and tucked up in a fetching cap. She came forward, reaching for the book. Rising to his feet, he controlled a mad impulse to hide it behind his back, but instead extended it to her. His fingers tingled as their hands touched. He put his hand behind his back, rubbing the fingers together as though to hold her essence a little longer.

"Are you enjoying it?" *Stupid question. Of course she was.* He suddenly wanted to keep her talking longer, despite the danger. The danger that in another moment he'd sweep her into his arms—what they had mutually decided they must not do.

"What?" Her eyes had darkened and become unfocused.

"The book. Are you enjoying it?"

"Oh. Yes. That is, not very much. It makes a fascinating topic rather dry. But reading about someone's journey isn't the same thing as actually getting to travel oneself, is it?"

"No." At luncheon, Great-Aunt Harriet, or he should say, Miss Sutton, had held forth on her recent journeys. Seeing the entranced expression in Harriet's eyes, he had wished Miss Sutton would shut up.

He had already lost her. Harriet gazed at him with the bemused expression he recognized from times he had held her, kissed her, but she would leave in the end. He might seduce her and persuade her to stay, but he didn't want to marry a woman who would always wish to be elsewhere.

He wouldn't be so weak. Besides, he had to remember, despite his inexplicable desire for her, she did not have the qualities he looked for in a wife.

"I think it's time for tea. Shall we go?" He held the library door and gestured for her to go ahead of him.

She gazed at him a maddening moment longer. "Yes, of course," she replied. She hurried into the corridor and away from him.

She couldn't bear his presence.

Nearly spitting with rage, Marianne tracked Beldon to his bedchamber before dinner.

"Good God, Marianne, is there nowhere I am safe from you?" Beldon grumbled. He stood stock still, head tilted at an angle and neck stretched, while his valet tied his neckcloth, and should have looked quite ridiculous. Even so, he managed to fix a glare on his cousin that would have made her run if she had been the least bit intimidated by him.

She glared right back. "No, when you break your promise to me, there is no place you can safely hide. You did not come to the rehearsal this afternoon."

"Rehearsal? Are we to that point already? Luchan is indeed a miracle worker."

"Stand still, my lord," Foote said. "You have made me ruin this neckcloth." He tossed aside the offending article and picked up a new one.

Marianne tapped her foot. "I should have said 'meeting.' We talked about what skills each person could bring to the production and discussed which room would be a suitable venue to turn into a stage. We are going to use the large ballroom. We still must decide on how we wish to handle the sets and costumes, but we made a good start at this meeting."

"So, you did well enough without me. I have no skills to

bring to this absurd farce, and no one missed me." Beldon's voice was muffled behind his valet's efforts to complete his toilet.

Just as she suspected, he intended to renege on the deal they had made. "No, Beldon, it is a pantomime, not a farce. They are quite different forms of comedy, I assure you. And you are mistaken if you suppose matters have progressed too far for me to call them off. I told you I would not lend myself to this entertainment without your complete cooperation and I meant it. There will not be a play unless you honor your promise."

"There, my lord. I will leave you to this interesting conversation," Foote said, bowing and backing from the room. He conspicuously left the door open behind him, as though to protect Marianne's reputation.

"I will do anything needed behind the scenes. But I cannot take part in the pantomime." Beldon fastened his cuffs, while at the same time fixing a pleading smile on his face.

It had no effect on Marianne. She balled her hands into fists and held them at her sides, resisting the temptation to use them on him. "Why? Do you fear making a fool of yourself? I assure you that is the point, and everybody else in the play will be as great a fool."

"That isn't it!" Beldon's glance darted about and his mouth twisted. "I can't . . . Well, I just can't."

"So be it, then. I'll tell everyone at dinner there will be no play." She whirled to leave.

Beldon pushed past her and shut the door. "Damn—dash it, Marianne, I can't work that closely with Harriet—Miss Vernon."

He swiped at his head, disturbing the neat hairstyle his valet had just arranged. "This betrothal was a mistake. I brought her and her family here for her to learn how incompatible we were so she would break it off!"

"What do you mean?" She narrowed her eyes at him. *What kind of rig was he running now?*

"Everything was going well, but you had to take a hand to

'fix' things. Another few days like the past two, and she and her family would have broken for home. I'd have been free!"

A laugh broke from her. "You—you *orchestrated* this whole thing? The houseful of guests with nothing to do? Everyone at odds? Grandmother pinching at Miss Vernon? I don't suppose even you can take credit for the rain." She sobered. It wasn't funny. Whatever his plan had been, Miss Vernon was the one suffering the most from it. "You can't do this, Beldon. It isn't fair to Miss Vernon. No matter what your feelings, you offered for her. You have to go through with it."

Beldon squeezed his eyes shut and said, as if it were forced from him, "She doesn't want to marry me, either."

Marianne frowned. "Did she tell you this?"

"No, she didn't have to. She's been throwing her sister at my head through the whole visit. When we first met, she told me her ambition was to travel with Miss Sutton, and she has dropped books about travel where I would find them. *A* book, anyway."

"If neither wanted to marry, how did the betrothal happen?"

His face reddened. "There is a certain—attraction between us, which resulted in some little intimacy between us. I believed a proposal was required. Why she accepted, I don't know. She clearly regretted it immediately after, as did I."

"By God, Beldon, you haven't ruined the girl already?"

"No, of course not. I wouldn't be planning to escape from marriage if I had."

Heart sinking, she asked, "Did you invite Mrs. Purvis? Is it she you wish to marry?" She would have to leave Langwell in that case. She couldn't live with Docilla Purvis as mistress.

"God, no! She came on her own. She's a predator. I wish I'd never made her acquaintance. I've had nightmares I'd wake up and find myself engaged to her instead."

Marianne stared at him, an idea forming in her mind that could resolve her own dilemma at the same time. Could she do it? She must! "I know what to do. Take the role of Harlequin in the play, as Mr. Luchan wants you to. I am to be Columbine.

We'll pretend to fall in love." In that moment her heart broke all over again, but she let no hint of it show on her face.

"*Us?* In love? No one will ever believe it! We've had all the chances in the world while we were growing up together."

"Yes, but now we finally see each other as a man and woman instead of practically brother and sister, working together where we play a man and woman in love. We'll have to be subtle, of course. If we're too obvious, it would be suspicious."

"Why do you think that would work?" He was considering it though, she could see.

"Because Mr. Luchan came here with the intention of wooing Miss Vernon. He'll take advantage of our 'growing love' and Miss Vernon's hurt feelings and win her over."

And Marianne would make sure that he did. With Miss Vernon's wealthy aunt here as well, Piers could turn the old lady up sweet and get enough money to better the lives of his dependents. He might even come to love little Miss Vernon. He already seemed to have an affection for her. She hardened herself against the pain this thought gave. Since there was no happy ending for her and Piers, she might as well ensure he was unavailable so she could start to heal.

"You believe it could work?" His eyes sparkled with hope.

"You know Mother drops hints that we are intended for each other. I would almost guarantee she has already filled the ears of Miss Vernon and the other guests with the tale."

"You'd really do this for me?" He looked like an eager little boy who had been offered a forbidden piece of candy.

"No, Beldon, I would do it for Miss Vernon. She doesn't deserve the low trick you have played on her. And you need not fear that you will find yourself betrothed to me when this is over. I wouldn't have you served up on a platter with an apple in your mouth!" Marianne said bitterly.

With that, she whirled and marched to the door.

Chapter Thirteen

The next morning Marianne sought out Piers in the library where she knew he would be working. Her heart hammering and throat dry, she closed the door and leaned against it. Piers looked up and smiled. "Darling," he said, starting to rise.

"No, don't come here, Piers, just sit and listen." She had prepared her speech but was not sure she could go through with it. She licked her lips. "There's no future for us, and I won't go on feeling this torment. It must end, *now*. You must carry out your original plan to court Miss Vernon. With Miss Sutton here, you can also flatter her. If she cares about her niece, she'll give her the money you need."

Planning an immediate escape after delivering her salvo, she opened the door and slipped through. Before she had taken three steps, Piers was beside her, his green eyes reflecting his pain. "You can't end it like this," he said desperately.

"I can." She jerked her arm away from him. "Let go."

"No, we must talk about this. Come back to the library."

"I am done talking, done hurting over this. I've decided to live a full life—without you." She strode quickly toward where the others waited for further discussion of the pantomime.

"Talk about it with me privately, or in the ballroom. You can't stop me from speaking for everyone to hear."

"You wouldn't!"

"Indeed, I would."

"Don't do this to me!" She glanced at his implacable face, then at the footman at the entry nearby. "Oh, very well."

She walked back into the library, shaking violently. Piers

took her in his arms, but she held herself rigid and turned her face away. "I can't change on this. It hurts too much."

"Darling, I hurt too. I'll find a way we can be together." He pulled her against him, but this time she refused to yield.

"We went over and over this five years ago. Why didn't you marry someone in the meantime and kill our love?" Tears spilled out, but she brushed them angrily away. "I'm through crying. I just want it to be over. Marry Miss Vernon. I am going to find someone of my own to marry and have a family."

He released her. "What about the betrothal between Beldon and Miss Vernon?"

"He told me he doesn't want to marry her."

Piers studied her with eyes that she feared could read her all too well. She made herself look back at him. "This is truly what you want?"

She nodded, not trusting herself to speak.

"All right, it's done. We are officially over." His face screwed hard against the tears she could see glimmering in his eyes, he walked out and left her standing in the library.

She covered her face with her hands. Despite her own words to the contrary, it wasn't over for her. It never would be.

And for a man reputed to be a fortune hunter and opportunist, Piers had proven the steadiness of his own heart. If he believed she was falling in love with Beldon, it would free him to love elsewhere. Could she enact a convincing charade? She fought to compose herself to join the others.

A giggling crowd of ladies—and one gentleman—fell upon the profusion of trunks in the attic that afternoon, looking for garments that could be adapted to costumes for the pantomime.

Harriet surveyed the space where generations of Mannings had deposited their unwanted goods—clothing, furnishings, and bibelots. Like the rest of Langwell, the attic was spacious and light-filled. She had a momentary pang, thinking this could be her home—if only she didn't care that Beldon didn't love her.

Pallas, Lettice, and Mrs. Purvis, recruited to play sea nymphs, scattered to separate trunks to rummage for the appropriate gauzy gowns.

Astraea and Lucy Willoughby had been granted permission to do a musical interlude to the pantomime and had no need for costumes, but hoped to find gowns that Astraea's mother and Lucy's stepbrother would approve and yet would look more sophisticated than their usual wardrobe.

The matrons, Lady Vare, Mrs. Willoughby, and Mrs. Manning, declined to participate in the attic expedition but promised to help with the sewing. Lady Beldon would do neither.

Luchan and Harriet searched for material to fashion the Mermaid Princess's costume. Luchan also wanted male garments to make over to suit Harlequin, Pantaloon, Clown, and any incidental males in the production.

The other gentlemen who had roles in the production declined to join this expedition. Eustace had submitted with good grace to the part of Grundige, father of Glissanda, the fair maiden who transforms into Columbine. Eustace would also play Pantaloon, Columbine's father. But he and Sir Bartram, who had agreed to portray Neptune, had no interest in the costuming of the production, claiming this was work for the women to do.

Beldon, although he had apparently acquiesced in the parts of Harlequin and Armedio, the sea captain lover of Glissanda, also refused to join the search for costume items. He claimed the press of other business but would attend when they met for further planning. Before he left, Mrs. Purvis cornered him, and he also maintained a whispered conversation with Marianne, but Harriet could not lower her pride to seek him out.

Marianne sorted through a trunk with dogged efficiency. Her cheeks had a high color and her eyes a brightness. Harriet could not tell if she was happy or upset. Had something occurred between Marianne and Beldon? What if they were in love, but he insisted he must carry through his betrothal to Harriet? Could she learn the truth, and what could she do? She did not want a man who loved someone else, whoever it might be.

Harriet pulled an emerald green satin gown from the previous century out of the trunk she and Luchan were sorting through. "Do you think this would make a mermaid costume?"

"It's possible. I am certain we might use it in some fashion, in any case," he said.

He continued to look in the trunk and set aside some other items. They moved on to another trunk—and another. Harriet grew bored with the process, but Luchan was tireless. He must have some vision in his mind that drove him to keep searching, when Harriet would have been content with the green satin.

Finally, he picked up a sparkling gown of iridescent colors. Harriet gasped. It must have been made for a very special occasion. Beaded, of a shade that hesitated between green and blue, with shimmers of violet. "This is it," Luchan said. "You will indeed be a Mermaid Princess in this."

"Oh, but it is so exquisite, it seems a shame to destroy it," Harriet said.

"Fabric is fragile," Luchan said. "It won't last forever, and why should it not have a renewed life in our pantomime instead of being buried in a trunk in an attic?"

"It's just—I've never seen anything so beautiful. I feel it is almost a sacrilege to cut it up."

"If the gown could talk, Miss Vernon, it would say it would much prefer to be recut in order to shine on a lovely woman again." He held it up to his ear and pretended to be listening. "Ah, yes, it says it wishes to adorn your form, and thinks you and it will make a ravishing combination."

She chuckled. "Very well, tell the dress that I look forward to wearing it."

He whispered some words to the dress while staring at Harriet as though whispering love words to her. She blushed and looked away, wishing he would not be so full of nonsense.

He put the gown into her hands and said, "I'm going to see if there are any old furnishings that we can use for properties." He walked around the corners of the large room.

The other ladies' conversations as they discovered treasures and shared their finds buzzed around Harriet. She folded all the objects Luchan had set aside from their trunk-diving, with the iridescent gown carefully laid on top.

Mrs. Purvis walked over and picked up the gown. "Oh, this is perfect. What an excellent sea nymph I shall make in this."

Harriet resisted snatching the gown back, not wanting to tear the fragile cloth. "It is s-supposed to be for my m-mermaid costume," she said, surprised at the fury bubbling beneath the surface of her mild words.

"Nonsense, it wouldn't do for your washed-out coloring at all. It will look much better on me." Mrs. Purvis whirled away with the gown, over to where Lettice was finishing gathering her finds, and showed her the gown.

Harriet gritted her teeth. Luchan had made it clear he wanted her to wear that gown in the pantomime. She could not bear the humiliation of explaining to him. She was not going to lose her gown to that narcissistic conniver.

She yanked the emerald gown from the pile and strolled over to Mrs. Purvis. "Look at this beautiful dress. I'm very eager to make a costume of it for me. It will bring out the green in my eyes. My eyes are hazel, you know. That is a mix of green and brown. But I find if I wear green they appear greener."

"Why should you imagine I care about the color of your eyes?" Mrs. Purvis said.

"No, I'm sure you don't. This is Beldon's favorite color."

"Really?"

"Oh, yes. This dress will make him notice me."

Mrs. Purvis raised her eyebrows. "It's the wrong shade of green for you, not the color of your eyes at all. If you wish to wear green, you should find a more, er, leafy color."

"This is the color Beldon likes. When we were in Town, he saw a woman in this exact shade and said she was beautiful."

"Very likely he did. That doesn't mean he cares for that emerald green color." Mrs. Purvis was losing interest again.

"Oh, but he particularly said that the color was flattering to any woman. I think it was Mrs. Higginbottom,"

Harriet said, naming a woman known for not being beautiful but having a great sense of style and hoping Mrs. Purvis did not know the lady in question well enough to be acquainted with her wardrobe.

"Hmm. Now that you mention it, I do believe I have seen Mrs. Higginbottom in a gown this color. Really, Miss Vernon, I have reconsidered about this gown." She held out the iridescent dress. "It really suits you after all. In fact, I think it is more flattering to your coloring than this emerald green."

"I don't know," Harriet pretended to dither. "Beldon said he likes that green."

"Sometimes men don't know what they like. I am sure when he sees you in this gown, he will be *bouleversé*."

"Do you think so?" Harriet made her voice sound doubtful.

"I am certain of it."

"Would you care to trade, Mrs. Purvis?"

"Yes, I think the emerald green will go very well with my more dramatic coloring." She handed over the iridescent gown and snatched the green one.

"Oh, thank you, Mrs. Purvis. I so appreciate your expert opinion on what would look best for me."

Harriet went back to the treasures she'd accumulated with Luchan. The others were moving toward the stairway, and she picked up her pile and joined them. Lettice fell in beside her. "I never knew you could be so devious," she said.

Harriet giggled. "Neither did I." She revised her thought that she would give up Beldon to anyone he loved. She would *not* give him up to Mrs. Purvis, no matter how she had to fight.

Back in the ballroom, Luchan spoke. "I have two copies of the script, and I need someone with a fair hand to make a copy for each of the participants. Who'll undertake this?"

Great-Aunt Harriet spoke up. "I've been told I have a nice legible hand, so I'll do that."

Luchan nodded and turned to the discussion of costumes. Harriet thrust aside thoughts of Mrs. Purvis's enmity. When this was over, she and Great-Aunt Harriet would be on their way to some exotic place. She recalled her aunt's stories the day before—the mighty Amazon River, thick tropical forests, bright-plumaged birds, dark-skinned headhunters. She sighed happily.

"Stand still."

Harriet stopped herself in the act of tugging at the mermaid costume. She watched in the mirror as Mary stuck pins in the skirt at Lady Vare's direction, making a narrow "fish tail" that would effectively hobble Harriet. She couldn't walk, much less dance. The gown was too snug all over, cut too low in front. "Mama, don't you think this is, er, almost indecent?"

Her mother considered the gown, tapping a finger against her chin. "Giving Beldon a preview of what he will have in marrying you can't hurt. And, should the other men in the party enjoy the view also, so much the better. So far Beldon hasn't been the most attentive lover. Competition is good."

Harriet's eyes widened. "Mama! That's—dishonest!" Mary, kneeling at Harriet's feet, gave a little snort.

Mama chuckled. "Certainly not! There is no fakery here. That is entirely you within this gown."

Her face felt fiery-hot. "I didn't mean in that way. But it is as if I set out to—to entice him."

"That's the natural way of things, dear. Women have been enticing men ever since Eve. There is nothing dishonorable about that, unless—you do intend to marry him, don't you? It is not the thing to toy with a man's affections, Harriet."

She avoided her mother's eyes—and the question of what she intended to do. "I love him, Mama." She blinked. She had never meant to reveal that, or even to acknowledge it to herself.

"I see."

And Harriet was afraid her mother did see, all too much.

"I don't think he wants to marry me," she added.

"Oh, my dear, that is very common. Men are strange creatures. They like to think themselves in control at all times. Love is the one emotion that resists rationalization or control. They run away from feeling something that defies their logic.

Lord Beldon strikes me as the very model of a man who believes life should be tidy, everything run according to plan. Such men are the worst at recognizing the state of their hearts when they fall in love. He'll fight it, but he will eventually come around. It requires only patience on your part."

"All done," Mary said, standing up.

"There is a section dragging on the floor," Harriet said.

"Yes, Luchan was quite specific about that. It will be folded up and make the fins at the end of the tail," Mama said. "Hmmmn. I do think this gown may be the very thing!"

"What 'very thing'?" Harriet stared at her reflection in the pier glass, squinting to imagine the costume finished and herself transformed into a lovely mermaid who performs magic.

"Why, the very thing to bring Beldon to his knees."

Mary began carefully unpinning enough of the costume so Harriet could be removed from it.

Harriet wished she had her mother's faith in such an event.

"We'll practice with the full cast today. On other occasions, I will call together only those needed for a particular scene." Luchan stood before the pantomime cast, his voice carrying over other conversations and noises.

He handed out the scripts, copied out the evening before. Great-Aunt Harriet, Lady Vare, Lettice, Mrs. Willoughby, and Lucretius Taber had been discovered to have a legible hand.

Harriet took her copy and began to read, trying to ignore the bustle taking place around her.

The ballroom was in chaos. Carpenters and footmen built a platform over the floor for a stage at one end of the room, and their hammer blows made it difficult to hear Luchan's voice.

Her insides quaking as she leafed through the pages of her script, Harriet marked speeches by her character, the Mermaid Princess, Halcyone. Her first speech was on the deck of the pirate ship which carried the fleeing lovers,

Glissanda and Armedio, away from Glissanda's pursuing father and suitor.

However, Halcyone first came on stage in the swamp where the lovers ran for refuge. Halcyone arose from the "water," green cloth covering a trapdoor in the stage, and sighted Armedio. By gestures and expressions, Harriet conveyed that Halcyone was enamored of Armedio and swam after his ship.

Since Armedio was played by Beldon, Harriet wasn't sure she liked this part. It was too uncomfortably real. She glanced to where he leaned against the wall, close enough to hear Luchan. However, his face carried a blank expression of boredom.

Luchan spoke loudly to be heard over the sawing and hammering. His usually relaxed demeanor had become an air of serious and competent command. "This is Neptune's Palace. On the ship our characters have been transformed into Harlequin and Columbine, Pantaloon and Clown. The ship has changed into a whale that conveys them to the Palace. The whale also holds the Mermaid Princess, Halcyone, and the ship's crew. After the footmen's carpenter duties are done, they will play the crew."

Marianne, reading her script, moved as if to step off a ship onto a solid surface. She held out a hand to Beldon, who took it and drew her close. With a protective arm around her, he smiled down at her. Marianne smiled coyly back at him.

Harriet's heart squeezed painfully. They were acting, she reminded herself.

Luchan spoke, taking Harriet's attention to the business at hand. "Halcyone, you move to stand beside your father."

Harriet only stared at him, not knowing who was her father.

"King Neptune is your father. Sir Bartram, you sit on the chair. We will have a chair that looks like a golden throne."

Sir Bartram sat in the chair. The natural dignity of his appearance made him an excellent choice to play a king. Harriet walked over to stand next to him.

"Halcyone, read the lines introducing the guests."

Shaking inwardly, Harriet read in a breathless, quiet voice that slowly strengthened as she finished.

"O Noble Sire, I commend to you
These travelers from afar, and their retinue.
Here is renowned Papa Pantaloon,
His good friend Clown,
Who wants to marry sweet Columbine
(aside, to Neptune) please send her to the shelf,
And she wants Harlequin, her lover true
(aside, to Neptune) I want him for myself."

"Good," Luchan said. "Neptune, read your lines."

Sir Bartram cleared his throat and proposed a competition between Clown and Harlequin for the hand of Columbine. They would sail to the Seven Seas and bring a treasure from each.

The script said that Halcyone pouted at hearing her father's words, so she mimed her anger.

They moved on to the ballroom scene celebrating Harlequin and Columbine's betrothal at the end of the play. Luchan asked Lady Vare to play the pianoforte. Then he spoke in a low voice to Harriet, "Keep in mind that I am Clown," he said, leaning in close. "I shall perform several outrageous tricks during our dance. You shall appear dignified and princess-like, no matter what ridiculous things I get up to."

She smiled. "You give me a most difficult task, sir, since I have little dignity to begin with."

She looked beyond his shoulder to Beldon, treading a measure with Marianne. He gave her his full attention, his expression intent. He seemed to like his role as Columbine's lover. Was it just acting? It seemed all too real. Harriet's heart thudded heavily, and an ache started behind her eyes.

"Don't be such a stick," Marianne whispered. "Remember, you are starting to fall in love with me."

Beldon couldn't remember why he had thought that a good

idea. He watched Luchan smiling at Harriet, showing her how to react to his extravagances as Clown. He stood much too close, and his manner was much too solicitous. Beldon growled under his breath. He might not be able to hold Harriet himself, but he would be damned if he would give her up to a fortune-hunting scoundrel! He let go of Marianne and started toward Luchan.

Marianne caught his arm and whispered, "Play your part, Beldon."

He stepped back, turning to his cousin and staring into her eyes, trying to act as though he were lovesick. He had no idea how to play such a part.

Harriet trod the steps with Luchan, laughing unreservedly while he engaged in clownish tricks, pulling shuttlecocks out of his pockets and throwing them toward other cast members. She had never laughed so heartily, nor looked so free, when she was with Beldon. Some wild beast ripped at his innards.

Harriet could not be interested in Luchan, despite Marianne's statement that those two would marry after Harriet parted from Beldon. She wanted to travel to exotic places.

Or so she had said. *Could* she be interested in Luchan?

"You're squeezing my arm, Beldon," Marianne protested.

"Your pardon," he muttered. He loosened his hold on his cousin. He hoped this torture would be concluded soon and the whole nightmare—the foolish attraction to Harriet, his hasty words that had started the trouble, and the misery he was going through to stay away from her—would be as if it had never happened.

Sir Bartram came into the room just as Harriet was finishing her morning meal. "Ah, good. I'd hoped I would find you here," he said. "Since there is a break in the weather, would you like to come to the stables with me this morning?"

Harriet looked out the window, needlessly since she had already noticed a watery sun shone this morning. She needed time to consider whether she might encounter Beldon in the stable, and whether it would be a desirable or unwanted outcome.

"Why don't you go?" Eustace said. "It's unlike you to remain mewed up indoors for so long, and you look wan."

"Are you going now?" Harriet asked Sir Bartram.

"Yes, just on my way."

Harriet sat, rubbing a spot on the white tablecloth. "I should change if I go to the stables," she said.

"If you wish to come along later, I shall be there for a good while." Sir Bartram left.

"Really, this isn't like you, Harriet," Lettice said. "Are you certain you aren't becoming ill?"

"No, I am fine. I shall probably ride if I go to the stables. I just want to put on my habit." She rose from the table and strolled casually from the room. Instead of going to her chamber, however, she wandered along the corridors.

Thoughts of her riding habit brought back memories of the last time she had worn it. She wasn't sure she could bring herself to wear it again, but that was foolish, really. The habit was not responsible for her embarrassment. And "embarrassment" was not the precise word, either. She only wished she knew what she felt. She had very nearly lost her virginity.

No, the problem, if Harriet were honest with herself, was that she could not stop thinking about what had happened between her and Beldon in the cottage, and every time she thought of it, her knees went weak and her insides heated. Encountering him in the stable would be too vivid a reminder for both of them.

Outside the ballroom that was still undergoing work in preparation for the pantomime, she saw Marianne. "Do you know where Lord Beldon is this morning?" Harriet asked.

"Yes, I believe he went to the village to recruit some more workers for the pantomime. Were you wishing to see him?" Marianne's eyebrows rose in inquiry or surprise.

"No, it's all right." Heat crept up Harriet's face. Beldon would not be in the stables and she could safely go there. She ran to her bedchamber, scrambled into her riding habit, and passed through the kitchen and out the door in back.

The weather was humid and warm, a high overcast obscuring the sun. No breeze stirred to relieve the stickiness. Still it felt good to be outdoors, and Harriet's spirits lifted. As she walked into the well-maintained stables, she again thought Langwell would be a delightful place to live.

The stables were built of whitewashed stone, with several grassy paddocks around the building. Inside, each horse had a roomy box stall. The stables smelled of hay, horses, and leather. Everything was clean, and supplies hung from hooks around the room, although Harriet could see a large tack room at one end, the door ajar, showing her saddles and harness.

In one corner there was a large, open area with clips for crossties for grooming. This was where Beldon and Witch had been that first morning.

Through a set of double doors Harriet found an indoor arena where horses could be put through their paces in inclement weather. The roughed-up soil in the area showed evidence of recent use. Doors at the end led to an outdoor arena, and here she found Sir Bartram, with a groom riding a tall chestnut colt with one white leg and a star on his forehead.

"Rein him in a little, Gilroy. That's better," Sir Bartram said as the groom held the young horse to a collected trot.

"Miss Vernon." Sir Bartram didn't turn to acknowledge Harriet, but his voice was warm. "Glad you came out. This is Pasha, the youngster I am working with. I'll be busy with him for a while yet, but I'll show you around when I'm finished."

Harriet watched awhile as Sir Bartram put the horse through his paces and then, with the help of some other grooms, set up low jumps and Gilroy took him over them at an easy stride.

Then she said, "Would you mind if I looked around on my own, Sir Bartram?"

"No, feel free to go wherever you like. I'll answer any questions you might have after I'm done here."

Harriet strolled into the main block and walked along the

rows of stalls, admiring the horses. Nearly all were hunters, tall, handsome animals, well muscled, coats agleam from regular grooming. They poked their heads over the doors of their stalls inquisitively, ears forward. Harriet patted their noses. A couple of then laid their ears back, warning that they were of a more temperamental nature, and she refrained from touching them.

She found Witch and offered her some pieces of apple and carrot she had begged from the kitchen before coming out.

"Did you wish to ride today?" Beldon's voice behind her made her jump.

Harriet whirled around. "Oh, I thought you were gone!"

"Just a brief errand. I am back already. I could ride with you if you wished."

Her heart was pounding out a warning, one she was all too willing to ignore. Did he really wish for her company? She gazed into his face for a clue to his feelings, and he looked aside as though already regretting his invitation.

She bit her lip, clinging to her wavering good sense. Her skin felt hot and she had a nearly irresistible urge to step closer, to touch him. She backed away, up against the stall door. "I—I—" It was on her lips to say she would ride with him when the stable door slammed open and three boys raced inside, coming to stand by Beldon. Calder and Lord Peregrine, and the third one must be Beldon's young half brother.

"Beg pardon for being late, sir," Calder said. They were flushed and panting, as if they had been running for some distance.

"Damnation!" Beldon said. "I forgot these imps of Satan. I promised them my time. My regrets, Miss Vernon."

"It's all right." She scanned his face to determine if he was sincere. "I can ride by myself." Her voice came out breathless-sounding, as though she too had been running.

"Very well. Take a groom along. You don't know the area."

"Of course."

He stood there a moment. Did he look disappointed? He reached out to touch a lock of her hair that had escaped and peeked out from under her bonnet. Her skin tingled all over her body. Then Beldon jerked his hand back as if her hair were hot. He cleared his throat. "Well, I must be on my way. Higgins!" he called. When his head groom came out of the tack room, Beldon said, "Put a sidesaddle on Witch for Miss Vernon and have one of the stable hands accompany her on her ride.

"All right, boys, let's go." He strode out the door and they followed like puppies.

Harriet watched him leave, her face flushed and heart pounding. Matters were becoming worse and worse. If she had to let Beldon go, she wasn't sure her heart would recover.

Chapter Fourteen

Mama sat on a bench before the piano. Harriet stood behind her, her legs trussed together at the knees, although the bonds were invisible beneath her muslin gown. Despite her protests, Luchan was adamant that she must get used to walking and dancing as if in the mermaid costume she would wear for the pantomime.

Luchan gave Mama the sheet music. "This is the 'Minuet in D' by Eccles. Would you please play it, Lady Vare?"

Harriet's mother nodded, studying the music.

Luchan stretched a hand to Harriet, and she took tiny steps to join him in the middle of the floor. Why had she agreed to play this part? She would never manage.

"Just relax. It will take practice, but you will become accustomed to moving about thus confined." Her hand on his arm, he supported her as the strains of the minuet began.

He spoke as they bowed, curtseyed, and saluted each other. "The king will be at the head of the dance. Sir Bartram will dance with the duchess. The next couple is the bridal pair—Beldon and Miss Manning. We will be third or fourth, depending on where the tricks will have the most effect."

He led her into the steps of the minuet. Fortunately, the dance tempo was slow, the steps mincing. Even so, Harriet stumbled. Her feet didn't want to obey her commands. Her thighs and hips felt huge and ungainly, throwing her off balance. She would have fallen if not for Luchan's support.

He said, "Follow the music and let your body tell you how it needs to move instead of trying to direct it with your mind."

She tried to obey his instructions. It made her hips sway in a most alarmingly conspicuous way.

"That's good," Luchan said.

Harriet glanced at her mother, but she was concentrating on the music she played.

Luchan followed her gaze and smiled.

"I have wanted to have a chance to talk with you, Harriet," he said, too low for his voice to carry to her mother over the notes of the pianoforte. "May I call you Harriet?"

"I do not think that wise, Mr. Luchan."

"Perhaps not, although it is how I think of you." He led her into the *Pas Bouré*.

She chuckled. "No doubt that is because it puts you in mind of my great-aunt."

"You are far too modest about your own attributes, Har— Miss Vernon. Nonetheless, I have never hidden the fact that my circumstances dictate that I marry a lady of means."

"Your pockets are to let, I understand." The fluttery skirts of her morning gown became tangled around her ankles, nearly tripping her, and she had to stop to straighten them.

"It is not as bad as that." His face was stiff as he caught the tempo and led her into the next figure. "For myself, I should do well enough. I must worry about more than myself, however. I own extensive land in the Highlands, which is not arable. It grows pasturage for sheep but little else. I have tenants living in desperate poverty. It is my obligation to attempt to bring some sort of prosperity to my holdings so my people can survive." His green eyes held sincerity.

"I apologize for teasing you, Mr. Luchan. I did not know the situation. All the same, I am a poor choice to repair the fortunes of your tenants. I have only a modest dowry. My great-aunt has assured me she intends to leave me something, but as you can see, she enjoys excellent health. I would much rather have her for many years to come than collect my inheritance."

"I agree. I have also noticed that she holds you in great affection, and it seems likely that she would give you money if you asked her for it."

"I would never ask, even were I to contemplate marrying you, Mr. Luchan, putting aside I am promised elsewhere."

They began the dance anew. Luchan bowed to her and saluted her hand, stepping into the *Pas Balancé*. "From my observations of you and Lord Beldon, it occurred to me you might wish to be released from your promise."

Harriet stepped away from him, in her haste forgetting the hobbles that impeded her movement. She toppled and would have crashed to the floor had Luchan not grabbed her by the arms and saved her. The music played on, Harriet's mother apparently not noticing the near accident.

She glared at him. "You have no business to 'observe' me, Mr. Luchan, or to speculate on my dealings with Lord Beldon."

"I beg your pardon." He took up the dance once more, leading her into the next figure. "I did not mean to offend. Whatever motives you impute to me, I have a care for you, and it has seemed to me you have been rather unhappy."

"I will acquit you of the intention to offend, but I do not give you leave to comment on my situation."

"Will you not even allow me the concern of a friend? Friends may inquire about each other's well-being, Miss Vernon."

Harriet sank into a curtsy. "If you will avoid bringing up subjects distasteful to me, I will be happy to name you friend."

The pianoforte music stopped, and Luchan applauded her. "You are doing much better, Miss Vernon. However, I think we must practice still more. If you do not mind, Lady Vare?"

Mama shook her head, smiling, and began the number again.

"Keep your fists up, Nick," Beldon said. "And you're hitting short. Move in closer before you strike."

"It isn't fair. His arms are longer!" Nicholas said.

"You have to judge your timing. Calder can't be hitting all the time. Watch for your chance and move inside."

The boys listened closely to Beldon's instructions, and he

relaxed. Perhaps he could teach the boys. So far, it hadn't been terribly difficult.

The boys' hands were encased in huge, bulky gloves. Although Beldon had heard of boxing gloves, he had never used them himself. Awareness of the need to keep his pupils from injury had led him to seek out the gloves, which were meant for men's hands. He had had to wrap the boys' hands so the gloves would stay on. They had complained, but Beldon was adamant.

"Calder, remember your footwork. Knees bent and keep on the go. It's harder to hit a moving target."

"Yes, sir." Calder didn't take his eyes off Nicholas. They feinted at each other, neither landing a solid blow.

Beldon was about to call a halt and allow Lord Peregrine to spar when Nicholas caught Calder a lucky clout to the face. Calder went down, blood gushing from his nose.

A feminine scream came from behind Beldon. "Oh, my baby!" shrieked the Duchess of Moorewood, running over to kneel at her son's side in total disregard of the dirt floor of the arena.

The Marquess of Calder's blood sprayed onto his mother's lavender gown as she held him to her breast.

"Lay him down," Beldon said, then summoned a groom. "Bring some cloths. Soak one in cold water."

He knelt at the boy's other side. "Stay calm," he urged him. "The blood will clot shortly and stop flowing."

A shadow fell across his vision, and he turned to see Harriet behind him. "Did you suggest that the duchess search for her boys here?" He reined in his anger. Harriet could not know what she would unleash—finding them engaged in a boxing lesson.

"I just thought . . . the boys were nowhere to be found in the house. The weather is too inclement for them to be out of doors. I thought they might be in the stables . . . with the horses." She was pale, biting her lip and frowning.

A groom brought cloths and a blanket for under Calder's head. Beldon made the boy more comfortable, wiping his face with clean cloths and laying a cold compress across his nose.

"Is his nose broken?" the duchess asked shakily.

After he had cleaned away the blood, Beldon checked the nose, under Calder's protests. "I do not believe so, but it will be sore for some time."

The other two boys stood, silent and chastened, in the background. "I didn't mean to hit him so hard," Nicholas said.

"I know," Beldon said. "It's all right, Nick. You must understand these things happen."

The duchess turned a tear-stained, grim face to him. "Perhaps this low brawling is suitable behavior for the son of a sea captain, but *not* for the sons of a duke! I cannot believe you allowed—nay, *encouraged*, this disgraceful spectacle!"

Still kneeling by the boy's side, Beldon straightened, affronted. "Madam, the *science* of pugilism is a pursuit any gentleman will recommend. A man never knows when he may be called upon to defend himself, or those he cares for. I am certain the Duke of Moorewood would say the same, as would any of the gentlemen who frequent Jackson's rooms in Bond Street."

Calder's nose had stopped bleeding, and he sat up, following the heated debate avidly. The other two boys stayed well back from the line of fire, watching with widened eyes.

Her color high, the duchess spoke in a low, venomous voice. "Don't quote the duke at me! He knows nothing about rearing boys. He spends no time with them. He may frequent that Jackson place with his friends trying to pummel each other to death. I will not allow my sons to emulate him!"

Beldon stared back at her. She was hysterical, not surprisingly. It was unfortunate that she had interrupted the boxing lesson just when her son's cork was drawn. No mother could like to see her child covered in blood. However, she was wrong, and if the duke did not take a hand in his sons' upbringing, Beldon must try to convince her to let them lead a more normal life.

"You do the boys no favors by trying to turn them into milksops," he said. "Duke's sons or no, they will have to defend themselves when they are in the company of other boys."

He looked at Harriet, trying to determine her mood. She stared back at him, her eyes narrowed and mouth tense.

"They do not associate with other boys. I allow *no one* to tell me how to rear my sons." The duchess stood up, brushing arena dirt from her skirts.

"You cannot keep them tied to your side forever, you know."

"And you cannot justify the fact that you went behind my back to foster this mean, vicious undertaking."

"We asked him to teach us to box." Calder's voice came out muffled and nasal with his stopped-up nose.

"That is no excuse. He should have known better." She beckoned to Lord Peregrine. "Come, boys, we are going to the house. I think I should have a physician to attend that nose." She glanced around at Harriet. "Are you coming with us?"

Harriet threw an agonized glance at Beldon. "I must go. My sister is upset." She went after her sister and nephews.

Beldon watched her leave. He suddenly remembered the scandal he had tried to recall when he had first met Harriet. At a ball, the duchess discovered her husband *in flagrante delicto* with a woman she accounted a friend. She flung a punch bowl and several dishes from a laden table at the duke when he followed her to plead his case. Dripping with punch, decorated with shrimps, caviar, and various other foodstuffs, their guests gaping at the display, the duke had objected to the insult to his dignity. They had been separated ever since.

Nicholas stood beside him, his hands behind his back and his body twisted awkwardly. "I apologize, sir."

"Never mind, Nick. Women don't understand. It most likely would have been much the same if it had been Mother who had found us." He looked down at his half-brother. "That was as neat an uppercut as I ever saw."

"Really?" Nicholas stood straighter, the beginnings of a smile lighting his face.

"Yes. However, it's probably just as well that the lessons have come to an end for now." He cupped his hand on the bony shoulder and gave it a squeeze.

* * *

Most of the ladies who were guests or who lived at Langwell Towers were in the drawing room. The Sheraton chairs and sofa, upholstered in a green- and ivory-striped silk, were drawn into a loose oval about the room. The occasion was a sewing session to turn the garments that had been found in the attics into costumes for the pantomime.

Great-Aunt Harriet had disclaimed any sewing skill and had gone out for a walk, accompanied by her servant, Aseem Singh.

The ladies in the room did not have the air of camaraderie that had characterized other such groups of women in Harriet's experience. Instead, the air was thick with tension.

Harriet, seated by her mother, sewed multicolored patches on a suit of extra-large pantaloons for Clown. Her mother had undertaken the alterations on Harriet's mermaid costume.

"What was Luchan about, Miss Vernon, casting you as a mermaid in that play?" Beldon's grandmother suddenly asked. She sat next to Marianne on the sofa, at right angles to Harriet's chair. "Mermaids are beautiful—I have always heard. Must admit I have never seen one myself. It makes no sense. Would have done better to make your younger sister a mermaid."

Harriet's eyes stung at this wound, but she hid her feelings. "I agree, Astraea would make a lovely mermaid. Mama will not allow her to play a role, as she is not yet out."

"Foolish to waste time on a trumpery play that will be seen only by the locals," Lady Beldon grumbled. "I don't know why Beldon is allowing it. The whole household is turned upside down, and it will not be worth seeing. Complete nonsense!"

"It isn't nonsense, Grandmother," Marianne said. She was creating her Columbine costume, a diaphanous, romantic design. "It is creating something pleasurable for our guests, and when we perform the pantomime, our neighbors and tenants will be entertained. It's a very worthwhile endeavor. And you know you will enjoy seeing it performed as much as anyone."

"Hmphh!" Lady Beldon said. She had a pleased smile on her face, happy no doubt to have stirred some controversy.

Mrs. Manning joined the fray, throwing down a male costume she was sewing. "It *is* nonsense. I do not see why we must have carpenters tearing up the ballroom, footmen running Heaven knows what errands, and all of us wearing our fingers to nubs making costumes." She leaped out of her chair, which was to the side and slightly behind the sofa, next to the French doors, and stalked out of the room. Marianne followed, throwing an apologetic look around the room as she left.

"The pantomime is demanding," Mrs. Purvis said from her chair in the corner nearest the unlit fireplace. "It is beyond the abilities of some of the guests to play their assigned parts." She stared at Harriet. "I think it foolish we must work so hard when the production is doomed to failure due to overestimation of some people's talents and to miscasting."

Harriet clenched her teeth to keep from tossing insults back at Mrs. Purvis. She was heartily sick of the woman's thinly veiled venom directed at her.

Lettice said in a sweet tone, "I am certain, dear Mrs. Purvis, that since you feel so strongly about being overworked, everyone would understand if you were to decide to leave." Seated next to Mrs. Purvis, she was working on Eustace's multicolored Pantaloon costume.

Mrs. Purvis sniffed. "Of course I will stay and do my duty. I spoke only as an interested observer."

Pallas, on the other side of Lady Vare, looked up from the sea nymph costume she made for her own role in the pantomime. "I must say I am sadly disappointed in our host. He used a want of judgment in allowing the boys to hit each other like low bruisers. His choice of leisure pursuits argues a want of decency and respect for the dignity of his position."

Mrs. Willoughby, sitting between Pallas and Lettice, bristled. "I have never cared for pugilism myself, Your Grace. However, boys will fight, you know, and it is no doubt better for them to do so with supervision than entirely alone."

Pallas's eyes flashed and she poked her needle through

the fabric with a stabbing motion. "*Boys* may fight, but I expect better of a man, especially a peer with a responsibility to model decent behavior for those younger than he. If the boys had a dispute, an adult who is present should intervene and find a peaceful solution instead of allowing the boys to pound at each other. Serious harm could have resulted from this ill-advised boxing lesson. As it is, my son has a very sore nose and great bruises around his eyes. I have grave doubts about Beldon's character." She sent a troubled glance at Harriet.

"My son is to be commended for stepping in when no other adult was keeping an eye on the boys. I understand that unless my nephew undertakes to look after them, they seldom have supervision." Mrs. Willoughby, her tone strident, set down her sewing and stood to face Pallas. "Oswald had gone to call upon a friend of his from the seminary. Where your boys' supposed tutor is, one can only speculate. I understand he spends his nights spying on you at the behest of your estranged husband. What behavior on your part has necessitated such a measure is something a polite person would hesitate to comment upon."

Pallas went dead white. "My sons are nearly always with me when we are in residence at the same house. If I were not helping with this play, I would be with them now. And my husband's unwarranted suspicions are not worthy of comment." She rose. "I do not know how such a rumor got about. However, I will not stay and listen to such slander. I pray you will all excuse me. Harriet, do you care to come with me?"

Harriet, shocked at the rapid explosion of enmity between the women, glanced around the room. Her mother's face was pinched, Mrs. Willoughby looked sick, and Lady Beldon seemed in good humor.

Lady Vare stood. "I do believe we have let our natural desire to defend our offspring override our good sense. Mrs. Willoughby, surely you did not intend to insult the duchess? Pallas, your father, as well as a number of other gentlemen of our acquaintance, enjoys a good boxing match. Unexplainable to a woman's mind, but considered quite unexceptional among men."

Mrs. Willoughby immediately spoke. "I apologize, Your Grace. I am inclined to be overzealous in the protection of my children. Since I am not happy with Beldon myself for teaching Nicholas to box, I perhaps reacted even more strongly."

"You are not to blame for your older son's actions, Mrs. Willoughby. I am sure, as any lady of sense would, you decry his teaching such a brutal sport to your younger son," Pallas said. "I must find a little privacy to compose myself," she added, looking once more at Harriet, but she shook her head, and her older sister left the room.

Harriet gazed at her mother, who calmly reseated herself and resumed sewing. How could Mama be so unruffled? Harriet felt quite ill herself. Her head pounded and her stomach hurt. She suddenly felt much too restless to sit and sew.

"Excuse me." She walked out of the room. Where to go? The brief respite from the rain, which had allowed her to go riding yesterday, had ended and the sky again dripped. She needed exercise. She rambled around the corridors of Langwell, recognizing that she neared the conservatory that she had only seen on the house tour and the one time with Beldon. Her face heated at the memory. Her brief times with him nearly always ended with the passion that flared between them so quickly.

Strolling in the conservatory might ease her restlessness. She opened one of the double doors and met with a wave of hot, moist air that almost immediately made her wilt. Still, the plants gave an illusory impression of wildness and privacy. She stepped in and spent the next few minutes identifying as many of the plants as she could. Several varieties of citrus, a fig, and, was that a banana tree with the long, flat leaves?

Behind her, she heard the sound of someone entering the room and footsteps approaching.

Beldon appeared around a squat, thick-trunked palm tree. He said, "I should have realized this place has an attraction for you." He stopped, some distance away from Harriet.

"Why should you realize that?" Her heart beat erratically and she felt breathless. She worked to control the happiness at seeing him, and the impulse to run to him.

"Because of your interest in travel. All these plants came from foreign places. . . ." He waved at the surroundings.

"Yes, of course."

"I'll go. I didn't mean to intrude." He turned.

"No, don't leave. I—I wanted to talk to you anyway."

He turned back, a frown on his face. "Yes?"

"About the boxing lesson. I apologize for my sister."

"That isn't necessary, Miss Vernon." He backed another step away.

Not "Harriet." She swallowed, tempted to let matters drop. He clearly did not want to talk to her. "It is, though. She is overzealous in protecting her sons. They are all she has, you see. But she is a good mother, and they truly are not becoming 'milksops,' as you said. They are perfectly typical boys."

"I shouldn't have spoken as I did. I have little knowledge of the matter." His remote expression did not change.

She forced herself to go on. "I noticed the boys were using some sort of gloves. I know little about boxing, but I believe the gloves are unusual?"

"They are, Miss Vernon. 'Mufflers' were invented some fifty years ago, but they are not in general use."

"I thought that was the case. I, well, I wanted to commend you for your concern. It was thoughtful, not just to protect them, but to teach them a skill they would enjoy as well."

"Thank you, Miss Vernon. I don't deserve your praise, however. I enjoyed the lessons I gave them." He unbent enough to smile at her, and her heart thudded wildly. She all but devoured him with her eyes, wanting so much more.

He stared at her, and she tried to interpret his expression. Did she read a hunger to equal hers? He quickly dropped his blank mask back over his face. Her momentary belief that Mama could be right about what he felt vanished.

"I will leave you to the enjoyment of your plants. I will see you at the rehearsal later." Quickly he turned about and rushed out of the conservatory.

Harriet wanted to cry.

Chapter Fifteen

Beldon escaped to the stables after another painful rehearsal, watching Piers Luchan make love to Harriet. He was tempted to plant a facer on Luchan and then carry Harriet off somewhere private to slake his passion and claim her for his own. He'd never felt so out of control. It was his frustration speaking, of course. He couldn't do such a thing.

He didn't understand why only she had the ability to send his libido soaring. With her hair, halfway between light brown and dark blond, and her pixie face, he could not say she was beautiful, yet she had an appeal he could not deny.

She had a curvaceous form that would tempt any man. Beldon had obtained a glimpse of the mermaid costume she would be wearing and wished he could forbid her to wear it in front of everybody. It would outline every curve. No even halfway red-blooded man could see her in it and fail to desire her. The thought brought out his need to claim her for his own.

However, that was only his lust speaking. He had never denied she had that effect upon him. It was not a sufficient basis for the kind of marriage he wanted.

A groom rode Pasha in the indoor arena. The outdoor arena, awash in mud, couldn't be used, or Beldon could have taken out one of the other horses which needed exercising. He walked back into the stall area. A curricle had just arrived, the horses streaming water. He could not identify the driver, concealed under a soggy many-caped driving coat and dripping hat.

"Beldon!" The newcomer leaped down from the seat as

one of Beldon's grooms caught hold of the horses. The man swept off his hat. "I decided to accept your invitation."

"Rayfield, you devil!" Beldon walked forward and greeted his friend. "Let's go up to the house and get you dried off. I imagine a hot toddy to warm you wouldn't go amiss?"

"I wouldn't refuse," Rayfield agreed. "I'm soaked through. It wasn't half bad in Biggleswade this morning. I didn't expect to encounter a downpour before I arrived at Langwell."

"Higgins, have one of the men see to the earl's horses," Beldon instructed, and then he and Rayfield walked to the house.

After Rayfield had settled and dried off, the two met in the library with their hot toddies.

"There was a bruiser in Biggleswade, issuing challenges to all comers. Big, rough fellow—they said he was a navvy. Took down a couple of the local lads while I was there. I couldn't help thinking you could beat him," Rayfield said.

"Is that so?" Beldon took a deep draught of the toddy, his heart rate accelerating at the thought of standing toe to toe with an opponent, slugging it out. He could almost feel the tight knot of frustration ease as he poured it all into his fists. The poor bruiser wouldn't realize he stood in for Luchan and had no chance. "How long was he going to be there?"

"Through tomorrow was what I heard. Are you thinking of taking up the challenge?"

"Sounds like just what I need. Are you game to go with me? The weather's settled down, but we'll take the landaulet just in case. If I get beaten, I'll want to hide inside anyway, so I don't scare the little children on our way home."

"You're serious? I thought you had a house full of guests. I heard people in the drawing room on my way by." Rayfield poured himself another cup of the toddy.

"There's a whole army of people. Enough so they'll hardly notice I am gone." Beldon hid his face behind the cup to cover this plumper. His leaving would create a fuss—with Marianne if nobody else. It would be worth it, however.

"I'll have Foote throw a few things in a bag for me and have the landaulet brought around. I'll be ready in an hour."

Now that he had determined on going, the last thing he wanted was to have anyone intercept him. He could feel the blood thunder through his body at the thought of pitting himself against another's skills.

Beldon had miscalculated in one respect. He had not realized that word of the challenge to all comers would bring the Fancy from every corner of England and there wasn't an available bed or berth anywhere in the village.

Beldon and Rayfield struggled through the press of bodies to make their way into the Mariner's Arms, a small tavern. There was not even a seat to be had, but they squeezed up to the barman and managed to get pints of ale.

They retreated outside with their mugs. The setting sun blazed into brilliance, casting red, orange, and violet streaks through the sky. Sipping their ale, they discussed what to do.

"Isn't that Hollesley?" Rayfield indicated the tall man walking toward them along the street.

The Hon. Philip Hollesley was the oldest son of Viscount Chithurst, a tall, well-made man who managed always to look elegant and a bit rough at the same time. "Are you here to watch or to challenge the Bruiser?"

"Both. Beldon plans to issue a challenge," Rayfield said.

"You have a place to stay?" Hollesley asked.

"No," Beldon said.

"I have room in a widow's house. Takes in boarders to stretch her income," he explained. "You can stay with me."

"Much obliged," Rayfield said.

Their problem solved, the three men set about finding dinner and a convivial place to spend the evening.

Next morning they rose just past dawn and set out for the meadow where the matches were taking place. Despite the early hour, others already had challenged the Bruiser. Beldon had to wait for the outcome of those matches to engage the Bruiser.

Beldon's first sight of the Bruiser nearly persuaded him to

rethink his challenge. The man was enormous, towering over Beldon's five feet, ten inches by a good six inches and outweighing him by four stone. Beldon's need to work off his frustration convinced him to go through with the match. He studied the fights with the early challengers, gathering clues to the Bruiser's style and looking for weaknesses.

The Bruiser dispatched two more opponents. Then it was Beldon's turn. His heartbeat sounding unnaturally loud in his ears, he stripped to his breeches and stepped in the ring. Noises from the crowd faded to nothing in his consciousness, his world narrowed to the ring and the huge man before him.

His opponent's torso was covered with sweat and the oils that had been applied to make him a slippery target. A powerful odor emanated from him, indicating that he had not bathed in recent weeks and his luncheon had contained liberal amounts of onion. Bruises just starting to purple marked the sites where the earlier opponents had landed punches on his body and face.

Over the next several rounds Beldon let his opponent hit him to get close enough to strike back. With his ability to follow up and his quickness, he usually got in five or six blows to every one of the Bruiser's. Although they did not pack as much punch, the cumulative effect showed on the other man. A couple of the rounds ended with the Bruiser taking a fall.

Finally, in the fourteenth round, tiring, Beldon packed the last of his strength into a hard jolt to the Bruiser's middle that doubled the man over, and followed up with several hits to his jaw and face. The big man went over like a ninepin, and the efforts of his seconds were unable to revive him enough to come up to scratch for a fifteenth round.

Beldon ached all over and longed for a good long sleep. He would not be able to sleep, though. His conquest of the behemoth fizzed through his veins, a powerful stimulant. He tried for a triumphant laugh, and found it hurt too much. So he contented himself with a wide grin—painful as well, with his cut lip, but he ignored that, filled with jubilation that blew away all the frustration he'd suffered.

Driving home, Rayfield said, "I have some champagne. What say we have a toast?" He popped the cork and, lacking glasses, the three took turns drinking straight from the bottle.

"By God," Hollesley said, "I never thought you'd do it!"

"I knew you could," Rayfield said. "There were times I was beginning to doubt it, though."

Beldon grinned wider. He'd never felt better in his life. He had pitted himself against an enemy he should not have been able to defeat, had borne up under inhuman punishing, and found the grit and determination to keep going, to prevail. Now he knew he could stand up to any test.

Except his aches now seeped through his euphoria, reminding him of every blow he had taken. "Have you any more of that champagne? I think I am shortly going to need an anodyne."

Harriet met Marianne on the staircase on her way to breakfast. "Did Beldon ever come home last night?"

"No. The weasel. He promised to make himself available for the pantomime. He'll hear from me when he shows up."

Marianne's sentiments did not sound very loverlike. They went down to breakfast together. As they approached the breakfast room, heated voices issued from it.

"Rolleston could not do so dishonorable a thing." Harriet recognized Beldon's mother, Mrs. Willoughby.

"I tell you, he and Marianne are to make a match of it. Marianne told me so herself." Mrs. Manning's voice.

Harriet looked at Marianne, who blushed. A sick feeling spread through her. It was not unexpected, but how it hurt. Tears came to her eyes.

"You are a liar and a conniver. He wouldn't forswear his promise." Mrs. Willoughby again.

"You always tried to stand in the way of my Marianne's getting her rightful place. If you hadn't been so opposed, our children would have been betrothed long ago, and this unfortunate affair with Miss Vernon never would have happened."

Harriet could not hear more. She turned and ran back up the stairs. She heard Marianne calling desperately, "Miss Vernon! Harriet!" but didn't respond.

In her room, she paced. Astraea had gone down early to practice her song, so Harriet was alone.

What was wrong with her? If Beldon and Astraea were not to make a match, this was nearly as good a solution, leaving her free. Her parents could not insist on her returning for another season after so embarrassing an imbroglio. She was *not* in love with Beldon, so his being in love with someone else should not feel like such a betrayal. Angrily she brushed the tears away, then set about repairing the ravages of her small storm.

Returning to the breakfast room, she found only Piers Luchan. Neither Marianne nor the two ladies whose quarrel she had overheard were in evidence. Piers jumped up when he sighted her. "How are you this morning, my dearest?"

"Oh, don't be silly, Luchan. I am *not* your dearest."

Harriet took a roll and a cup of coffee and sat down.

"I'm crushed. You seemed willing to give me a chance to win you just yesterday."

"Then, you spoke of friendship. That's all I granted you."

"Until you are married, I may still hope for something more than friendship between us, I suppose?"

"I tried to discourage your pretensions, Mr. Luchan," Harriet's patience had run out. "But you will hear only plain speaking. You may not hope for more. I will never marry except for love. I like you, but not enough for marriage. Even to save your starving crofters. If I should fail to marry Lord Beldon, I will travel with my great-aunt."

"Do you love him?"

"Of course not. That is, I don't know. I have always supposed it to be a mere infatuation that I would grow out of."

"So, you shall marry him, and let both my starving crofters and your aunt go beg."

"No. It looks as if he and Marianne will make a match of it. If they are in love, I won't hold him to his promise."

Luchan's face screwed as if he would cry, and Harriet had

a momentary wish to comfort him, but she could not think what for. What did he have to be sad about—other than Harriet's refusal? He could not have put much stock in that possibility, nor was his interest in her sincere.

"You are so easy to talk to, Luchan. I hope, no matter what happens, we can be friends."

A laugh was startled from him. "Friends it is, Miss Vernon. I shan't importune you any more."

She smiled. "What have you planned for rehearsal today?"

He gave a grim smile. "Well, it appears that our Lord Beldon is still missing, so it must be something that doesn't involve Harlequin. I should like to rehearse our scenes again, and then perhaps the musical interludes."

Harriet had an enjoyable ride on Witch after breakfast. At luncheon, Mama announced, "I had a letter from Clytie today. She and Lord Robert will not be coming here after all. She had good news. After more than five years of marriage, she is finally *enceinte*. But the dear girl is not feeling well, so they are returning home to Ashburton."

The rest of the day, Harriet sewed, then rehearsed. Green cloth had arrived, and she was given the task of creating scenery. Green ocean for ships to sail upon, green walls and ceiling for the cavern that was King Neptune's Palace. Yards and yards of green cloth to be assembled into a vast ocean.

She felt easier in her role than at first, but knew she would never be a true performer. As rehearsal drew to a close, Usherwood came to the door. "Miss Manning, you asked to be informed when Lord Beldon returned. He is here."

"Thank you, Usherwood. Excuse me," Marianne said to the assembled cast members who were rehearsing.

Harriet followed her to the ballroom door, drawn by the need to see Beldon. She gasped at the sight that met her eyes.

Beldon climbed the stairs toward them, flanked by two strangers who appeared to be holding him up. One of his eyes was swollen nearly to invisibility, and he had several cuts and bruises on his face. His hair was tousled, his neckcloth askew, and he stumbled as he reached the top of the stairs.

He came to a stop. "Greetings, ladies. You know my friends here, Hollesley and Rayfield. Oops, I said it backwards. Precedence, you know. It's the Earl of Rayfield, and Hollesley's just the heir to a viscountcy. Should say Rayfield's name first." He grinned.

"You're drunk!" Marianne said, disgust in her tone.

"You've been brawling!" Harriet added, shocked. Her first rush of sympathy at seeing him injured had turned to aversion when she realized the state of affairs. Her stomach twisted, as if she felt Beldon's pain, and despite her anger she had to restrain herself from running to him.

"Certainly not. I was exhibiting my expertise in the science of pugilism."

"Your expertise must have deserted you," Marianne said, "judging by the state of your injuries."

"On the contrary, I won!" he exulted.

"I would hate to see your opponent, then!" Harriet said.

"Indeed you would, Miss Vernon," said Rayfield. "An extremely ugly customer." The three men laughed, and Beldon began to sing loudly, "A-rovin', a-rovin', since rovin's been my ru-i-in, I'll go no more a'rovin' with you, fair maid."

His friends hustled him up the stairs and to his room.

Chapter Sixteen

Pain. Everywhere. Beldon tried to think whether there was one muscle somewhere in his body that didn't ache, but such contemplation increased his pain and he gave it up.

His hands were swollen. His head throbbed. His mouth felt like venomous beasts resided there. His stomach roiled.

He remembered finishing the bottle of champagne with his friends. That had begun to numb the pain of his cuts and bruises, but to complete the cure, they had decided to stop at a roadside inn and down a considerable quantity of rum. In fact, he recalled they had made several stops along the route home.

He groaned.

Even that hurt.

His groan apparently alerted his valet to his now-awakened state, for Foote entered. "Ah, good, milord. I am glad to see you restored to consciousness." He opened the draperies that darkened the room. Brilliant light flooded in, hurting Beldon's eyes. No, make that eye. He could not open the left one.

"I shall return instantly with my little remedy."

Beldon groaned again. It did no good, for Foote had already shut the door behind him. The only way to avoid Foote's vile hangover cure was to be gone before he returned.

He strove to roll over and arise. He couldn't move.

He tried again and rolled off the side of the bed. Now he was on the floor, nausea pulsing through him at the jolt from the long fall. Perhaps, if he could just hold on to the side of the bed, he could push himself up. His hands refused to open, close, or grip. He turned over and hauled himself semi-upright, grunting and perspiring.

And then, proving the god of wine had a malicious sense of humor, Marianne walked into his room. Beldon checked with his one eye to see if he wore any clothing. Ah, one bit of luck, at least. His breeches must have been too tight to pull off his unconscious body last night.

"Go away." He knew his cousin would pay no heed. He hoped Foote would hurry with his brew and complete his demise.

"You're in luck, Beldon." Furious though she was, it almost gave Marianne a pang to see him in his pitiful state. "I came to ring a peal over you, but I see you are suffering almost as much as you deserve from your escapade."

He peered up at her with his one operating eye. "Good. Then you can take yourself off again."

"Not yet. I have something to say. Our pact is off, Beldon. I won't pretend I'm falling in love with you any more."

Foote came in with a steaming mug. "Miss Marianne, you shouldn't be in this bedchamber. It is most improper."

"I'm not leaving until I finish what I came to tell him." She stood, tapping her toe while Foote knelt down and almost literally poured his concoction down Beldon's throat, saying, "Shall we get you back into bed, Milord?"

Beldon drew back from the mug. "No, we shall not. I'm going to get dressed and go about my business. And I'll not swallow any more of your poison, so take it away."

"My, we *are* rather testy this morning, aren't we?" Foote tipped the mug up to Beldon's lips again, ignoring his protests. Beldon choked and thick brown goo dripped down his chin. Relentlessly the valet held the mug in place until his victim swallowed the remainder. Foote wiped his mouth with a towel.

Beldon said, "You may as well put me back to bed. It will make it easier to lay me out, for you have killed me."

Marianne grinned. "No, I think you will live. You're not as green as you were." Suddenly, she was enjoying this.

Oswald walked in. "Marianne, you shouldn't be here. It isn't proper. Could I have a word with you, Beldon?"

"Now isn't a good time." Beldon looked green again.

"But since you are here, Master Oswald, perhaps you could help me get milord off the floor." Foote moved to one side of Beldon and gestured to Oswald to take the other side.

"Er, oh, of course." Oswald took his position and reached down to grab Beldon's arm. Beldon yelped.

"A little more gently, Master Oswald," the valet reproved.

"Beg your pardon, Beldon." Oswald blushed and looked down.

Foote slipped one arm under Beldon's, his other around his waist. "Now, let's lift together," he said. Oswald lifted his side and they got Beldon on his feet. He stood, swaying.

Sir Bartram tapped at the door. "I brought some liniment. I'm sure you have sore muscles this morning."

"That's kind," Marianne said. Beldon had a bilious expression, and she could imagine the effect of having his skin coated with the foul-smelling stuff concocted for hunters' sore legs on top of Beldon's tender stomach and Foote's brew.

Rayfield and Hollesley poked their heads in. "We wondered how you were this morning," Rayfield said.

"You're having a family discussion," Hollesley said. "We'll come back later."

"No need to leave," Beldon said.

"Yes, do," Marianne said at the same time.

His two friends stood uncertainly, blocking the doorway.

Marianne had had enough. "Everyone, go. I have something to discuss with Beldon, and I won't leave until I do so."

"You're outnumbered and outmanned," Beldon pointed out. "We can simply carry you from the room."

"You couldn't carry me in your present condition. None of the rest would dare try."

"You mustn't be alone in his room," Oswald said, shocked.

"You can stand just outside. If he tries to ravish me, I'll

scream and you can rush to the rescue. Not that I think he's in any condition to ravish anybody."

"Really, Mari!" Oswald blushed again.

"We'll come back later," Rayfield said, and he and Hollesley disappeared.

"It won't take long. Then you can have him to yourself with your liniments and cures." Marianne made brushing motions.

The three men in the room looked at each other. Uncle Bartram shrugged. "Can't fight it. Woman always wins." He waved his dark brown bottle. "I'll bring the liniment later."

"Let's at least make you decent," Foote said. He took a dressing gown out of the wardrobe and put it on Beldon, who winced when he put his arms into the sleeves.

Foote and Oswald left, Oswald casting a last doubting glance over his shoulder.

"What was so important to say right now?" Beldon asked as soon as the door latched shut. "You already said you weren't going to continue our charade."

"What are you about, Beldon? Miss Vernon has no notion of ending the betrothal." Marianne faced him, hands at her waist.

He frowned. "Did she tell you that?"

"No, she's not likely to confide in *me* right now. She overheard our mothers fighting and mine told yours that you and I were going to marry. Miss Vernon ran away, crying."

"Are you sure?" He rubbed his forehead. "God, I can't think right now!"

"I'm sure. I saw her tears as she turned away."

"I swear she's been throwing her sister at my head. Why would she do that if she wants to marry me?"

"Did she tell you that she wanted to end the betrothal?"

"No, of course not. How could I ask her such a thing? But she's made it clear that she wished to travel."

"Why wouldn't she just tell you the betrothal is over if that were what she wanted, Beldon?"

"Lord, I don't know! Her parents won't allow her to see the world with her great-aunt. Perhaps she hopes some dramatic event will change their minds. Couldn't you have waited until I was better to talk to me about this?" He moved away stiffly.

"You need to see your betrothal through. Whatever she thought at one time, she was devastated to hear my mother."

"Who gave your mother the idea that we would marry?"

"I'm afraid that is my fault. She was uncooperative about the pantomime, and I told her that I had changed my mind about you and working with you on the pantomime would make you realize you wanted me also. I couldn't have her sabotage the project."

"How do you plan to call her off?" He raised his eyebrows.

"I don't know." Marianne scraped a hand at her hair, disarranging its neat style. "She and your mother are at daggers drawn almost constantly lately. And another thing, Beldon. Your mother and the duchess nearly came to blows about the boys' boxing. Your mother accused her of being immoral."

"Immoral? Where would my mother get such a notion?"

"She said something about the boys' tutor spying on her. I don't know where she would learn of that, if it's true."

"Heard it from Nicholas. Lord Peregrine mentioned it. I must talk with Nicholas about keeping confidences. I believe I'll go back to bed. Come and get me when everybody's gone!"

"You can't do that!"

"It was a joke, Marianne. I'll have to do something about all of this, but I can't think now. Let me take my punishment from Uncle Bartram and Foote and see if they can't make me functional. I'll see you later this afternoon."

She eyed him. She really did feel a little sorry for him. He was clearly suffering. "Why did you do it, Beldon?"

"To which 'it' do you refer? Never mind. I don't think I have committed one rational act since I met Miss Vernon."

"Perhaps you're in love with her."

"Hah! Don't make me laugh now. It hurts too much!"

Marianne stopped at the door. "I'll ask Cook to send up a piece of beef for that eye. It will take a great deal of greasepaint to restore your masculine beauty for the pantomime."

* * *

Later in the day, Beldon was up and moving, although he could not have said he felt better. Oswald waylaid him again, and he forced himself to listen to his cousin.

"I saw my friend Walters the other day. He knows of a vacant living, but I need someone to put in a good word for me."

Beldon stared at the younger man. "I never knew you had a strong calling to have your own church."

"I never pretended to have a calling. Grandfather ordered me and I obeyed, just as you did. But I'll do a good job. The thought of living a useful life helping others through their troubles and joys appeals to me. I have no purpose staying here. You'll be marrying, setting up your nursery."

A sense of guilt pervaded Beldon's thoughts. He should have acted to see Oswald set up in his own life. His grandfather had drilled into him his responsibility for the lives of his family and his other dependents. He had thought it his duty to allow everyone to live on his bounty and make no shifts to care for themselves. It had never occurred to him that the status quo should change.

It was unfortunate that the relative who was leaving his protection was one of the few who never caused him a problem. Could he arrange for others to move from his house? Thinking about it, he realized that Captain Willoughby's dependency on him must add to his gloom. A sea captain, used to command, reduced to an indigent supplicant. Gads, he likely would have put a period to his existence long since in such a situation!

"I'll be glad to promote your appointment. I have one condition, though. You must take your mother with you. She can help you with your parish duties until you marry."

"Agreed. I had intended to offer to take her off your hands."

Harriet watched Beldon during the rehearsal. He moved stiffly. His face was a mass of purpling bruises, although the swelling around his left eye had diminished. Clearly he was in pain, and she ached for him despite her anger at his becoming embroiled with his cousin while still betrothed to her.

It appeared he had quarreled with Marianne also, as she acted cool and avoided touching him in their scenes together.

Luchan frequently gave the pair puzzled glances and several times instructed them to stand closer or behave more like the lovers they were supposed to be in the play.

Their estrangement affected the whole cast and there was a noticeable strain throughout the rehearsal.

Beldon's friends Lord Rayfield and Mr. Hollesley observed the rehearsal. Although matters had progressed too far to give them roles, they quickly volunteered to help out in any way they might. They seemed to suffer less than Beldon from the effects of overindulgence the previous evening. Beldon's other injuries might have contributed to his green looks today.

Mrs. Purvis was quick to notice the estrangement between Beldon and Marianne. She hung on Beldon's sleeve much the way she had at the beginning of the house party, in fact until he and Marianne had begun showing their closeness. Lord Rayfield showed her a flattering amount of admiration, however, and Mrs. Purvis seemed a little inclined to entertain his suit.

The cast scattered after rehearsal, most of the women gathering in the drawing room to resume the major task of sewing the costumes and backdrop.

Harriet's fingers were stiff from hours of sewing and tender from numerous pinpricks. She wanted to speak to her great-aunt about going with her next time. So far her aunt had not spoken of her future travels, but she always became restless after staying in England for a few weeks and would undoubtedly soon wish to be on her way again. At the moment, however, Great-Aunt Harriet was in the drawing room with the other ladies.

Harriet wandered toward the ballroom to see how the work to construct the stage progressed. No sounds of hammering or sawing issued from the room, so perhaps the workmen had left for the day. They might even have finished. Only a few more days remained until the day designated for the performance.

She walked through the door and stopped dead at the sight that met her eyes.

Marianne and Piers Luchan were enwrapped in a passionate embrace, exchanging a fevered kiss.

Her reflexive intake of breath must have warned them they were observed and they broke apart. She could scarcely believe what she had seen. Marianne and Luchan?

"Harriet!" and "Miss Vernon!" they said, both at once.

"I don't understand," Harriet said. Were they rehearsing a scene for the play? But there was no scene requiring Columbine to kiss Clown. She had a raw, sick feeling in her stomach.

"I have felt terrible about deceiving you," Marianne began. She was flushed, with a glitter in her eyes.

"Deceiving me?"

"Yes. Pretending a romance between me and Beldon. Piers and I have been in love since my London Season five years ago."

"I have explained my situation," Piers said. "The poverty of my village and the need they have for an infusion of money."

"My parents had no money of their own, so I have no dowry. Beldon has said he would settle money on me when I married, but he is under no legal obligation. And he dislikes Piers. In any case, Beldon could not give me enough to help Piers's people without impoverishing his own estate," Marianne said.

"But why did you act as though you and Beldon were to marry? You even told your mother you would." Harriet was just realizing the full ramifications of the deception they had practiced. Heat flooded her face, followed by the sting in her eyes that presaged tears. "You acted like my friend when I came. Why would you do such a thing?"

"Oh, Harriet, I beg your pardon! I have been in such a state of confusion since Piers came, I haven't known what to do. There were too many barriers to our happiness, and I thought it best to end things. But Piers would not listen, and I decided to pretend I was falling in love with Beldon to convince him." Marianne gave Luchan a look full of exasperation, and of love.

"I see. Didn't you think of how I would feel?" Marianne and Beldon had played her for a fool—and whatever Marianne's motives, Harriet would vow Beldon had his own reasons.

Marianne bit her lip. "Beldon said he believed you wanted a reason to break things off between the two of you. He said you wished to travel with your aunt. Was that not true?"

"Yes, but . . . " *Didn't you think how humiliating I would find it to be treated thus?* But it would only add to the humiliation to reveal her feelings.

"I hoped you and Piers might be happy together. And now that your great-aunt is here, I thought she might settle enough money on you for Piers to help his village."

"I tried to woo you, but you refused me, Miss Vernon. Luckily Marianne and I have settled things. I was so jealous that I finally declared myself. I don't know what we will do, but we will find a way," Piers said, clutching Marianne's hand tightly against his chest and looking down at her with a grin.

"Oh, that is . . . wonderful for you." And indeed, as the two looked at each other with patent love in their expressions, Harriet hoped they would find a way.

Something Marianne had said gave her an idea of how she might help the lovers. At least one happy outcome might still occur from this strange house party.

After the afternoon sewing group broke up, she sought out her great-aunt and explained. "Isn't there something you can do for them?" she asked.

"You say it's a village in Scotland that he owns?"

"In the Highlands. It's poor land, good only for sheep to graze. The people have lived in poverty since the forty-five, Mr. Luchan says." Harriet looked hopefully at her aunt.

"Sheep, eh? What do they do, sell the wool?"

"I think that is their only income, or perhaps they spin and weave some of it. He looked at some sheep Mr. Taber has, but he cannot even afford to buy more at the present."

"Is there a source of water nearby?" Her great-aunt looked interested.

"I do not know. I could ask Mr. Luchan."

"Never mind. I'll talk to him myself. I have an idea that there could be an investment opportunity."

"Oh, thank you, Great-Aunt Harriet!" She threw her arms around her relative's ample form, and smiled at Aseem Singh, standing impassively in the background.

Chapter Seventeen

Harriet entered the rehearsal room to practice with Luchan, as he had requested. He met her exuberantly, lifting her and swinging her around. "I'll never be able to thank you enough. I'm to meet with your brother-in-law, Harborough. He and Miss Sutton may both invest to build a mill on my property. Harborough is an advocate of Robert Owen's reforms, so I won't be selling my people into servitude. They'll have jobs, real prosperity. Marianne and I can marry." He gave her a sound kiss for good measure, and Harriet laughed aloud.

Hearing a strangling sound, she turned to see Beldon, his face a twisted mask, rushing at them. Luchan let go of her and pushed her behind him, but she sneaked past and intercepted Beldon. "Stop it!" she ordered.

He brushed her aside and let fly with his fists. Luchan did not even try to defend himself but took the blow to his chin and went down. Beldon stood over him. "Won't you fight me?"

"Regret I cannot oblige," Luchan said, remaining on the floor.

Beldon stared, then turned to Harriet. "This is the man you prefer?" He wheeled about and strode out of the room.

She paused to say to Luchan, "I apologize for Beldon," and ran after Beldon. "Wait!"

He didn't stop until he got to his study; then he threw her a brief glance and stood examining the floor. "Do you wish to be released from your promise?"

She felt light-headed all of a sudden and reached out for support. Beldon remained still, not taking her hand. This was it.

What she had expected almost since her arrival at Langwell. "I don't know," she said at last. "But things aren't as they appeared with Luchan. He had good news and was just happy."

"Yes, I could see that you were both happy. What do you want to do, Harriet?"

"Could we discuss this after the pantomime?" She wished to ask what he wanted but didn't dare. He'd say he wanted to be free—even though she knew now it was not to be with Marianne.

She desired him to hold her in his arms and say he wanted her. *Oh, it was so confusing!* No, she couldn't say what she wanted until Beldon told her his feelings. She remained silent.

"As you wish." He walked into his study.

What had she seen in his face in the moment before he shut the door? Just for an instant, she thought his eyes were moist.

The day of the pantomime finally arrived. Benches, hastily thrown together for the spectators, were set up in the ballroom. Families with small children sat in front. Harriet, peering out from behind the stage curtain, could see her small nephews, Eustace's sons, in the front row, being minded by their nursery maid, as their parents were both in the cast. A few rows back Lord Calder and Lord Peregrine sat beside young Nicholas Willoughby. Their mothers had made up their quarrel sufficiently to allow their sons to associate again.

The audience must have been upwards of fifty people.

Harriet tried to ignore the state of her nerves—the fast heartbeat, the nausea, the moist skin. She tugged at her gown, which seemed much too tight and much too low in front. She could hardly move, since the skirt narrowed into a fish tail just above her ankles. She had endlessly practiced her dance and hoped she could manage to avoid falling on her face.

She backed away, as the production was about to begin and her part didn't come onstage until things were further along.

The musicians Luchan had sent for from London began to

play. The curtain opened to show a wooded scene, painted on a canvas backdrop.

"Within this salubrious sylvan bower . . . "

The pantomime was under way.

The lovers met and were parted by Glissanda's angry father, who introduced her to Carporo, the suitor he wanted for her. Glissanda angrily refused. The lovers fled to a swamp where a ship, made of wood and canvas, awaited. The musicians played music that matched the mood of each event.

Harriet crawled under the stage to the trapdoor through which she would first appear as Halcyone, her heart pounding so loudly the audience must surely be able to hear it over the orchestra. One of the footmen, serving as stagehand, lowered the trapdoor, and she emerged into a green, cloth-covered "sea" and watched, hand on heart and eyes, enhanced by stage lashes, batting at Armedio.

Beldon's bruises had faded to a greenish purple which was almost unnoticeable under his stage makeup. The cut over his eye had left a reddish mark which would probably become a scar and looked rather dashing. Even clad in the ordinary clothing of Armedio, he was as handsome as ever. And in the skintight costume of Harlequin, which he wore underneath his suit and would be revealed later in the pantomime, he was devastating.

Therefore her role's requirement to stare in a lovesick manner at Armedio needed no acting ability on her part. She needed only to conceal that her stares were all too real. The orchestra played "The Lass That Loves a Sailor."

The lovers boarded the ship and "sailed." The ship did not actually move, but a canvas backdrop was unrolled and moved across the stage to simulate motion accompanied by "Heart of Oak." Harriet made swimming motions, then "dove" back under the trapdoor.

Grundige, the father, and Carporo appeared on the scene, gestured wildly at the escaping ship, then boarded another, hidden in the tall "grass" of the swamp and sailed in pursuit, with stirring music to accent the action.

The curtain came down to the orchestra's fanfare, ending the first act.

The stage was quickly rearranged to show the ships in mid-ocean. Grundige's ship, the *Silver Treasure*, overtook Armedio's, the *Golden Lady*, and fired on it. Armedio rang up a skull-and-crossbones flag on his mast, then returned the fire. Realistic booms by the drummer and puffs of fire issued forth.

Harriet could hear the children in the audience shrieking in delight. She was on the far side of the *Golden Lady*, out of sight of the audience, preparing to mount up into the ship, magic trident in hand. Then as the ships began to "sink"—the green cloth ocean being lifted higher to cover the bottoms of the ships—Grundige and Carporo boarded the pirate ship. The musicians played "The Bay of Biscay-o." Their ship disappeared under the waves, and as the waves prepared to engulf the *Golden Lady* as well, Halcyone appeared on the deck and waved the trident. The pieces of the ship broke apart and were raised to the flies overhead, revealing a dark gray "whale" made of papier-mâché, with the cast standing on its back, and the song "Married to a Mermaid" playing.

The audience gave an appreciative sigh, then cheered. Halcyone waved the trident at each of the major characters, who "transformed" into Harlequin, Columbine, Pantaloon, and Clown. All slid down the whale's blowhole, and the whale turned slowly to reveal the inside. The characters sat decorously on cushioned benches. Glittery curtains framed the "window" which looked out at fish swimming by in the ocean. The musicians played a rousing version of "The Jolly Young Waterman."

Wild applause.

Harriet suddenly realized she was having fun.

The curtain dropped again, then opened to show Neptune's Palace, a cavern formed of the green cloth Harriet had worn out her fingers sewing. The cavern glittered with glass "jewels," strings of seaweed, fisherman's netting. Mozart's Symphony No. 41 in C, Molto Allegro highlighted the splendor. A number of Luchan's property fish and other sea creatures "swam"—suspended from thin wires that did not show to the audience. For the comfort of the denizens there were green carpets and soft lounges.

Beldon could hardly wait for the pantomime to be over. He would rather climb back into the ring with the Bruiser than leap about a stage in tights. The curtain lowered again. There were interminable scenes to go through. He and Luchan—Clown, that is—were charged by King Neptune to go to each of the Seven Seas and bring back a treasure to decide who would marry Columbine.

The one compensation this whole experience offered was the sight of Harriet in her mermaid costume. The curves it revealed conjured up the image of those same curves with nothing at all covering them. No, this wasn't exactly a pleasure, more of a pain-and-pleasure mix, and one he had to deny himself as much as possible, given the snug fit of his Harlequin costume.

As the mermaid who wanted him for herself—what irony!—Harriet sabotaged Harlequin's efforts to find the treasures of each sea, and aided Clown. But with Harlequin's magic bat and the power of True Love, Harlequin and Columbine triumphed and sailed back to Neptune's Palace, victorious.

The pantomime progressed to the Wedding Ball scene. He saw Luchan leading Harriet as the minuet began. His fists tightened and Marianne protested the squeezing of her fingers. "Beg your pardon," he murmured and embraced her for the audience.

For all his jealousy of Luchan's closeness to Harriet in the past fortnight, he acknowledged the man was inspired. The marine properties he had conceived and ordered from theatrical friends in London added much to the play. They transformed Neptune's Palace into a magical setting, and now . . .

While Luchan and Harriet performed the dainty steps of the minuet, a veritable parade of the denizens of the deep swam out of Clown's pockets. Fish, octopus, eels, crabs. Some sailed out on their own, fins wriggling, and swam away. Others, Clown pulled out and threw—all contrived with the aid of nearly invisible wires. An octopus cast its fishy arms around Mrs. Purvis. A long, slimy-looking eel popped into Pantaloon's mouth. The contrast of the stately minuet by Eccles with the nonsense taking place on the stage added to the merriment.

Harriet, the mermaid, played a part in distributing the marine missiles. Luchan dropped some of the properties onto the mermaid's tail, and she flipped them with her fin. A large lobster grabbed Neptune's nose with its claw. Several beasts came Beldon's way, a few landing on his person with an audible splat. The audience laughed immoderately at their antics.

All the while, Harriet and Luchan danced. Beldon had perceived Harriet as awkward and prone to accidents. She had metamorphosed into a supple, sinuous creature, much as the pantomime's characters and properties changed into completely different things than they had been at their first appearance.

Beldon could not remember the elegant lady he had always imagined as his eventual wife.

Would it have been a problem being married to Harriet? He thought not. In fact, he couldn't remember why he had been so opposed to the idea. She was everything he wanted. Warm, giving, and gallant, an excellent horsewoman, and with a beauty he had been far too slow to appreciate. Indeed, he almost believed she was a fairy changeling, a being made of magic.

His realization came too late, after he had lost her. She was to give him her answer after the pantomime. Whether he had lost her to Luchan or to travels with Miss Sutton, he had little doubt she would refuse him. He had wasted the time that should have been spent fixing his interest with her.

He went through the motions of acting, scarcely noticing what he was doing. A couple of times he had to be reminded by hissed directions from Marianne, dressed as Columbine.

He hoped it would be over soon. The time passed in a blur.

With a flourish of grand music and percussion, the final curtain fell.

* * *

The cast was jubilant after the pantomime. The audience had cheered and clapped for a long time.

Outside the sun was hanging low in the sky, and the tenant families took their leave. Other neighbors stayed to congratulate the cast and partake of refreshments laid out in a room adjoining the ballroom.

Harriet's euphoric mood gradually evaporated in sheer fatigue. She wished for nothing so much as her bed by the time the last of the guests invited to watch the pantomime had departed.

As the exhausted pantomime participants progressed toward the stairs to retire for the evening, Mrs. Purvis edged closer to Harriet. "I wish to give you a word of advice, dear." Her voice was pitched just so it would seem to be intended for Harriet alone but was perfectly audible to everyone nearby.

Whatever Mrs. Purvis had to say would not be kindly meant. Harriet pasted a polite smile on her face and waited.

"You really should not wear clothing that clings so to your, er, figure. I suppose with several eligible bachelors at hand, you thought you must take advantage of the situation. But such a strategy only redounds to your disadvantage. Indeed, you will give the gentlemen a disgust of you."

Harriet's smile became even more fixed. Mrs. Purvis continued to behave as though she were not perfectly aware Harriet and Beldon were betrothed, though Lettice assured her she had told the woman even before they all came to Langwell.

"Everyone knows how desperate you were to secure a husband," Mrs. Purvis continued, her voice sounding sugary sweet, but her eyes glowing with venom.

Every moment Harriet had swallowed an insult during this wretched house party coalesced and fed a wave of rage that she no longer wished to control. "A trousers-chasing widow such as you should certainly know about desperation. At least I have never been reduced to appearing uninvited at a house party and pretending to believe I had an invitation."

* * *

Several shocked murmurs followed upon this pronouncement, Lady Vare's scandalized "Harriet!" among them.

Beldon heard only Mrs. Purvis's first comment about Harriet's revealing costume. And although he believed Mrs. Purvis was not motivated by kindness, he could not help agreeing with her sentiments. Even now, looking at Harriet, still clad in the clinging gown, he could feel the stirring in his loins. Luckily, after the pantomime had ended, he had donned the suit he had worn as Armedio, which did not fit as snugly.

Mrs. Purvis flushed. "You owe me an apology for that."

Harriet stood her ground, speaking with a quiet emphasis Beldon could not help admiring. "The truth needs no apology."

"I have never been so insulted! Beldon, make her apologize to me." Mrs. Purvis laid a beseeching hand on his sleeve.

He shook her off. "Harriet, could I speak to you alone?" He was through with subterfuge, looking for excuses to talk with her. He should have been more forceful from the start. He had behaved as he had because of his belief he could still wriggle out of the betrothal and salvage her reputation at the same time.

"This is not a good time, Beldon. I am very tired."

Hollesley said, "You don't intend to take her to task for the mermaid costume, do you, Beldon? I tell you, that was the most enjoyable part of the play."

Harriet flushed and cast an irritated glance at Hollesley.

"If you intend to make her apologize, Beldon, I think we all should hear what is said," Mrs. Purvis put in. "And I especially should be there."

"This concerns only the two of us, and it can't wait. *I* can't wait." He begged Harriet with his eyes. He couldn't go through the night with the uncertainty he had gone through ever since he had caught her and Luchan together.

"Very well," she said, "but *not* alone." She preceded him back to the ballroom, where the servants were disassembling the stage. Their efforts made enough noise that he and Harriet would not be overheard from the other end of the room.

He shut the door in the faces of any interested observers.

"What did you wish to speak to me about?" Harriet's face was anything but welcoming.

Dusk had fully descended, and the workers had lit every candle in all the chandeliers and candelabra in the room to light their work. Thus harshly illuminated, Beldon could see the lines of fatigue in Harriet's face, and his conscience pinched at him for insisting on this interview. "I apologize. It can wait until you are rested."

"You made such a to-do, only to tell me that we can wait?" Her tone was annoyed.

"I was wrong. I should have waited. You tried to tell me you were tired. We can talk tomorrow." What a slowtop he was. First he took so long to realize how important she was to him, and then he rushed his fences.

"No, since we are here, let's get this over with. You want your answer?"

No. Now that it was upon him, he didn't want to hear her pronounce the end of his hopes. At the same time, he didn't know if he could stand the suspense any longer. "Yes, I'd like to know what you want to do," he acknowledged.

"I haven't had much time to think about it," she said. "I agree we should settle things between us one way or the other." She hesitated, her eyes searching his. "What do *you* want, Beldon?" she asked softly.

"You don't get to hear my answer before I hear yours. I asked you first."

"My answer depends on what you say."

Fresh hope sprang alive in him. If he admitted he wanted her, would she stay? Was it fair to bind her when she wanted to be free? He couldn't stand to think she might marry him and spend their time together longing for what she had forsaken. He had to allow her the freedom to make her choice. "I am, as I always was, willing to accept whatever answer you give."

Was that an expression of disappointment that flitted across her face? He must have imagined it, as she said in a formal tone, "In that case, I ask you to release me from my promise to marry you."

"Very well." Beldon felt tears stinging his eyes. He had to get away before he revealed his emotions. Next thing, he would fall to his knees and beg her to stay. He had chosen to act unselfishly, and now he must carry it through.

He bowed, then pivoted and walked from the room, as straight-backed and controlled as he could manage.

He'd never had a chance to try to win her. Or rather, he had thrown away his chances, not knowing what he wanted. He knew now.

Harriet watched him go, tears blurring her vision. She wiped her eyes with her hands, then found an outward composure to take her back through the crowd of relatives who would be curious about what they had said to each other. The betrothal was finally over. She would never forget the cold voice that had said, "I am willing to accept whatever answer you give." Yes, he would have honored his word if she had insisted. He was a man of honor. She could not live in such a cold marriage!

Chapter Eighteen

Beldon had to leave Langwell. He supposed Harriet and the other Vernons would depart as soon as they could pack, but in the meantime, an encounter with any of them was to be avoided. Such a meeting would be embarrassing for them as well as for himself. And for him, seeing Harriet would be unbearably painful and, he supposed, nearly as much so for her.

He had already taken time, during the last week of preparations for the pantomime, to give his endorsement to Oswald's appointment to the vacant living he had described to Beldon. Oswald would take up his duties at the end of August, at which time the vicarage that went with the living would be vacant and ready for him to occupy, along with Mrs. Manning.

Now, he decided to attempt a solution for the problem Captain Willoughby presented. He left for London early the morning after the pantomime.

After debating a request for a breakfast tray in her room, Harriet decided to face down anyone who would try to embarrass her over the matter of her broken engagement. Accordingly, she and Astraea entered the breakfast room precisely in the middle of the allotted time. There was an awkward moment of surprise; then the occupants of the room opted to act as if nothing unusual were happening.

Hollesley arose to hold her chair for her, and Oswald performed the same office for Astraea. Lucy Willoughby was somewhat reserved but eventually unbent with Astraea. After they ate, the two girls went off arm in arm as they had since the beginning of the house party.

Lettice gave Harriet a searching look when she first entered the room, but there seemed more of sympathy than reproof in her manner. Eustace, however, began, "Is it true that your agreement with Beldon is at an end, Harriet?"

"This is not the time or place to discuss the matter, Eustace," she said.

"Oh, er, well . . . " He glanced about him as if realizing for the first time there were others present. "Yes, of course. Well, I wish to talk to you about it after breakfast."

"There is nothing to discuss," she said flatly. She had always been in awe of her oldest brother, despite his tendency to be bombastic. Denying him power over her gave her a surge of strength.

She would have to talk to Mama though—and when they were back at the Grange, there would be Papa as well. She sobered. Both discussions would be exceedingly difficult to get through. It didn't help that she was nursing what she suspected was a broken heart. At least, she had a distressing tendency to break out in tears at the slightest thing.

Marianne came in as she was finishing her meal. "Harriet—Miss Vernon—my grandmother requests an interview with you." She was pale, and looked stiff, as if she expected a refusal.

The old witch wishes to gloat. Why should I give her that opportunity?

Because this time, I will tell her what I think of her.

"Very well, take me to her," Harriet said, adding, "We were Harriet and Marianne, at the beginning of our acquaintance."

Marianne's mouth opened in a little O. "I thought you might not wish for any further acquaintance."

"We will be connections, of a sort. Your husband will be a business partner of my great-aunt and brother-in-law. And I bear you no grudge. This was an ill-advised business from the start, but Beldon and I are equally to blame, and no one else needs to shoulder any remorse over it."

Harriet had not seen Lady Beldon's rooms. In fact, as she looked around, she reminded herself that this was the master suite, which would have been hers if she had married Beldon, and if they succeeded in moving his grandmother out. If it were ever to have been hers, she would have redecorated before she ever spent a night in it. She shuddered. The rooms were stuffed full of ugly rocaille furniture, overheated, and dim, the draperies drawn against sunlight and few candles lit.

"Sit down, Miss Vernon." Lady Beldon had dressed in some state for this interview, no doubt with a view to intimidating Harriet further.

She sat and waited for Beldon's grandmother to begin. The silence stretched unnervingly.

"My husband was an astute man," Lady Beldon finally began.

Harriet blinked at the unexpected topic.

"You wonder why I say this. He had the raising of the present Lord Beldon, my grandson. He made sure Rolleston—Beldon—was no fool, either. In fact, from early in his boyhood, Beldon was unusually bright, with sound judgment."

"No doubt you are wondering why he abandoned his sound judgment in my case," Harriet contributed.

"Indeed not. I understand it very well. I wonder, however, whether you do. In my experience, Miss Vernon, which is quite lengthy if not especially varied, there is only one reason why a man loses his ability to reason."

Harriet's throat went dry. "And that is?" she whispered.

"Love, of course. You knew the answer already."

"My mother said something very similar," Harriet admitted.

"You disagree."

"I don't disagree. I just don't believe it." With an effort, Harriet controlled the tears that tried to spill forth. She did not trust that this devious old woman had no spiteful reasons for this conversation.

"Why don't you believe Beldon loves you?"

"He told me he didn't."

"I see." Lady Beldon gave her a long, considering glance. "Men may lie about love, or may tell the truth, or they may not know the truth themselves until it plants them a facer. Did you end the betrothal, or did he?"

"You know it wasn't Beldon. He could not do so."

"I was not completely sure. He spoke to no one before he left this morning."

"He's gone?"

Lady Beldon did not answer, and again the silence lengthened. "I know you consider me an insufferable person, but I wish to ask a favor of you."

"Why would you suppose I would grant you a favor?"

"Perhaps because it would be to your advantage to do so?"

This time Harriet let the air deaden between them before she finally answered. "What do you want of me?"

"Your family is packing. Do not go until Beldon returns."

Harriet jumped up. "No! That is too much to ask! Do you think I'll change my mind?"

"Would you not change your mind if you were assured he loves you?"

"That's ridiculous." Harriet dashed away the tears, uncaring this time whether Lady Beldon saw. "I don't know why you wish to torment me, but I won't stay to listen." She whirled and made for the door.

"I am a dreadful old woman, but I desire my grandson's happiness, Miss Vernon. Sometimes I have resorted to very devious means to assure it."

Hand on the doorknob, Harriet looked back. "I'll think about it." She went out.

Her interview with her mother was as painful as expected. Now, in addition to explaining how the betrothal was broken, she had to report the strange conversation with Lady Beldon.

"I rather imagine you do not want to hear it, Harriet, but Lady Beldon is right."

"How can she be? He said when he proposed that he did not love me. Nothing changed while we were here. If anything, he cared less for me by the end than at the start. I *asked* him what he wanted, Mama. He was so stiff. I know he wanted me to break off the betrothal, but of course he couldn't say that!"

"You owe him a hearing. Imagine if this broken betrothal became known in Society. It could have a most damaging effect."

"What Society thinks is immaterial to me. I shall be traveling with Great-Aunt Harriet. I intend to have nothing to do with the *ton* in the future."

"Your sister is making her bows this next Season. You are not ignorant of the ways of Society, Harriet. Any scandal you become embroiled in will reflect upon her. Surely you do not wish to harm her chances?"

"Who would—" Harriet bit her lip. Mrs. Purvis. How unfortunate that someone so inimical had witnessed the events.

"Very well. I will discuss it with Great-Aunt Harriet. I believe she is eager to be on her way, but I'll stay as long as she remains here. After that, Beldon will have to travel to where I am if he wishes to speak to me."

Harriet marched down the corridor to her great-aunt's chamber. As she approached, Aseem Singh left the room.

"Oh, good, my aunt is up," she said.

"I suggest you not disturb her yet," the servant said, bowing. "She is not at her best this early in the morning."

"Oh. Will you inform her that I particularly wish to speak with her as soon as possible?"

"Yes, mum."

Harriet went to her room, frustrated to be remaining at Langwell. She had awakened convinced that they would be leaving today, and she wished to be gone.

Her mother obviously still hoped for a renewal of the promises between her and Beldon. Harriet could not explain to her how the betrothal had begun and how little of genuine affection existed between them. She had hoped something more might grow, but it had not. She had been spared one of those marriages like Pallas's, where so much bitterness existed that husband and wife could not be in the same house.

Later in the morning, Harriet sought out her great-aunt

again. Great-Aunt Harriet was back in the familiar Indian clothing she had worn for years—a colorful sari and a turban.

"Good morning, dear. Do we travel to the Grange today?"

"Apparently not. Lady Beldon has asked us to stay on until Beldon returns, and Mama says we must do so."

"How extraordinary. Parents cannot like to see their daughter whistle down such a good match as Beldon. I hope you will not allow them to influence your decision."

"No, I shan't do that. May I go with you when you leave on your next journey, Aunt?"

"If you are certain that is what you wish, you may accompany me. I am eager to be on my way," Great-Aunt Harriet said. "I shall leave in the next few days for the Outer Hebrides. Will your parents not object?"

"I think not, after what has happened. In the future, they will not find me so biddable as I always have been." Indeed, Harriet felt quite strong.

She did not feel so strong where Beldon was concerned. She vowed not to be persuaded to marry him. What if Lady Beldon and her mother were right and he loved her? But that was perfectly ridiculous. Why would he not say so?

The Outer Hebrides also was not where her adventurous imaginings had taken her. She pictured India, China, the Silk Road, Egypt—all the exotic places to which her great-aunt had traveled in the past. Perhaps a return to South America.

However, advancing age had made her great-aunt more cautious, no longer willing to risk traveling beyond British shores.

Of all the ill luck, just when Harriet finally was able to join her great-aunt on her travels, the exotic places she dreamed of were closed to her.

Over the next days, as Great-Aunt Harriet made preparations to leave, Harriet also packed her belongings, but doubts had set in. She thought, with the passing of time, her feelings of grief and loss over Beldon would dissipate. Instead, what dissipated was her anger, only a little fed by his continuing absence.

Pallas and Astraea were gratifyingly partisan and advised her to stiffen her pride and refuse even to listen to his entreaties. Mama, however, believed Beldon truly cared for her.

Beldon's family were all quiet. Oswald and Mrs. Manning were readying themselves for the move to Oswald's new living. Harriet had the impression Mrs. Manning did not like this descent in her circumstances.

Lady Beldon was strangely silent. Harriet thought the old lady had even looked upon her with approval once or twice.

Luchan had gone to meet with Harborough to determine whether his land was suitable for a textile mill. Marianne waited for Luchan's return. They had decided to travel to Scotland with Great-Aunt Harriet and Harriet, to be married across the border, then continue on to Luchan's lands and begin readying everything for the mill that would be built. Their leaving awaited only Luchan's return.

Mrs. Purvis stayed on, also. Apparently Harriet's break with Beldon had renewed Mrs. Purvis's hopes to attach him. Rayfield and Hollesley waited a day or two for Beldon, then left.

Luchan returned from a successful meeting with Harborough. Harriet's brother-in-law could not go to Scotland to initiate building the mill because of the imminent birth of Genie's baby. He would go as soon as matters were safely resolved at home.

And so, they would all leave tomorrow.

"Are you really resolved on this?" Mama asked Harriet.

"I am," she replied. Only, she wasn't. The longer she thought about it, the more wrong it seemed to leave before Beldon came back.

Only he didn't come back. It had been four days.

Harriet couldn't sleep. A strong feeling of oppression gripped her, growing stronger day by day.

Astraea slept beside her, undisturbed by the emotions that seemed to fill the room. Harriet slipped out of bed and put on a dressing gown, deciding to find her way to the kitchen and make some hot milk if there were coals left in the stove.

False dawn lightened the room, and she decided against lighting a candle, which might awaken Astraea.

In the corridor, she saw a ghostly figure come out of one of the chambers and glide toward the stairs. Her throat went dry against the urge to scream. Heart thumping madly, she watched the figure moved toward her. Just when she thought her heart would leap out of her chest, she recognized Aseem Singh. His eyes widened when he saw her. He hurried down the stairs.

He had come from Great-Aunt Harriet's room. Was she all right? She rushed to the room and flung open the door.

"Yes, darling? Did you forget something?" Great-Aunt Harriet said.

Darling? At the same time Harriet realized the word was meant for Singh and recognized what it meant.

She stood in the doorway, stunned.

Great-Aunt Harriet sat up. "Oh, Harriet, it is you. I must have been asleep. Did I say something?"

"No," Harriet managed.

"Are you all right?"

"I'm fine, Aunt. I'll talk to you in the morning." She backed away and ran to her own room. She curled up in the bed, covers pulled up high, shivering.

Why had her aunt's indiscretion shocked her so? Aseem was her servant; he was a different race; he was far younger than she. They weren't married. She was *old*. All of these things would have made society whisper and turn aside from Great-Aunt Harriet if they became known. They played a factor in Harriet's shock, but they weren't the real issue.

Did her aunt love Singh, or was he just a convenience, like the mistresses some men took? Did she merely see herself growing older and lonelier and know finally that she had missed her chance at the true treasure life had to offer? She had no one with whom to share her life and grow old beside.

Would that be Harriet's own fate?

What did Beldon feel toward her? Why had he left it up to her to determine their future? When she examined his words, she realized they contained no clue to his feelings. Could he have concealed them because he thought *she* wanted to be free?

Harriet did not want to travel with Great-Aunt Harriet now. Perhaps it was never as much of an aim as she had believed. Her aunt's life had seemed romantic and adventurous—but it was frightening, also.

Not as frightening as navigating the vast seas of emotions since she had met Beldon. Perhaps those seas were her home now.

Harriet lay in bed, shivering, and watched the morning come. She rose with Astraea when her sister awoke.

"You are leaving today," Astraea said. "I shall miss you."

Harriet didn't answer.

Great-Aunt Harriet knocked at the door and entered. "I must talk with you, Harriet. Could you excuse us, Astraea?"

Eyes wide with curiosity, Astraea left the room.

"You saw Singh last night." Her aunt wasted no time coming to the point.

Harriet nodded.

"You think I'm a foolish and wicked old woman."

"Oh, no! I have no right to judge you." Harriet threw her arms around the woman. Pillowed against her favorite aunt's breast, all the storms and anxieties of the last few days overwhelmed her and she burst into sobs.

"Perhaps it will help to tell you Singh and I are married."

"What?"

"It is a secret. We could not live in either world if our relationship were known. But Singh's religion is very strict. We could not have a relationship at all without marriage."

"Are you happy with him, Aunt?"

"When we are together, I am very happy. You are in love with Beldon?" Great-Aunt Harriet said.

Harriet nodded. "I won't marry him if he doesn't love me. Long ago I promised myself I wouldn't have a loveless marriage."

"But if you leave without talking to him, you'll never know for sure."

Harriet nodded again.

"So you aren't coming with me?"

She pulled back and looked into her aunt's eyes. "I can't. I'm sorry."

"No need to be sorry." After a little pause, she said, "You haven't unpacked."

"I'm still leaving, but not going far. There's a little cottage on the estate, Beldon and I were there once."

"Is it wise to meet him all alone?"

"Maybe not. We need the privacy. It's the one thing we've had almost none of since I came to Langwell. And I'm strong enough not to let anything happen unless he swears his love."

"You know best what you need."

Harriet smiled. "Yes, I do."

After four days in London, pressing hard to accomplish his business, Beldon urgently rode back to Langwell.

Harriet would not be there, likely had gone home to the Grange, but he had to know. Wherever she was, he would follow, pour out his feelings, and try to win her back.

He strode into the drawing room direct from the stables. Several blurred faces stared at him, but not the one he was looking for.

His gaze found Lady Vare. "Harriet?"

"She's not here."

Ice gripped him. "Where's Luchan?"

"Gone."

"When did they leave?" God, was it too late?

"This morning."

"On their way to Scotland?" Lady Vare nodded. He wheeled and dashed out of the room.

"You implied Harriet went with them," Lady Beldon remarked.

"I thought he should suffer a little," Lady Vare said.

Lady Beldon nodded. "He's had everything his way so far. Striving to achieve his desire will surely be good for him."

The two ladies smiled at each other, in perfect charity for the first time.

Beldon rode north. A huge, empty pit yawned inside him, and his head pounded. Since Harriet ended the betrothal, he had scarcely slept, and in his weariness he several times nearly fell off the horse. Darkness fell not long after he started. He couldn't stop, couldn't lose her to that Scottish fortune hunter. Traveling with an elderly woman, Luchan and Harriet no doubt would stop for the night, giving him a chance to catch up.

If he were too late, or if she refused to change her plans . . . he couldn't consider that. He had taken every step he could think of to make her his again. Changing horses when needed, he learned the party he sought was ahead, and as he progressed the gap kept narrowing.

At mid-morning, he saw two carriages proceeding ahead of him. He recognized Miss Sutton's, and the other must be Luchan's hired chaise. He galloped to Luchan's carriage and yelled to the driver, "Halt!" The man plucked a blunderbuss from under the seat and lifted it to aim.

"Good God, man, I'm not robbing you. I just have to stop this carriage from getting to Scotland."

Luchan let down the window. "Beldon! Why are you here?"

"I came to stop you."

Luchan turned back inside the carriage and exchanged words Beldon couldn't hear, then looked out again and called the coachman to stop.

Beldon jumped off his horse, yanked open the door, and stood in shock. Marianne, not Harriet, was inside with Luchan.

"Where is she?"

"Who?"

"Harriet. Is she in the carriage with Miss Sutton? But—why isn't she riding with you?"

Marianne spoke. "Beldon, old dear, you are befuddled. Harriet didn't come with us. She is back at Langwell."

"Her mother said she was gone. And that *you* were gone." He looked accusingly at Luchan, his head awhirl with confusion.

Luchan shrugged. "She didn't come with us or Miss Sutton. Marianne and I are on our way to be married."

"You and Marianne? Why were you making up to Harriet the whole of the time?"

"Only part. The rest of the time, I made up to Marianne, and she has agreed to end my days as a fortune hunter." He grinned and exchanged a heated look with Marianne.

All the frustration and desperation of Beldon's last few days rose up in him. "How could you mislead Harriet, hurt her that way? By God, I ought to smash you."

"Harriet cares nothing for me, never has. We are friends, nothing more. Go home, Beldon, and find your own bride."

"Wait!" called Miss Sutton, attempting to exit her carriage. Her servant assisted her, and she strode over to Beldon. "She has not forsworn touring with me. She plans to join me later. Don't put any stock in her not being here now."

Late that night, Beldon arrived back at Langwell. A sleepy groom, rubbing his eyes, came out of the stable to take charge of the rented horse.

Stumbling with fatigue, Beldon walked to the house. It turned a dark face toward him, no lights within. Everyone was abed. Where was Harriet? Her mother had said she was gone. She did not elope with Luchan, or travel with her great-aunt. Had she returned to the Grange? To one of her sisters? Why didn't she accompany her aunt to Scotland? It must be she couldn't bear to witness the man she loved marry another.

Grandmother and Lady Vare had conspired to send him on a wild goose chase. Beldon had no idea why, or when they had reached accord. He didn't even know why Harriet's family remained at Langwell. He would confront Lady Vare and get the truth, but he could not awaken her at this hour. Although he had been unable to sleep since his break with Harriet, he would rest a little, wash off the road dirt.

In the morning, he was prevented from seeing Harriet's mother by her habit of spending the mornings in her room and receiving no one. Beldon might as well take the opportunity to speak to the various members of his family about the arrangements he had made. Then, when he finally spoke to Harriet, he could explain how he had taken the house back, for them. Perhaps, added to the other steps he had taken to persuade her, it would carry the day. He quelled his urgency to see her, to beg her to undo their break.

He met with his mother and Captain Willoughby first, asking them to join him in his study for privacy. Standing in front of his desk rather than sitting behind it, he placed his hands on their shoulders and leaned forward.

"I talked with Cage at the Admiralty. They have a position for you. You will have to live in Town in order to take it up."

The Captain waved his empty sleeve at Beldon, his face belligerent, his eyes reddened from the excesses of the night before. "I won't take some damned desk job! I'm a seaman."

Beldon kept the pity from his voice, speaking in a matter of fact manner. "You'll not have a ship again. You can either take this position, where you can at least help the war effort, or go on feeling sorry for yourself and drinking yourself into oblivion. It's your choice."

"You are forcing us out?" Mother asked, her voice shaky.

"No, I will never do that. But for your own good—both of you—I hope you will take the position, sir, and care for your family again." He looked the captain straight in the eye.

"Nicholas should be in school. I realized it while the Duke's sons were here. I've been selfish," Mother said, her voice still quavering. She looked at her husband. His choice would determine how the rest of her life proceeded, and Beldon's heart went out to her. The last few years, seeing the man she married—perhaps loved?—become a shadow of the dynamic man he used to be, must have been hellish.

"I won't dictate the choices you make, but I think it wise

for Nicholas to go to school. It wouldn't come amiss for Lucy to have a year or two of school before she comes out, as well." Privately, he vowed to pay for Nick's schooling at least, but now, when his stepfather needed to believe he could take command of his family again, was not the time to bring it up.

"Yes, you're right." Captain Willoughby almost visibly pulled himself upright. "I've been feeling a worthless relic. But I have knowledge that could be useful to the Navy. I'll take the position. Regret I have been such a burden on you."

Beldon shook hands with his stepfather, hoping the Captain would take advantage of this opportunity. Perhaps the chance of once again controlling the course of his life would inspire him.

He felt a thousand pounds lighter. Grandfather had never explained, perhaps had not known, that taking care of one's dependents sometimes meant helping them to become independent. Whatever the Captain chose to do, Beldon knew he had performed a very fine, perhaps even a noble, act.

Next came Grandmother and Sir Bartram. This was for Harriet, who could never be happy living in the same house as Grandmother. A spacious dower house sat on the property, and Grandmother's brother could provide company for her.

He met with them in the drawing room for her comfort. She sat in her favorite chair, and Sir Bartram stood behind her. Grandmother didn't take the news well, her face reflecting anger and fear as Beldon stood before her, explaining.

"We will visit often. There can be only one chatelaine of a house, and you will not be she."

"You can't send me away from Langwell! I've been the mistress here for fifty years!" Her voice thundered with a semblance of its old authority.

"It's time you rested from your labors. You won't be far away. Sir Bartram can accompany you, so you won't be lonely."

"You'd turn me out?" Grandmother's eyes filled with tears.

"You cannot be surprised, after the way you treated the woman I chose to wed."

Her manner transformed in an instant. She gave him a

glance full of mischief. "I shall keep some of my belongings in the dower house, and visit it from time to time. However, I had already decided to move to Bath. These last weeks, with all the activity and people, I flourished. I'm not ready to sit in a chair and gaze into the fireplace.

"In Bath, I shall always find someone to gossip with, interesting goings-on. I think I'll offer to take your Aunt Manning with me if she wishes. I suspect she will. I think Bath will suit her better than a vicarage in a small village."

"You, Madam, have been bamboozling me." Beldon shook a finger at her, a smile forming despite his wish to be stern. "How many times have you tricked me?"

"Often enough, you foolish boy. You used to be easy to lead by the nose. It seems Miss Vernon has been good for you. Go, win her back, and see you don't lose her again."

"I intend to do that." He didn't reveal the stab of doubt, of panic, that struck him at the thought of failure.

"I've made my own arrangements," Sir Bartram said, a little sheepishly. "My own horse farm. Thoroughbreds, my first love, but don't worry I'll ruin myself again with gambling."

"How will you pay for it, sir?" Beldon asked.

"Docilla will buy a nice little farm for us. She and I have decided to marry."

"You and Mrs. Purvis?" He heard the shock in his voice.

"Yes. I know I'm quite a bit older than she. I managed to prove to her that I didn't at all suffer from the same, er, impairment as her first husband. I'll make her happy."

"The greater question is whether she can make you happy."

"There's no doubt of that." Sir Bartram had a smug grin.

The house would be emptier than he planned. Marianne, also, had arranged her own life. If he could persuade Harriet to marry him, they could fill it anew with their own family.

At last Lady Vare came down. Beldon had been hovering, waiting for her. In his eagerness, he met her at the bottom of the stairs. When she caught sight of him, her lips lifted in a pixyish smile which was a sharp reminder of Harriet.

"You sent me on a chase nearly to the Border for no purpose," he accused.

"You led Harriet on a chase for the past fortnight. It seemed reasonable for you to run a bit." Her smile was still in place, but a glint in her eye warned of her seriousness.

He nodded his acknowledgment of a fair hit. "It won't happen again. If I get another chance with her, I intend to make her happy."

"You do that." She nodded in return.

"Where is she?"

Lady Vare told him.

The cottage. His heart beat faster. She must be thinking of what it meant to their relationship, or was she? Still, optimism stirred in him for the first time in days.

Beldon rode up to the cottage, his pulse jumping erratically. Witch stood in one of the stalls. She had fresh straw bedding and was glossy and well-cared-for. He looked behind the feed bucket for the key, but as he expected, it was gone.

He turned toward the house. Front door or kitchen door? In the years he had made use of the cottage, he always entered into the kitchen, closer to the barn. But this occasion seemed to call for a formal approach.

Heart thumping and mouth suddenly dry, he walked around the house and rapped the front door knocker. Harriet opened the door herself. Unexpectedly, she was not wearing a riding habit, but a green gown that brought out the matching shade in her hazel pixie eyes, with a necklace of peridots fastened around her neck. "C-come in," she said, her voice breathless.

He stopped just within the door, suddenly diffident, his future uncertain. Harriet looked pale and twisted her hands before her, her patent nervousness twisting his heart. Silence lay thick between them, threatening to go on forever. Peripherally, he noted a shaft of light from the sunny kitchen slicing the darkness of the hallway. The air in the house had changed, lost its sense of unoccupancy.

"I thought you'd gone."

"No, I—" Her voice cracked, and she cleared her throat and started again. "I planned to go with my aunt on her tour of the Outer Hebrides when I realized it wasn't what I wanted."

"What *do* you want, Harriet?" He held his breath.

She studied his face for a long moment. "If I said I wanted not to be betrothed, would you accept that?"

His stomach plummeted. Could he change her mind? He moved closer, where he could smell the hyacinth fragrance of her hair, and feel the warmth of her body. "I don't know if I could. I would try, if that is what you truly want."

He wanted to hold her, to beg her not to go, but was afraid he would certainly lose her if he pushed too hard. "Is that it, then? You wish to remain free?"

"No! Oh, Beldon, I do love you. But I can't marry someone who doesn't love me."

She glowed, love and desire shining out of her eyes, and he wondered how he could ever have thought her less than a beauty. He closed the remaining distance between them and swept her into his arms. "God help me, Harriet, I love you so much. I couldn't stand it if I couldn't have you."

He bent to kiss her and realized he was still wearing his hat. He flung it off and yanked off his gloves as well. Then they were kissing passionately, her arms belted tight around him. He pulled her against his body, relishing the feel of her. He had to claim her, all of her, make her his.

He drew away just a little, to say, " 'Beldon'? Can you still not call me Rolleston?"

She bit her lips. "You really do love me?" She had waited so long to hear those words, and now she didn't know if she could ever get enough of them.

"I do. I intend to show you just how much. Now I have you, I'm going to make sure I never lose you again." He picked her up and swung toward the stairs with her cradled in his arms.

"Beldon—Rolleston, what are you doing?"

"We are going to make use of that bed!"

She smiled and snuggled against him as he carried her up the narrow staircase. He smelled of soap and his unique scent.

He looked down at her, passion glowing from his eyes. "No protest from you? I am going to ravish you!"

"I have wanted you to ravish me ever since, well at least since the park!" She flushed and looked away.

He set her down, nearly at the top. Only two more stairs, and the bedchamber a few steps beyond. She protested. "What? Have you already changed your mind? I have been in love with you that long. That's why I said we should not be alone together after our first visit to this cottage. And when you saw me kissing Luchan . . ."

He touched her lips, quieting them. "I know. He explained he had just learned he and Marianne could marry, and that you were in large part responsible. I was jealous at the time, but it's a logical reason to kiss."

"When did you talk to Luchan?" She still stood within the circle of his arms, aching to have him closer.

"When I caught up with him on the way to Scotland."

"You didn't!" She touched his chest, running her fingers over his coat, wishing it were his skin.

"I thought you had eloped with him."

"Mother didn't tell you otherwise?"

"I suppose I didn't really give her a chance."

"How delicious!" She laughed. "I can just see you hot-footing it to Scotland to save me from the fortune hunter."

"No, to save you for myself. Harriet, I think I've loved you since I nearly ran you over with my curricle. I only regret that I wasted the time we could have been together."

"We have our whole lives now."

"Yes." He stepped back, no longer contacting her, his eyes hungrily staring. "We should go back to the house."

She reached toward him, needing his touch. "Oh, no. We were on our way upstairs." Why was he suddenly becoming proper?

"Perhaps we shouldn't do this. I have a special license at the house. We can be married this afternoon."

"You were that sure of me?"

"I wasn't sure of you at all. I thought of as many ways as possible to convince you to step back into my trap—and to shut the trap door as soon as you did."

"Very wise. You never know when I shall suddenly take a notion to travel."

He swept her up again and leaped the remaining stairs.

Once inside the tiny chamber, he kissed her thoroughly, igniting her. She played with his mouth, using her tongue to tease his lips. He tasted like mint and coffee. He made an incoherent noise and worked his own tongue inside her mouth. She moaned and went limp against him. She was meant for this.

He fumbled with the ties of her dress, undid them and yanked off the gown, tossing it aside and kissing the exposed flesh of her neck and bosom above her chemise and stays. She shivered. They had somehow progressed to brush against the bed.

With the last of her coherent thought, she whispered against his ear, "We could fix up this cottage. We might still wish a retreat from your family at times."

"They will all be gone. We will have the whole house to ourselves—except for servants, who are hardly likely to interfere the way our families have."

"Gone? What have you done with them?"

"Actually, except for Marianne, they are all still there, even your family and Mrs. Purvis. Everyone is packing, however, and will be gone after we celebrate our marriage."

She wrenched at his coat and slid it off his shoulders, panting. "Let's hurry so we can get to the wedding."

He tore off his shirt. "Help me with the boots?"

He sat on the bed and she straddled his legs, tugging off his boots. "You are so beautiful," he murmured.

She threw a glance over her shoulder. "You are looking at my back."

"All of you is beautiful. I thought I would go crazy when that back and, er, the rest of you was captured in that mermaid costume." He picked up the coat from the floor and plucked some papers from the pocket, running his fingers over the creases.

"Not now, Rolleston, we have serious business here." She nuzzled his neck, smooth from recent shaving, her need urgent.

"But I want you to see. I had more ammunition to persuade you to marry me."

"Very well." She took them, then frowned. "What's this?"

"The passenger list of the Sea Star, sailing two weeks from now. For India. See—it says 'Lord and Lady Beldon.'"

She squealed, "Rolleston! I can't believe you did this! More bait for the trap?"

"Yes, whatever it took. I don't want you to give up what you most desire for me. It's our honeymoon trip."

She wrapped her arms around him, threw herself against him, putting all her love into a passionate kiss. Now she truly believed in his love. She had been prepared to give up her dream for him, but he understood its importance to her.

He rolled with her onto the bed, and braced himself, his arms on either side of her. "I know you want to see the world. We'll see it together."

Laughing, she pulled him down. Just before her lips joined his, she whispered, "Then hurry and make love to me. You are my world."

Celebrate Romance With One of Today's Hottest Authors

Amanda Scott

__**Border Fire**
0-8217-6586-8 $5.99US/$7.99CAN

__**Border Storm**
0-8217-6762-3 $5.99US/$7.99CAN

__**Dangerous Lady**
0-8217-6113-7 $5.99US/$7.50CAN

__**Highland Fling**
0-8217-5816-0 $5.99US/$7.50CAN

__**Highland Spirits**
0-8217-6343-1 $5.99US/$7.99CAN

__**Highland Treasure**
0-8217-5860-8 $5.99US/$7.50CAN

Available Wherever Books Are Sold!

Visit our website at **www.kensingtonbooks.com.**